ALSO BY KATT ROSE

BUILDING IT UP
A FATHER'S DAUGHTER
FORGET ME NOT (Coming Soon)

THE LOSS

KATT ROSE

Country Roads Publishing
Vancouver Island

ISBN-13: 978-1-9993994-0-5

THE LOSS

Copyright © 2019 by Katt Rose

Country Roads Publishing are trademarks used under license and registered in Nanaimo, Vancouver Island, Canada.

www.countryroadspublishing.net

Cover design by BespokeBookCovers.com

Formatting by Polgarus Studio

Author Photo taken by Kyle Trienke

PROLOGUE

"Didn't I tell you? It's amazing here, isn't it?" I could almost hear the excitement in his voice.

"You're right, I love it! Thank you for bringing me here."

A broad smile would appear on his face. "You're welcome. I'm getting to know you pretty well." I could see him extend a hand. "Come on, follow me."

And I would. I would have followed him anywhere. In this particular scene, I knew where we would end up; sitting on the tailgate of his truck, music pouring from the open windows. He would hop up and pat his hand for me to sit next to him. I would. And there we would sit, taking in the view around us. It would have been the perfect day. But I was alone. I found myself staring into the vast openness around me and grew cold. I looked into my viewfinder one last time and took the final shot. I made my way back to the truck and slid inside. I flicked the music on and listened quietly. I stared out into the still confinement around me and let the tears fall. For today, I had come to a place where no one could find me for a reason. I let my mind wander and felt the ending of a life. Today, I was trying my best to let go.

I turned on the engine and carefully drove back to the main road. I had nowhere in particular to be, so I made a last minute decision to take the back roads home. As I drove past miles upon miles of farmland, I came to a crossroad. I pulled off slightly to the side and got out of the truck. I breathed in the sweet air and heard the faint mooing of cows in the far off fields. The large maple trees swayed in the breeze, the tall green grass shone under the late sun. My GPS lost it's signal, but today, it did not bother me. To the right, a herd of horses grazed peacefully, their tails swished in unison, trying to keep the early spring bugs at bay. I watched them for a long while. I stared out into the fork in the road. Where do I go from here? Will this ache, this hurt ever truly go away? I knew I was lost, the question was, would I ever find my way to where I belong? Or am I one of the unlucky few destined to always be left searching for a way on my own?

CHAPTER 1

My name is Ryleigh Carter. I am twenty-five years old and probably have more patience with the world than I should. There is nothing special about me other than the fact bad things seem to happen to me wherever I go. I am a dreamer. I have high hopes for my future and that everything will somehow work out in the end. They say good things come to those who wait, and well, I have been waiting for quite sometime. My life has not been easy. Everyone has a story. And this, well…this is one that nearly broke me to the point of never coming back. I'm not sure where it comes from, but somewhere deep inside, I possess an unwavering strength. Perhaps there is something special about me after all. Like most good stories, mine involves a very special man. But before I can introduce him, we need to go back to the beginning. The very beginning.

⌘

My life wasn't going as planned, but this is not unusual for me. I was fresh out of University and work had been hard to find. I grew restless in my daily life and struggles. Change was on the horizon, I could feel it brewing from within. I was stuck working a job I hated, and my hours had been cutback, yet again. The routine was always the same; once my shift was over I would race home, kick off my shoes and curl up on the couch with a steaming mug of tea. Today was no different.

I closed my eyes and listened to the world outside. The noise from the city filled my ears and I sighed heavily. I was a country girl who was stuck living amongst the madness. The concrete buildings and house to house neighbourhoods held no draw for me what-so-ever, it felt slightly suffocating. The lights were always on, and the noise never stopped. Nothing ever stopped. The world I longed for was no longer here. For me, freedom comes from the peace and quiet nature has to offer, somewhere you can hear the frogs croak in the summer and the crickets sing their night song. I ached for a place where I could see the stars at night, and let the horses run. That was home for me and always would be. I tapped my fingers impatiently against my mug. There was nothing holding me here; I could pack up and leave at anytime, and that's what I chose to do. I muttered a silent prayer, packed up my truck with only the bare essentials and decided it was time to go to Alberta and start my life. I arranged with my mom to look after my horse, Tess, and my blissfully happy dog, Maggie, while I ventured into the world in search of a new beginning. Before I left BC, I got in touch with an old high school friend. and arranged to stay at her place while I searched for work and sorted out a new home. It was now time to set off into my own little adventure. It was just after 4:00 a.m. and the world was still dark. I hopped into the truck's drivers seat, plugged my Ipod into the stereo, and away I went toward the open road. Unfortunately for me, my 'little adventure' would turn into a nightmare that would set me back a whole year, but I did not know this at the time. Thirteen hours later, I appeared to be in the middle of nowhere. I drove along the lonely gravel road until I came across a long, winding driveway. The address matched what Katie had given me, so I pulled in.

"I don't see a white barn anywhere," I muttered under my breath. I stopped the truck and checked my text message from Katie one last time. "Head down the driveway and you'll see a large white barn. Keep going past it. There's a white house on a hill. That's us."

I pressed the gas and proceeded down the drive. This had to be the right place. All I wanted at this point was to eat and have a good sleep. As luck would have it, a large white barn stood in the distance. It over looked fields that appeared to go on forever. I made out a herd of a dozen horses in the distance. Ahead sat a cute, white house up on a hill. Next to the house stood a chicken coop and a large dog run. I recognized Katie's black pickup. I had finally made it. I opened up the truck door and stiffly stepped out. Fresh air hit me like a good hug from an old friend. I clasped my hands together and stretched out my tight muscles.

"Ryleigh!"

I turned to the excited voice and smiled brightly. Katie hopped her way toward me, blond hair bouncing, blue eyes brightly shining.

"Katie!" I met her halfway and we gave each other a quick hug. We hadn't seen each other since high school, and that was nearly six years ago now.

Katie's eyes sparked. "Do you want to go for a ride?"

I tapped my finger against the side of my cheek. "Hmm," I said slowly, "do you even have to ask? Yes!"

"Excellent! Let's find you a horse!"

Katie and I caught up with each other as we wandered the fields and chose our horses. I settled on a steel gray gelding who seemed like a good guy. He was honest enough and he knew the lay of the land. We saddled up quickly, and as I placed my boot in the stirrup, I wondered if I was making a terrible decision. I had just spent nearly thirteen hours stuck in the confines of a vehicle. I should be stretching out my muscles with a good walk. However, once I swung myself into the saddle and heard the creak of leather beneath me, my earlier thought was forever erased. We turned the horses down the treed lane and picked our way up the hill, letting the horses into a gallop along a flat stretch. I leaned forward in the saddle, settling into the rhythm of the horse beneath me. Life could not get any better than right now in this moment.

Four hours into the ride we let our feet hang out of the stirrups and laughed as we talked about old memories. The horses walked in unison side by side down the range road. For miles, I could see nothing but farmer's fields and trees. The sun began to set and a shade of bright pink filled the dimming sky. A small lake nearby pulled my attention. The reflection of the glowing horizon set the water on fire. Mosquitoes danced above the surface and sent the pink water rippling softly below. Crickets began to sing, welcoming the promise of night. It was a perfect ending to the day.

Since Katie's house was quite small, I got to bunk in the barn loft, which was rather large and suited me just fine. The loft had a decent kitchen, a bedroom that led into a sunken living room, and a sitting room. There was next to no furniture, except the fold out couch that would act as my bed for the next few weeks. Many pictures hung proudly along the walls of champion race horses bred and raised on the farm many years ago. I admired the photos one by one. A lot of love and dedication had gone into those horses, that much was clear by the smiling faces looking back at me within the frames.

As charming as the loft was, there was one downfall to the lay out; the bathroom. It was nestled downstairs in the main barn, two flights of stairways below. Not exactly fun in the dark, especially in an unknown setting, and with more than half of the light fixtures not in working condition. But I was not complaining. At least it was a place to stay, and so close to horses at that. It didn't take long to figure out that phone reception was pretty spotty around these parts. There were very few places on the farm, the loft included, where I could get cell service. There was one particular spot, if I laid in bed, arm outstretched at the perfect angle, I could get a live feed. It was nice to keep in touch with those I had left behind.

I landed an interview, actually quite a few of them. It was so nice to be able to pick and choose from which job I would want rather than waiting for months on end to hear from someone, anyone. I landed my dream job at a Vet clinic. I was head over heels. Now it was time to find a place of my own, one that must be dog friendly. I also had to find a spot for Tess to stay. If I was really lucky, I could find a place to rent on acreage and kill two birds with one stone. Life looked good. I had a new social circle, a fantastic job, and I was in the province that had my heart. What could go wrong? Well, apparently my body had a mind of it's own.

⌘

It was a great day. We had spent the entire day at a nearby ranch and most of it was spent in the saddle or behind the lens of the camera. I settled down for the night when out of nowhere I began to throw up. And I couldn't stop. It was odd, I didn't feel sick. The motion finally settled and I got slammed with a sudden, splitting headache. I shuffled my way back to the bed when a sharp, tearing pain hit my lower stomach. It knocked the very breath out of me. This was bad. It was unlike anything I had ever felt. A voice deep inside said to call for help, that this would not end well. Another sharp, fluttering wave tore through me that caused me to hunch over and grab my side. The pain intensified at an alarming rate. I reached for my phone only to find there was no service. I took a few agonizingly painful steps in another direction. Nothing. I tried another spot, no dice. I yelled out in frustration. *Work! Work for me, baby!* And then it happened. A sharp spasm ignited deep inside. The pain was too much, I cried out in surprise. The next thing I knew, my world went black, and I hit the floor.

Ow. Ow. Ow. I opened my eyes groggily and spit dust out of my mouth. I pressed my hands flat onto the cool floor below and began to lift myself upwards. I could still feel the stabbing aches as they tore through my gut. My eyes landed on the bed and I proceeded to delicately make my way toward it. I gingerly sat on the edge of the mattress and let my head fall onto the pillow. I was out like a light.

The warmth of the sunlight caressed my skin. I opened my eyes and saw it was morning. I wiggled my toes, and to my dismay it sent a lightning charge throughout my stomach. I gasped in pain. I attempted to sit up but couldn't on my own. I held onto the edge of the mattress and slowly, painfully I pulled myself on to my side. It felt like my stomach muscles were being torn out of me, piece by piece. *What's going on? This has got to be the strangest flu I have ever had.* My mouth was dry. I had a stash of fluids by my bedside and I reached for the orange juice. I took a long, cool sip. Something didn't feel right as the liquid settled into my gut. I let the drink fall to the floor. I studied the room around me and something was off. The room swayed side to side. I rubbed my temples and closed my eyes, and took a long, slow deep breath. Bad move. A stab of pain kicked at my ribs. I laid my head onto the pillow and closed my eyes once more. I needed to sleep this off, whatever it was. *When I wake up, please let the pain go away. Sleep, take it with you.*

"Ryleigh? You alive up there?"

I blinked my eyes a few times. "Katie? Is that you?" The stairs squeaked from someone's weight.

"Yes. Are you okay? You've been up here for two days."

Two days? That can't be right. "Ugh, I think I have the flu. I am down for the count. I feel terrible."

Katie furrowed her brows together, and studied me. "You look awful. Can I get you anything?"

"No thanks, I just need sleep."

"Okay. I just wanted to check on you. Jamie and I are taking off for a few days so the place is yours."

"Thanks," I mumbled from under the pillow, "have a good time."

"We will. Call us if you need anything, okay?"

I waved my hand in acknowledgment and closed my eyes, letting the tiredness wash over me. Sleep was peaceful, heavy, and strangely comforting. The pain was now constant and growing worse. Breathing became difficult, and my heart rate climbed. I grimaced as cold sweat soaked through my clothing. I needed a shower. I sighed in defeat as I thought of all those stairs I'd need to go down, but it wasn't just the stairs that would be the problem. There was no shower in the barn washroom. The only shower was nestled away in Katie's house. So that meant not only would I have to get down all those stairs, I'd need to make my way up the little hill, which was more like a mountain in my current state, to reach the house.

Almost twenty minutes later I had only conquered going down the stairs. I wrapped my arms into my sides and continued to place one foot in front of the other. Every once in awhile I'd see a flash of blinding white light as the pain intensified. I took small, quick breaths and continued to move forward until, finally, I stepped into the safe confines of the house. I fell on top of the washing machine and pressed my damp skin against the cool metal. I was in trouble, and I needed help. My eyes landed on the calendar, it read September 15th. *That can't be right.* I counted the days in my head. I had lost seven days, a whole week. I closed my eyes in defeat. I needed to go to the hospital. The shower lay six feet in front of me. I just about burst into tears for those six feet seemed like an eternity. And that's when I broke down. Sobs escaped my lips and the salty tears streamed down my face. I was scared. I had no idea what was wrong with me. I had no appetite what-so-ever, I did not even have a thirst. I felt weak. My limbs trembled with each movement I took, my heart rate shot up by even the slightest jostle. Not to mention the pain, the blinding, constant pain. It felt as though someone repeatedly stabbed my gut with a burning hot blade.

I managed to take a hot shower. I collapsed my tired body against the wall and let the steamy water caress my aching muscles. At one point I had dropped the conditioner, and as I reached down to pick it up I screamed out in pain as the jolt tore through me. I couldn't move, and for ten long minutes each breath was a struggle. Getting dressed was no easy task either. I had to mentally prepare myself to lift each leg, for I knew the pain it would send shooting through me. Finally, with clean clothes I made the slow journey to the barn. I stopped at my truck and leaned helplessly against the hood. I needed to head back up to the loft to gather my things and load up the truck. *Could I do this? I really don't have a choice, do I?* Suddenly, in that moment I wished Mark was here next to me. Mark and I went way back, we met just over two years ago on my birthday. He had caught my eye from across the room and I his. The moment I saw him, I knew he would always be in my world. And I was right. We grew close over a summer I wished would never end. However, the timing just wasn't right. Life took him in one direction, and I went the other. We had both decided to stay in touch, neither of us felt right about cutting each other out of our lives. We made plans to meet up in the coming few days. He lived an hour away from where I was currently staying, but for the time being, he was gone on yet another work project.

I gave myself a pep talk and pushed my head off the hood. This was it, it was now or never. By the time I reached the top of the stairs, I felt like I had just completed a marathon. My heart pounded against my chest and I was drenched in sweat. *So much for my shower.* The bright lights appeared in my field of vision and I was forced to sit on the edge of the bed. I felt nauseous. I bent forward and let my head fall between my legs, breathing slowly. I stayed in that position until I could see straight once more. Standing slowly, I gathered my belongings and headed downstairs. I sighed loudly and leaned helplessly against the truck door. Damn, my door sure looked high. I sucked in another careful breath, opened the door, and grabbed on for dear life to the handle that lay above the window. I hoisted one half of my body inside and let it fall against the seat heavily. *Oh, shoot me.* That hurt. I stared helplessly as my left leg still hung outside my door. Shaking my head, I wrapped both hands around my leg and swung it inside, squeezing my eyes shut tightly. At last, I was in.

⌘

Screw you GPS. If you tell me to make another U-turn when available you are going out this god damn window. I gripped onto the leather steering wheel tightly and muttered some choice words under my breath. I was lost. How hard could it be to find a hospital? Apparently a lot harder than I thought. I had left the small town I started to think of as home almost two hours ago; it was a long drive into the city. And now that I was apparently ten minutes from my destination I found myself circling the block aimlessly, growing more and more impatient. Like a shining bright light ahead, there it was. The tall, off white building loomed over small houses nearby. My beacon of hope, the hospital. I pulled into the parking lot and found a space to pull into. I paid for my parking in somewhat disgust, and shuffled my way through the main doors, arms wrapped tightly against my torso. I glanced at the time on my phone, 8:30 a.m. Hopefully I beat the rush. I registered at the front desk and a nurse called me over to take my vitals. She asked me a long list of questions and I answered somewhat hopeful that this would all be over soon. A good dose of antibiotics and I should be out the door to get back to my new life.

"Hmm. I think we're going to draw some blood. I'd like a urine sample too." The nurse looked at the thermometer and shook her head slightly. She bustled to the cabinet, handed me a cup, and gestured me to the washroom.

"Okay," was all I could manage.

I came out of the washroom and a tech stopped me to draw blood. As I waited for my results I sent my mom a quick text, sending her a brief, reassuring message that all would be okay. In and out. I sent Mark one too as he would be in town later this evening and hoped to see me.

"Ryleigh Carter?"

I looked up toward the man calling my name. "Yes?"

"Come with me, we're sending you for an x-ray."

"Oh?" I furrowed my brows in confusion. "Um, sure."

I followed slowly as he led me into the diagnostic room. A few minutes later I was taken into a waiting room with a bed. I was assured a doctor would be in soon to examine me. With each minute that passed my suspicion began to grow. The curtain flew open and a chipper, gray haired man walked in.

"Hi, Ryleigh. Can you please lay down. Let's see what we have going on here."

The doctor took my hands and helped lie me down. He lifted my shirt and gently pressed my torso. I flinched in pain and glanced down, my eyes widened in horror. My stomach did not look my stomach. It jutted out like a pregnant belly. I couldn't resist the temptation, I let my hand gently rest on top of my midsection and pressed down. It was hard as rock.

My voice filled with panic. "What's happening to me? That's not right."

"Unfortunately, the x-ray didn't give us a clear image. Your urine and blood show your white blood cell count is very high, which usually indicates an infection. We're going to send you for a CT scan and hope that gives us a clearer picture of what's going on."

My heart slightly dropped. This did not sound good, so much for a good dose of antibiotics and out the door. "How high is high, exactly?"

The doctor pursed his lips. "Well, the average persons white blood cell count remains at ten or eleven. Yours is twenty-three."

Crap. "I see."

The doctor gave me a small smile. "Don't worry, we'll figure this out."

With that, he gave me a quick tap on the shoulder and left. I lied back onto the hard bed and stared at the white, bland walls around me. I had a very bad feeling.

CHAPTER 2

I was once again alone in a waiting room, a different one this time. This room was more official; instead of curtains separating the beds it was a solid wall. My heart sank, this could not mean good things were coming my way. My CT scan was completed and I was left to wait for the GI specialist. All the waiting was maddening, no one would tell me a thing.

The door creaked open and a stern looking man stepped inside. "Ryleigh Carter?" His eyes didn't leave his clipboard.

"That's me for the time being." I tried my best to be chipper. He did not seem to appreciate it.

His cold eyes left the paper and met mine. He glanced at me quickly and his lips pursed together. "I see. Well, this is where we're at. You're being admitted and we'll be starting you on a hefty dose of very strong antibiotics. I don't like the look of your white blood cell count. That tells me that there is a massive infection brewing or it could be cancer."

My blood ran cold and my head snapped up toward his. The doctor continued on in a matter of fact manner, and I held up my hands quickly. "Whoa, whoa, whoa, stop the bus here. Did you just say cancer?"

He stopped and looked at me quizzically. "Yes. But that's not a sure thing as of yet. The CT revealed your abdomen is filled with abscesses. We're going to insert drains to help relieve the fluid build up, and then we'll run more tests. We will figure this out and see if surgery is needed."

"Oh," was all I could muster. I blinked my eyes a few times, I would not cry in front of this man.

He looked at me once more and then his eyes settled on the door, looking for his escape. "A nurse will look after you. I will be in touch."

I watched him leave. *Ass*. Moments later a nurse walked in. She smiled warmly and helped me to a small, somewhat private waiting room. The room held three leather chairs and a television on the wall. I settled deep into the cushion and bit my lip. This was a lot of news, a lot of 'what ifs to digest.' It wasn't too long ago my world looked so bright, so happy, so full of....life. How so much could change in a single day. The room was fairly quiet. Another woman sat in the chair next to mine, her eyes glued to the television, her arm hooked up to an IV.

Purposeful footsteps came into the room and a nurse entered with an IV pole and two bags of fluids. "Ryleigh Carter?"

"That's me," I smiled weakly.

She smiled. "Great. Can you please roll up your sleeve?"

I nodded, pushed up a sleeve, and held my arm to her. She knelt in front of me and her eyes narrowed, examining me. "Hmm. Well, isn't that cute. You have such tiny veins. This may be a bit challenging."

Her eyes studied my arm and she worked quickly."There! Got it. The nurse clapped her hands in a moment of quick pride, and hooked up the IV bags. "Would you like something for the pain?"

I noticed the other woman in the room looked up quickly. "I would!" she called out.

The nurse looked at her absently and focused her gaze on me, waiting for an answer. "Um, no. I'm okay for now, thank you."

The nurse gave a concerned look. "Okay. If you change your mind, just give someone a shout in the halls. We'll take care of you."

I nodded. "Thank you."

As the nurse turned to leave, the woman beside me grabbed at her stomach. "Ouch. I'm in so much pain. It really hurts."

The nurse nodded slowly. "I'll get you something."

She turned and briskly left the room. The woman settled back happily into her chair and began to entertain herself on her phone, a smile upon her face. I shook my head, people never ceased to amaze me. I glanced at my own phone to check the time. It was now 1:00 p.m. This was going to be a long day. I decided to text a few people to give an update. I told them almost everything. I decided to leave out the cancer.

My mom was the first to respond. "Surgery!? What the hell is happening? I'm on the next flight out."

I smiled, that was mom. She was hands down one of the strongest people I have ever had the honor to know. Not only did she seem to have all the answers, but she had to act as both a mother and a father for most of her adult life. She did it with ease.

I glanced impatiently at the time once again. It was now nearing 7:30 p.m. and I still waited for a bed to be available on the floor. My pain grew steadily worse and I could no longer get comfortable. I tentatively adjusted my seat when the nurse who had been looking after me for the past few hours walked in. He carried a glass of apple juice alongside a can of ginger ale. "This is for you. How about something for the pain?"

"No thanks."

He shook his head almost impatiently. "I'm sorry, but I won't accept that answer. You are getting something, I can't watch this anymore," he reached into his pocket and pulled out two syringes. "One is Gravol, the other is Demerol. It will help. Trust me."

I nodded slowly. "Okay." *Honestly, what do I have to lose at this point. It certainly can't get any worse.*

The nurse winked. "Good. It's about time."

My eyes closed in relief. Gravol and Demerol combined can take you to magical places. Or at least it did for me. I didn't realize how much pain I was in until those two wonderful concoctions worked their charm. I smiled slowly, I felt nothing. Absolutely nothing. It was bliss. As I opened my eyes, the room began to spin softly. I leaned my head back onto the chair and let my eyelids fall shut. It felt like someone bundled me up with a warm, healing, magical blanket. The feeling washed over my head ever so slowly, all the way down into my toes.

I giggled slightly and reached for my drink. "This is amazing. I can't feel it! I don't feel the pain!"

The nurse chuckled. "Bet you wish you would've said yes a few hours ago, eh?"

I looked up at him. "You're cheeky. I like that."

He grinned and shook his head. "Enjoy."

"I will. Thank you." I settled back into my seat, and for the first time in quite awhile, I was comfortable. Lady no name glared at me from her chair. I grinned back at her. "I'm not going to lie, I feel fantastic!"

My phone jingled and I glanced down at the screen. It was a message from Mark. "You're at the hospital? Which one are you in? Are you okay?"

I wrote back slowly, the medication made me feel very loopy. I had to reread my message to make sure that it came together clearly. "I'm at the Red Deer Hospital. I'm not quite sure what's wrong yet, but I'm sure it's nothing." That was a bold face lie.

"I'm coming to see you soon. Please let me know what room you're in."

"I will. I promise."

"Good. Keep me updated. xoxo"

It was now 11:30 p.m., and they had a bed for me at last. I settled into my new room and began to fear the diminishing effects of the Demerol. It scared me. I could feel the numbness slowly dissipate and the pain began to take over like a disease. I didn't remember the pain being so...so....unbearable. How the hell did I live with this for a whole week? I thanked the nurses politely for their help and they gave me another dose to keep the pain at bay. I felt the wave of the medicine hit me and I slipped into a quiet slumber.

Strange voices next to me awoke me. My eyelids flew open and I found myself staring at two unfamiliar faces. "Sorry to wake you, dear. We're trying to fix your IV."

I looked toward my left arm in confusion. My mouth fell open in horror. "My arm!" I gasped. "What happened? It's huge!" It was nearly three times the size of my right arm.

The nurse patted me comfortingly. "The IV slipped out of your vein and it's been pumping the medication just under your skin. We need to fix it."

I watched in slight disgust as they touched my arm. It was like someone tapping onto the mattress of a water bed as it slightly jiggled from the fluid

15

build up. The one nurse muttered apologies under her breath as she tried for the third time to get a vein "It's not catching. Her veins are so little."

"Let me try."

I tore my focus from them. I didn't want to watch their attempts. I winced as another miss took place.

"Sorry, hun. Here, let's try propping your arm up. Bev, can you grab Anne? She's usually pretty good at this. I'm going to give it another go."

Bev, I assume nodded and left the room. Another pinch marked another miss. Bev came back inside followed by a woman, at which I'll assume was Anne. Anne gave me a small smile. "Sit tight. We'll get it right for you."

Sit tight. Where else am I going to go? Anne leaned over me and studied my arm, which now throbbed from being used as a pin cushion. I noticed the time on the wall, 2:00 a.m. *What a fun day this has turned out to be.*

"I think we'll have to use an infant sized needle for her. The adult ones are just going to slip out," Anne mumbled, deep in thought.

Bev's voice rose. "Oh, that's a creative idea."

Anne got to work, and to my relief the woman got it in a vein. First try. "All righty, my dear. That should do it. Have a nice sleep."

I mumbled quietly. "Thank you." I watched as the women left the room. I took a deep breath and the medicinal smell of the hospital filled my lungs. The steady, rhythmic *beep beep* from my IV pump ran rather noisily. I closed my eyes and let myself drift off into the dark.

⌘

"Ryleigh? Ryleigh, honey."

A quiet, warm voice met my ear. A wave of comfort washed over me. *Mom.* I opened my eyes and was met by my mother's big blue eyes that were brimmed in concern.

"You're here!" I cried out.

"Of course I am. I told you I would catch the first flight out. James is watching the animals for me. I'm staying at his dad's house, which isn't too far from the hospital. No hotel fees for me, which is a lifesaver."

James was my stepfather. I could only imagine how hard it must be for him to stay put while all of this was going on "That's nice of him to look at all the critters," I offered.

My mom nodded. "Yes. He knew I couldn't stay put. I'd go crazy." My mom pursed her lips. "I spoke to the nurses about you. No one knows what's going on yet, but they tell me you're getting your drains put in today."

I grimaced. "Drains put in. I sound like an appliance."

My mom smiled. "James and I were talking before I left. You really can't go anywhere without something happening can you? Bad luck follows you wherever you go."

I couldn't help but smile. It was true. No matter where I went, no matter what I did, things always managed to happen to me. Throughout high school, especially when it came to sports, I made a point of staying away from large, fast objects. I could be off the field in a corner and you guessed it, that damn ball would get me every time. Even simple tasks like walking up the stairs to my locker somehow ended up with me flat on my face in the hall, my binder contents scattering every which way. These special talents had followed me ever since.

"I'm sorry, Mom. I can't help it."

She laughed quietly. "It's part of your charm."

Her eyes settled on my arm. I followed her gaze and groaned. The swelling was still there, but not to the degree it was last night. Today however, it was very colorful. My arm was marred in large bruises; purples, blues, and a yellowish green. Not it's finest moment. *Would you look at that, I have my own personal rainbow.*

A nurse walked in at that moment. "How are you feeling this morning?"

"Sore," I admitted. She nodded and looked over my arm.

"Hmm. That little bugger is going to slip out again. We're going to get a PICC line put in for you as well."

My mom sounded concerned. "What's a PICC line?"

The nurse turned to her, every once in awhile throwing a glance in my direction. "Essentially it's a catheter that acts as a portable IV. We can administer her medications through the line and it goes right where it needs to go. She will get it put in at the same time as her drains. They will run the line through a large vein near her upper shoulder and thread it to the heart."

My jaw dropped slightly. That did not sound like fun. The nurse turned to me with a sympathetic smile. "It's not as bad as it sounds, and this way there will be no more IV's slipping out. It'll stay put." She hung new IV bags and took my vital signs. "In about half an hour we'll send you for your procedures."

I nodded. "Okay. I just want to get this over with."

True to her word, half an hour later someone came to get me. I was wheeled into a radiology room with three men waiting in white coats. They explained the procedure in great detail and began to prep me. I had hoped I would be knocked out, but no, I was awake. They numbed the area and they first put in the PICC line. They positioned the screen so I could watch the catheter being threaded through my veins. I chose not to look, for I was feeling queasy enough as it was. Next were my drains. On the lower left quadrant of my stomach they placed in two drains, right next to each other, and threaded the tubes into the right half of my stomach. It was not a pleasant procedure, it hurt me a great deal. The first drain felt like a slight pinch, however the second drain caused me to scream out in pain. The nurse standing near my head told them to stop and she gave me another dose of pain medication. Once the nurse gave the nod to carry on, they proceeded swiftly. I sucked in a sharp breath, it still hurt. I closed my eyes and pressed my lips together in a hard line as the tears ran slowly down my face. After it was over I was taken back into my room. I excused myself to the washroom and stood in front of the mirror. I stared back at my reflection and studied the left side of my body in disgust. A large tube hung out of my left arm and ended on the inside of my elbow crease. Two clear drain bags the size of a small purse hung down the front side of my body for all to see. A reddish, milky fluid dripped steadily into the bags. I watched the girl in the mirror closely as her green eyes widened in horror. Could this really be me? Was this actually happening? I pressed my back against the cold wall and began to cry.

⌘

My mom spent every day, every minute by my bedside. On top of daily blood draws, getting my drains flushed and scans, they added Heparin shots to my morning regimen. I was to be given a shot into my stomach that would thin out my blood for the time being, minimizing the risk for blood clots. I was basically immobile at this point. Food was no easy task. It didn't feel right in my stomach. I was placed on a clear fluids diet, my meals consisted of Jello and broth. The cancer scare was just that, a scare. For the first forty-eight hours of my hospital stay, I was on sepsis watch. That danger, luckily for me, came to pass. They decided my appendix had ruptured, and when that little sucker burst, it released a whack load of poison throughout my system. I had been marinating in it for just over a week. Stupid appendix. Stupid, stubborn me.

I was alone in my room. My mom spoke to a nurse in the hall. When she came in, she was teary eyed. "Mom? What's wrong?"

My mom smiled sadly. "They're not sure how much damage is done. Your stomach is too full of fluids to tell but, honey, you may not be able to get pregnant. The concern is with your fallopian tubes."

Devastation hit me like a ton of bricks. Not able to get pregnant? Sure, I had no need for kids right now, but it had always been a part of the plan to become a mom one day. A wave of panic hit me as there was nothing I could do to fix it. *Please, don't take this right away from me. Please.* I didn't know who I pleaded to, but whoever it was, I sure hoped they could hear me. I sat back against the pillow and stared blankly at the walls around me. How did I end up here? How could this happen to me? My body didn't feel like my own anymore and there was nothing I could do to stop it. I looked up sadly as I heard footsteps enter the room. Mark stood unsurely in the door holding a teddy bear along with a bouquet of the most beautiful blue, white, and blue roses I had ever seen. A wave of happiness rippled through my sickly body, and for the first time in awhile, I felt a smile stretch upon my lips.

"Mark! You're here," I said warmly.

My mom smiled and gave him a hug. "I'm going to grab some food. I'll let you two catch up."

He nodded at her and his blue eyes fell on me. He studied me slowly and carefully. His features fell and the color drained from his face. I shifted uncomfortably and suddenly felt very self-conscious. I tugged at the drains quickly and slipped them under the blanket. Mark's hands slightly trembled as he set the roses on the table next to me.

He sat down heavily, blew out a breath, and began to run his fingers against his facial scruff. "You said you were fine. This does not look fine." His blue eyes burned into my own.

I cleared my throat and pulled down a sleeve to hide my swollen, bruised arm. "I'm sorry, I didn't want you to worry about me." I shrugged helplessly. "They say my appendix ruptured and because I was so stupidly stubborn, all of this," I gestured to the tubes that hung out of me, "is damage control."

He smiled softly, pulled his chair closer, and placed the stuffed bear gently in my arms. "You are too stubborn for your own good." He ran his finger against my cheek. "Somehow you're still sexy as hell."

My eyes grew wide and I laughed loudly. "Oh, I doubt that very much."

He leaned closer. "You are. If only you could see yourself through my eyes."

I looked up at him and felt the sting of tears. He gazed at me with his playful smile, god how I had missed him.

"Come here," he whispered softly and his lips met mine. He pulled away slowly and gently lifted my bruised hand up to his lips to kiss it softly. He slipped his fingers through mine, interlocking them, and held on tightly. My head grew heavy and I let it fall to his shoulder. Mark ran his fingers through my hair and I felt his lips meet the top of my head.

"I'm glad you're here," I whispered.

"There's no where else I'd rather be." He held me in his arms until I fell asleep.

⌘

It was now day twelve of my hospital stay. The doctor said I would have a long road to recovery and so it was decided I would go back to BC, back to my mom's house where homecare would be arranged. A home nurse would come by every other day to check on me and flush out the drains. Ah, the drains. Those lovely things had to stay in me for nearly two months. My medication would be switched from IV form to oral. Pills. *Fantastic*. I have this odd relationship with swallowing pills, as in I can't. Even a tiny Gravol I have to break in half, or, as gross as it is, chew them, and then chug some water to force them down.

My world had been turned upside down. Goodbye bright, new life. Just like that, my new future was ripped away. I found myself saying goodbye to Mark once more and the new friends and contacts I had made. I was given the choice of an ambulance transfer or my mom could drive me home in my own vehicle. I chose to go with Mom. Waiting for an ambulance transfer would mean I would be stuck here for another three days. If I was going to leave, I wanted to leave now.

My last lunch was brought to me. Over the past two days I was finally able to eat something other than broth. I chatted with Mom, and as we ate an odd sensation washed over me. The pain in my stomach had always been low before, but this one was higher. It lied just below my breast bone and it tightened like a vice. I attempted another bite. I chewed slowly and swallowed. The sensation happened again. This time it didn't stop. Tears streamed down my face and I hugged my mid section.

At that moment one of my favorite nurse's walked in and she looked angry. "The doctor gave you T3's for your drive home. T3's! That's not going to do anything for you." Her expert eyes looked me over quickly. "What's wrong?"

I spoke in bursts as it hurt to take in a fluid breath. "I don't know. This is new."

My mom looked upset. "Maybe we should stay here for a few more days…"

"No," I said quickly, "I can't stay in a hospital anymore. I want my bed. Fresh air. Peace and quiet at night. Please, let's go," I begged.

The nurse and my mother exchanged a glance. Nurse Suki nodded. "I'll tell you what. I'll help you load her in the vehicle. Right before you take off, I will give her a shot of Demerol and Gravol, that should give her six hours of comfort."

My mom looked so grateful as she wrapped Suki in a warm hug. "Thank you."

The truck waited downstairs for me. My mom made a cozy bed in the passenger seat out of sleeping bags. The women helped me inside and Suki gave me my last dose. She squeezed my hand and concern filled her eyes. "Take care of yourself."

I smiled slowly as the drugs took over, erasing my pain. "Thank you for everything."

We drove out of Calgary at a decent speed and the Rocky Mountains came into view. "It's so beautiful here," I sighed softly.

At that moment Paul Brandt's 'Alberta Bound' played over the radio station. I sniffed back tears. "We're going the wrong way," I sobbed. With that, we began the thirteen hour drive back to BC.

⌘

"Wake up honey. We're home."

I opened my eyes and was greeted by concerned, loving faces. The trip had been hard on me. Once the drugs wore off, I was in agony. Every bump, every uneven surface was intent on killing me. The T3's did nothing to ease the pain, but now, here I was, home. My step-dad, brother, and Oma stood together, waiting to embrace me in careful hugs.

My brother held the best expression. When he saw the drains hanging from my midsection his eyes widened and his jaw dropped. "Oh, good god." His eyes then focused on the fluids swishing around inside. "What the hell. Is that shit coming out of you?" My Oma looked horrified. "Skyler!"

I laughed. "It's okay, Oma. That's just Sky. Yes, yes it is coming out of me."

"That's disgusting." He wrinkled his nose. "So, you're telling me that my appendix could just blow up at any given minute?"

I managed a grin. "You betcha. Any time, any place."

James laughed and gave me a gentle hug. "I still say the horses did this to you. All that riding, getting jolted up and down, that can't be good for you."

I rolled my eyes. He always blamed the horses. My mom left to go to the pharmacy, our family doctor had written me a stronger prescription for the pain, and she needed to get my antibiotics as well. I was so weak from having been in bed so long that my leg muscles were gone, any effort would cause them to shake uncontrollably. I had to hold onto my step-dad and brother as they helped me up the steps into the house. I saw my horse, Tess in the distance. I called out to her and was greeted with an excited whinny. I smiled, but was so exhausted I needed to lie down.

"Tomorrow, big girl. I'll see you tomorrow," I called to her.

The men led me to my old bedroom. My Oma and aunt had made the room cozy and warm for me. They placed a bar fridge next to my bed and filled it with drinks and light snacks I could tolerate. Pictures of my friends and family were on display upon the nightstand, and they lined the front of the bed with fluffy pillows. I sighed. It was good to be home. Something was missing though.

"Where's Maggie?"

My Oma spoke. "Your aunt has her. We didn't want her to knock you over in excitement."

I smiled, yes, that sounded like Maggie. She wasn't a small dog either. I fondly referred to her as my little black bear. My aunt owned Maggie's sister and they lived a short distance down the road.

As I slipped into bed, the soft mattress felt like a cloud to my aching body. Hospital beds were certainly not the most comfortable things to rest on, especially for an extended length of time, which was rather ironic. My Oma busied herself as she tucked me in, like she used to do when I was a child. I had noticed her suitcases in the kitchen. She planned to stick around for quite awhile.

She pushed the hair out of my face and pretended to look stern, wagging her finger at me. "Don't you do that again, young lady. You nearly drove me to drink."

I smiled. "Sorry. I'll do my best."

"That's all I've ever asked. I'm so glad you're home safe and sound." She leaned forward and kissed me on the forehead.

⌘

I hated the morning ritual. I had to attempt to swallow three giant horse-sized pills two times a day. It was quite the production, and since there was no way in hell I could swallow them, I crushed them into a fine powder, or broke them into tiny pieces and took it with pudding. The pills made my stomach turn; they were so bitter and strong. Nothing could mask it. I was not a happy camper. The new pain medication did a good job for the most part, at least it let me sleep in peace. Something new was beginning to happen and it made me uneasy. I kept it to myself for I knew I would be sent back to the hospital, and I was not ready to go back. Over the past few days, I started to have night terrors where I was chained to a hospital bed and no one would let me leave, no matter how much I begged and pleaded. Mad doctors stuck needles in me and performed crazy rituals. They promised to let me go, but they never did. I became their play thing. I often woke in a cold sweat with my heart racing.

However, I couldn't hide things from those who loved me. Breathing had begun to get difficult and that new pain made itself known. I had started to throw up again. The pills I had spent so much time forcing down came up fully intact, as did anything else I attempted to eat. My mom wanted to take me to the hospital, but I kept refusing. One particular night, things got really bad. The darkness of my room was lit by flashing lights. I was greeted by paramedics taking me back to the hospital. They helped me outside to the ambulance, and I watched as the faces I loved the most were etched in worry. My own face fell, as I too, was scared.

So, there I was yet again, in a hospital bed. My stay wasn't nearly as pleasant as it had been in Alberta. Back there, only one other person shared the room with me. Here, there were four of us, and they were not quiet. My room smelled sour. I winced as the sound of dry and wet coughs came at me like surround sound, followed by the lullaby of dry heaves and moans. I was in no better shape. My health kept crashing. Apparently, my stomach was now kinked over. Nothing could get in, nothing could get out. Lovely. I could keep nothing down, not even water. I'd try out a small sip, but it had nowhere to go but back up.

The heavy tiredness was back in full swing. I wanted to do nothing but sleep. It was so easy there, so quiet, so still. I could have stayed in that quiet, happy place forever. My body was shutting down, I could feel it. My pain had gotten so bad, the nurses put my pain medication on their chart to be routine every five hours. There was no magic here of Demerol; I got Morphine instead. I hated Morphine, or I should say, it hated me. Sure, it eased the pain, but it made me violently sick, more so than I already was. I had gone over my daily limit of Gravol so they hung an IV bag of an anti-emetic called Zofran. It was supposed to help ease the nausea, I needed it now on an almost twenty-four hour basis. Friends and family came to see me, I was only vaguely aware. I could see the fear written on their faces. I knew I looked awful. I was as white as a sheet, the color was gone, and I was beyond weak. I was no longer allowed to have anything by mouth, including water. My nutrition came from a large bag filled with a fluorescent yellow liquid. The doctor decided I needed a nasal gastric tube. I dreaded the upcoming procedure, for it did not sound pleasant. A long clear tube would be threaded through a nostril and settle into the bottom of my stomach, pumping out all the poison inside of me. My body needed help to perform a very basic function. Their hope was it would eliminate the need for me to throw up. Here's to hoping.

A nurse entered the room. "Ryleigh? We're going to perform your procedure later in the day. Right now, we're sending you downstairs. The doctor wants to drain the fluid from your ribs."

I nodded weakly. "Fine."

The pain in my ribs had gotten so bad it felt like they were being cracked, one by one. Since I had been immobile for so long, fluid had settled between the spaces of my ribcage. They were to drain the excess and send some to the lab to be sure nothing new was happening. I felt like a science project. Take a little here, take a little there, add something here. I was too tired to care.

I was wheeled to a surgical room near radiology. "We're just going to numb the area. We'll make this quick," said a friendly man who held a very long, thick needle.

"Okay." I nodded quickly, "let's get this over with."

The man smiled warmly and lifted my hospital gown upwards to reveal my right side. He pricked a small needle in the area he wanted to numb and waited a few seconds before proceeding. He then tapped at my side. "Do you feel this?"

"No." I responded.

"Good, let's begin."

He pulled out the long needle and I looked away, trying to keep my breathing quiet. I closed my eyes and began quietly counting to myself. *One. Two. Three. Fou-…holy hell! This hurts!* My eyes flew open and I gasped. I looked at my side and not even half of the needle was in.

I met the man's eyes in horror and he winced. "I'm sorry. I missed the area I froze. I can pull it out and try again."

Of course you did. This is me. "No, it's in already, just finish. Please make it quick." I pleaded.

His eyebrows shot up. "Okay," he let out a quick breath. "Women are definitely stronger then men."

A small smile tugged at my lips. "Can I get that in writing?"

He chuckled and began to draw a pale red fluid from my ribcage. I looked away and squeezed my eyes shut. The pain medication had begun to wear off. I could feel the wave of a new monster coming and it was ready to come out and play. *When will this be over?* Fifteen minutes later, I sat in an upright position on my bed. The nurse was next to me. A long, thick clear tube coiled neatly on my lap. That terrible thing would soon be sitting inside me.

"All right. It's time," the nurse said. "Please tilt your head back. Oh, and here," she handed me a glass of water. "As I insert the tube, continue to take small sips throughout. It will make this a little easier." *I thought I couldn't drink water.*

I didn't buy that for a minute. "Okay," was all I said. There was no getting out of this one.

I tilted my head back and begun to take small sips. My left nostril burned as the tube made it's way down. The taste of plastic filled my mouth, and the back of my throat felt irritated. The sips were getting harder and harder to swallow. With my free hand, I squeezed onto the blanket tightly.

"All right, it's done."

I looked down and saw she had hooked up the tube to a machine behind my bed. She flicked on a switch, and like turning on a vacuum, the tube filled with sludgy green liquid. It pulled contents of my stomach into two containers behind me. I tried to take a deep breath but the tube burned the back of my throat. I attempted to swallow but my throat felt swollen.

Someone began to scream in a slightly hysterical voice. "What the hell is this? What's wrong with me? Get it out! Take it out!"

It was me. I felt like I was having an out of body experience. This entire time I had been nothing but a polite, and quiet joy to deal with. I never complained, I let them poke and prod me to their hearts content. But this was too much, this sent me flying over the edge. I hadn't felt my outburst coming on. I felt calm, cool, and collected. In a matter of seconds, I transformed. My heart began to race, I was entering hysterics. I tried to rip the tube out of my nose and another nurse ran into the room.

"Get her Ativan now. Honey, it's going to be okay. Look at me, Ryleigh. Look at me." The nurse's hands gripped my forearms and I met her eyes. "Good," she nodded. "Take a deep breath with me. Breathe. Focus."

The other nurse entered the room with a pill in a tiny cup. She gave me a concerned look and extended her hand. "Stick this under your tongue. It will help you relax."

I did as was told. It didn't take long to kick in. I was now mildly sedated. My heart slowed, and I welcomed the peaceful slumber that quickly became a very close friend. I awoke to a rather unpleasant scent. Something smelled sour. I shifted my body position and it felt wet. My hands felt the bed beneath me and it was soaked. My gown was damp on the right side. *Oh no. Did I wet the bed?* I flicked on the night lamp by the bedside and my eyes widened in horror. I was covered in my own stomach bile. The tube had loosened from the suction cups and had begun to leak throughout the night. I pressed the call button and waited for someone to come to my aid. I was mortified and disgusted all at once. What else could go wrong? A little while later, I was assisted out of the shower and the nurses helped me dress. I held onto them as they helped me into the freshly cleaned bed. I thanked them politely and stuck the ear buds into my ears. I flicked on my Ipod and cranked up the music and counted silently. *1, 2, 3, 4.* Four tubes were now inside me. I looked out the window vacantly, and wished I could be anywhere else but here.

⌘

The days dragged on. My Ipod worked 24/7. I let the music transport me to another place, somewhere where I didn't hurt, somewhere where I could be me again. I felt like a caged animal on display at the zoo, and I wanted out. I wanted out so badly. On a more positive note, the NG tube seemed to be doing it's job. The first day it was put in was very disappointing for I still spent most of the day throwing up. Can you imagine how uncomfortable it is to throw up while you have a tube coming out your nose and sticking to the back of your throat? I certainly don't wish that experience on anyone. Well, that's not entirely true...maybe my worst enemy, maybe. Certainly no one I cared about. I had grown so fed up with the burning, and the taste of plastic, I attempted to rip the tube out myself. I was given a stern talking to and was once again sedated. I kept myself busy through music, and texting friends and family. I asked for them to stay away. I did not want to be seen like this. However, most of them ignored my plea and swung by to visit anyways. Today had been a particularly bad day for me and the nurses had given me a sleeping aid so I could get a decent night's rest. While waiting for it's effects to kick in, I sent my brother a text.

"How are you holding in there, sis?"

"I'm okay, I'm on a lot of different drugs right now. They gave me a sleeping aid tonight, I think I'm starting to feel it kick in."

"Wow, I've never taken one before, that must be strange. Let me know how it works out!"

"Haha, sure thing. I've never had one before either. I'm starting to feel really dizzy and the world's spinning. I should try to sleep now. Goodnight, little brother."

"Goodnight. Go chase rabbits into the woods and such."

On day twenty, give or take, I was finally released from the confines of the hospital. Fresh air had never, ever, felt so good. I was a tube free woman once again. My freedom was short lived as I ended up back there a week later, but this time I only had to stay for five days. For the next year and a half, I was a frequent patient, but my trips became shorter and shorter, they usually ended up only being a day or two. My appendix was never found. That still sounds so strange to me. How could it not be found? Where did it go? It's a mystery.

I still suffer from the odd bad days, my stomach will never quite be the same, but that is such a small price to pay. A very small price considering the alternative.

My recovery was frustrating. I was quite weak and fragile, but I was at home, in my own bed, with the freedom of fresh air. It was mid October, and we were blessed with an abnormally sunny one. I would often sit on the deck, overlooking the horse pasture and barn. Tess would graze nearby and stand as close as she could while I spoke softly to her, venting my limitations to someone. Although I was tube free, I was watched like a hawk by the family, they didn't trust me to not over do it. I had a problem sitting still. I had spent close to two months lying in a bed, and I was ready to feel useful again. Unfortunately for me, my body did not receive the memo. I could take thirty steps safely, anymore than that and my stomach would receive sharp, shooting pains that would threaten to knock me off my feet. The world around me would sway and grow fuzzy until I sat down to let it pass. It was so frustrating. I was banned from doing barn chores, and that I understood. I could not picture myself hauling a full wheelbarrow and tossing hay bales. The thought alone was enough to make me faint. I stared down at Tess, her large eyes stared back at me, begging me to go see her. I leaned back in my chair, looking for those who would stop me. My mom was at work, and my Oma was in the kitchen sewing. I glanced at the clock outside. Almost noon, Tess's lunch time.

My step-dad worked from the home office this week and had been placed in charge of feeding Tess. He was a little skittish around horses and Tess liked to have fun with that. She was a very large horse and she knew it. She would often watch quietly as my step-father would enter her domain. For the most part she would follow him politely until she grew bored of being well behaved and then all hell would break loose. She would heave her massive haunches off the ground in one swift motion and dance, making the ground shake in protest. Tess would toss her large, beautiful head and simply begin to run as fast as she could, sliding to a stop at the last minute. I had often watched this scene break out time and time again from the confines of the deck. It would always play out the same, my step-father would jump to high heaven, yelping, and run behind a tree, cursing all the while at the large horse. I would shake my head and laugh, even though it hurt my stomach.

"Tess! You silly, evil girl. Get over here now!" I would call. And she listened. Tess would slam her massive body into a stop, raise her head, and flick her ears in my direction. I would cluck to her, and like a large dog she would trot toward me, eyes dancing. I would bet my life on the fact that she was laughing.

I smiled at the memory and carefully got up off the chair. I took a few slow steps to the house, I did not hear my step-dad getting ready. He was never in a hurry to feed the 'dinosaur' as he called her. I gingerly looked at the barn, it was a good sixteen feet from the deck. I really shouldn't try, it would max out my daily step limit. But my eyes fell to my horse. I missed her so much and I knew she had missed me. I had raised her from a foal and we had developed a very strong connection. Tess felt my eyes fall on her. She let out a very loud neigh.

"Shhh!" I shushed her. "Don't give me away just yet."

I grabbed the railing and held on with all of my might as I headed down the stairs. My leg muscles were nonexistent and quivered uselessly; I needed to bring them back. Once I had both feet on the solid ground, I picked my way to the barn. I felt very unsteady as I had nothing or no one to hold on to. I kept my gaze on my destination and kept moving forward, stopping to catch my breath here and there. *Stupid body, work with me here!* I finally arrived at the main gate that led into the large treed paddock. Tess was waiting for me, nickering.

"Shh, big girl. Let's keep this our little secret okay?"

I let myself in and Tess lowered her lovely head. I pressed my forehead against hers and breathed her in. This was where I belonged. I looked back at the barn. My heart fell into my stomach. This was going to be hard.

I looked up at my big horse, studying her. "You have to help me out, girl. If you want me to feed you, I need your patience."

I shuffled closer to her, and tossed my arm to her withers, and grabbed onto a chunk of her mane. I pressed my weight against her side and held on. "Okay, big girl, let's go to your stall. Walk slow."

To my surprise, she did. She seemed to sense I wasn't my usual self; she was very careful around me. The upward stretch of my arm sent my stomach into a frenzy, it hurt so much. I let out a gasp and faltered. Tess stopped and waited for me to collect myself. "Good girl, Tess," I cooed. "Good girl, we're almost there."

Tess stopped in front of the tack room door. I let my arm fall to my side and gave her a hearty pat. Before I could start the task that lay ahead, I had to wait for my heart to slow and my breath to grow steady. *This is ridiculous, I feel like an old woman. Slow and steady I suppose.* Once my breathing returned to normal, I opened the door and stepped inside the tack room. I walked past the row of saddles and made my way to back corner of the room. I opened another door, and stepped inside the hay barn. I glanced down wearily at the large hay nets scattered below my feet. This would be a workout and a half. There once was a time when I could carry four at once, two slung over each shoulder; I would be lucky to manage even one at this point. I bent over, and with a moan, I picked up one of the nets. I began to make my way out of the barn into the paddock. Tess waited for me eagerly, and when I stepped outside, her nostrils quivered in a silent nicker.

"Go to your tree," I motioned to her with my hands. Tess had a few favorite trees in the paddock that she claimed as her own. We had hung hooks on them so we could tie the hay nets securely to her 'special' spots.

Tess did as asked and I envied the speed in her step. "I'll be there sometime tomorrow," I mumbled.

I lagged behind slowly. Confusion was heavy in Tess's eyes, yet she waited. I finally arrived and reached up toward the hook, grimacing as the pain tore through my mid section. "Oh, hell!" I cursed out. Pushing the pain aside, I finished what I had set out to do. I settled onto the dirty ground and watched my happy horse pull at her hay. I wrapped my arms tightly around the middle, and rocked myself slowly side to side. *Pain, please go away. Do not come again another day.* A loud, slightly angry voice captured my attention. I looked over to see my step-dad marching to me. *Uh oh, I'm in for it now.*

"Ryleigh! What do you think you're doing out here? Your mom is going to kill me for this!"

I looked at him, eyes wide with slight amusement. "She will not kill you. I won't say anything if you don't."

My step-dad's eyes took me in. "You all right?"

"No," I sighed angrily, "I am sore."

"You pushed yourself too much. Here," he extended his hand down and pulled me up.

"Thanks." I looked back at Tess. "See you later pretty girl."

I hooked my arm around my step-father's and used him as a crutch as he led me to the safety of the house. I knew where I would be heading; to the comfort of my bed and the relief of pain medication. And that's exactly what I did. I slept well into the next day.

⌘

After the stunt I pulled at the barn the day before 'Ryleigh' watch was now in full swing. Those in the house watched me like a hawk, even the neighbors conveniently stopped by to make sure I behaved. They had nothing to worry about. The walk to the barn had done me in. I had nothing but pain for the next three days. I was stuck in the confines of the bed, and I began to sulk. The sun peeked through the blinds, taunting me, yet I was stuck, motionless, and popping pain medication like candy. Finally I felt a little better and was able to go outside. Maggie followed me like a shadow and I knew she missed our daily hikes. "One day, girl. One day soon, I hope." I ruffled her ears as I pouted.

After everything I had been through, you would think I would have learned my lesson. I blame my family genes. Stubbornness runs strong throughout my mother's side of the family, and I am no exception. My eyes once again fell to the barn and my horse. Over the past few days, I had been feeling a little bit stronger and I wanted to push the boundaries. Without a second thought, I got out of my chair and began the journey to the barn. Tess again neighed loudly at my arrival. I waved my arms frantically and begged her to stay quiet. I stepped inside the paddock when I heard my mom's voice behind me. I froze.

"Ryleigh."

I turned, guilty to face her. "Hello, sweet Mother of mine."

With her hands placed on her hips she sighed heavily. "What am I going to do with you girl?"

I looked down at my feet and said nothing.

She sighed loudly. "Fine. I can't tie you to the bed, though I would like to. I know once you set your mind to something, that's it. But what I will do," she paused to take a semi frustrated breath, "is this. I will do the heavy lifting, and you will watch. Does that sound fair?"

I smiled brightly. "Sounds like a plan!"

And so began our daily adventure. The days passed and turned into weeks. I had slowly but surely gotten stronger. I was able to carry one hay net without nearly passing out, and one hay net slowly turned into two. By the time I was nearly three months into my recovery, I was able to start slowly with barn chores. I started with the little things like sweeping the barn aisle and filling waters. That eased into scooping horse poop and cleaning stalls. Five months into recovery, I was able to move a wheelbarrow by myself. I also began to take Maggie for short walks. They started down the driveway and back, and then progressed with short trips down the road. All of these happened slowly, and the few bad days that found me would keep me in bed for a week at a time. It was my body's way of shaming me for pushing too far too fast. I had grudgingly, learned to accept limits and tried to listen to my body's warning signs before they reached the point of no return.

Eight months into recovery, I was able to complete one of my and Maggie's favorite hikes. It was a 5K hike around the lake. The terrain was varied, flat stretches, steep hills, and bridge crossings. What normally used to take me under an hour had taken two. But I did not care. As I cleared the last stretch of the trail and saw my truck in the parking lot, I nearly burst into tears of happiness. I could have shouted to the moon and back, for I had done what I thought I would never be able to do again. There was one last thing that I needed to attempt before it was time to move forward with my life.

"Are you sure you want to do this?" My mom asked, worry in her voice.

I rubbed my hands together in anticipation and looked up at Tess. "Without a doubt."

"Okay, but I don't like this idea."

"I know." I stepped toward the big horse with a halter and a lead rope in one hand. "Head down," I clucked. Tess did as was asked, she dropped her head to my shoulder. *I am glad I taught you that when you were still a wee little thing.* I slipped her head into the rope halter and clipped on a set of reins.

"Okay, big girl, don't throw me off, please. You're a long way down, and I don't bounce like I used too." I led Tess next to the large mounting block that was more like a small picnic table.

"You should at least put a saddle on, don't you think, Ryleigh?"

"It doesn't feel like a saddle day, Mom. This feels perfect."

"Well, at least the hospital knows who you are at this point," my mother muttered to no one in particular.

I shot her an exasperated look and rolled my eyes. I stepped onto the top of the mounting block and got ready to swing a leg over Tess's wide back. She side stepped away and I was caught off balance. My mother took a sharp gasp in, but I steadied myself quickly and stepped off the block toward Tess. I repositioned her and placed my hands on the side her head. "I know, girl. It's been awhile. You know what to do. Be a good horse for me."

Once again, I stepped onto the large block, swung my leg over, and with a quick hop, I launched myself onto Tess. I grabbed a handful of mane and let my heels hang freely. My heart burst into a happy song. I tapped my heels lightly against her side. "Walk on." She did. I felt every muscle, every powerful fiber move beneath my seat. It was pure heaven. I smiled so hard, my cheeks hurt, but I did not care. I was once again sitting atop my horse. I was home. It was now time to pick up the pieces and move forward to bigger and better things. I had been given the green light healthwise, and applied for jobs on the mainland. I was lucky enough to get hired for a reputable company. It was now time for me to move, once again. And that's where this story really begins.

CHAPTER 3

It was a cool, crisp November evening and I was in the process of settling into my new place. The move had been a bigger task than I expected. I would be quite content to never have to look at a moving box ever again, or unload in the pouring rain for that matter. Tonight was a big night; Bryce and I would finally meet face to face. After a lot, and I mean a lot of coaxing from friends, I finally joined in on the whole online dating craze. It was kind of fun, a little bit like online shopping really. Narrow down age, height, postal code, build, hell, even hobbies. I did get a kick out of reading how they chose to, let's say, "advertise" themselves. I must admit, I did not have a lot of faith in the procedure but a few close friends of mine had success so I thought, what the hell, what do I have to lose? A few bad dates ahead of me I'm sure, but who knows. I was in a new town, and at the very least, it got me out there meeting some new people.

I was still on the island when Bryce and I began our daily conversations. We had been talking for over three weeks now, and though it was only over the phone, he left me with a very good impression. We shared many of the same interests and goals in life. I liked that he made an effort to get to know me, it wasn't all about him, there was already a give and take. I was definitely intrigued. Now that I was living in the same area, it was finally time to look each other in the eyes. I was in the midst of unpacking, attempting to make my new house a home, when my phone jingled.

"Is it bad that I'm nervous to meet you?"

I read the text across my phone and smiled happily, the butterflies growing in my own stomach.

"Nope. I must confess I'm nervous too. So you're not alone in this."

"Good. See you soon!"

Bright headlights lit up my small basement suite half an hour later. The crunching of gravel in the driveway sent shivers down my spine, he was here. I ran to the bathroom to give myself one last inspection in the mirror. I gave my long auburn hair one last tousle and sent the loose waves dancing down my back. I was ready.

"I think I'm here?"

I ran to my phone to respond. "You're here. Maggie and I will be right there."

I slipped into my boots and clipped the leash to Maggie's collar. "Here we go, girl!"

Maggie followed me, her long tail wagged happily. I stepped into the brisk night air and watched my breath float in a white cloud. I took a deep breath in, and rounded the corner, stepping into the drive. A dark blue pick up truck was parked near the mailbox. A silver tool box in the back reflected the glow of the streetlight. I smiled to myself. *He drives a truck.* That's one big check off the wish list. The driver door swung open and Bryce stepped out. He stood about 5'10" and had an athletic build. My eyes lingered on his broad shoulders, I had a thing for a good set of shoulders. His short brown hair was tucked under a hat, and he wore blue jeans with a pair of boots. Bryce had a military look about him, with his chiseled face, and high set cheekbones. His features, while strong, were warm and slightly lit with nerves.

He gave a small, crooked smile and strode toward me. "Hi, it's nice to finally meet you in person." His voice was smooth and quiet. His brown eyes were lit with a gentle kindness.

My heart begun to beat unevenly. I grinned in what I hoped looked like a confident manner. "It's nice to meet you too."

There was already something about him that had me thinking he was going to leave an imprint. He was going to have some sort of an impact on my life. I couldn't find anything specific to pin point. It was merely a gut instinct. He gave me a careful study before he wrapped me in a quick hug. As his arms encircled me, I took him in, he smelled good. I returned the embrace and we stepped back. His eyes fell to Maggie and he reached out to pet her. Maggie pressed herself against my right leg and I laughed, giving her a light smack.

"I'm sorry," I began, "Maggie's a big chicken. It takes her awhile to warm up to people she doesn't know. She's got 'stranger danger' down pat."

His eyes studied her and he smiled slowly. "Ah. Gotcha. That's cute."

We stood for a moment, each of us a little unsure where to go from here. Both of us were on the quiet side. I was not used to being around a man who was almost as quiet as I could be. Normally I dated men who were forward and generally took hold of the conversation. It drew me out of my shell rather quickly. I felt comfortable around those who liked to talk as it balanced out my own silence. Bryce was different, we were on an equal playing field and it made me a little uneasy.

His eyes fell to my truck. "Ah," he began and walked toward it, "you drive a Ford."

I laughed. "Don't you even start that."

He chuckled, eyes shining. He drove a GMC, I drove a Ford. Friendly war had been declared awhile back when we were on a phone only basis.

He made his way around my Ford and he looked back at me. "I'll admit, it's a nice looking truck."

I placed my hands on my hips and smirked. "I know, but thank you." My eyes lingered on his own vehicle. "I think I need to give yours the stamp of approval." I walked purposeful to his and whistled. "It's a nice looking vehicle," I nodded to a large dent on his driver door. "What happened here?"

He stroked his jaw. "Ah, yes. That. A deer ran into me early in the morning, didn't see it until it was too late. It scared the crap out of me."

I laughed. "Aw, I can imagine. Was the deer okay?"

"I don't know. I hope so. It took off running."

"Hmm, poor thing." I looked up at him. "Do you want to go for a walk? Admire some Christmas lights?"

"Sure."

"Okay. This way." I gestured to the left. He followed along quietly. We walked side by side in silence. I felt him steal glances my way. Tonight was not a planned meeting, it had been a last minute idea. Bryce got his son every other weekend and he was in my area, as he had to drop off his little boy to the child's mother. I had suggested if he wanted to get together on his way back home for a quick meet and greet. He agreed. We made small talk throughout our night stroll and soon enough we were back in front of my house. We stood beside his truck. "This was nice," he said.

I smiled back shyly. "It really was. Have a good night, and thanks for coming out."

He gave me another hug. "It was my pleasure. I'll talk to you tomorrow," he paused before getting in his truck. "You have a very pretty voice." With that, he slid inside and fired up the engine. I turned, heading back to the house with a smile on my face. I had a good feeling about him.

⌘

"Good morning, beautiful."

"Good morning!"

"I had a lot of fun last night. I'm so glad we finally met. I'm going out for drinks with coworkers tonight. Can I see you tomorrow?"

"I'll be free. What time were you thinking?"

"The earliest you want me there I'll be there…with bells on. Of course, since I'm the morning person I'd even suggest we watch the sunrise together. But I know you don't enjoy mornings so you might think I'm crazy."

I laughed and rolled my eyes. Morning's weren't all that bad for me, especially if I had something to wake up for. I thought silently to myself for a moment when an idea flitted through my mind.

"Haha, okay. How about we meet up at 10:00? I have an idea. Come to my place, I will take us the rest of the way. We can save some of your gas."

"Sounds good! This will give me motivation not to drink too much tonight. I'll tell them all I've got a hot date."

"Glad I could help. Enjoy your day!"

"I will. You too. Can't wait for tomorrow."

I busied myself most of the day with setting up all of my things. Kitchen, check. Bedroom, check. Bathroom, check. Living room, check and check.

The radio played my favorite country station when I flopped onto the couch. The clock read 8:30 p.m. The day had flown by, which suited me just fine. I looked around at my progress and smiled, the house was beginning to feel like a home. The entertainment center was now set up, and below the main window I placed the couch. Next to the couch was an end table which held a lamp, and my precious radio. The walls were no longer empty, I hung what little art work I owned along with personal photographs. I pulled back the curtain to peek outside at my new surroundings. Under the glow of the streetlight, snow fell lightly. Excitement bubbled within me. "Come on, Maggie. I think we need to go for a walk."

I ran up the first flight of stairs that led me to the main back door. I stepped onto the deck, locked the door behind me, and let myself through the gate. Maggie and I hopped around the corner, both filled with excitement when I nearly collided into Brian. The house that I now called home was a fourplex. Three other people lived here, and we all had our own suites. Everybody in the house was in their mid twenties and we all got along fairly well. I often saw Brian, who lived in the attic suite. We shared the back door, as the other two tenants had their own entrances and decks in the front portion of the house. It was rather perfect really, as Brian was my 'cowboy' as I called him. He was in school to become a Farrier, a specialist in horse hoof care. Brian was a laid back type of guy, and we both shared a love for country music, and horses, of course. Not to mention Brian was very easy on the eyes. He had sandy blond hair and possessed the most amazing set of blue eyes I had ever seen. I often found myself lost amongst them, I really had to pay attention to our conversations and remember to respond when appropriate. "Whoa!" Brian stepped back, smiling. His dark blue eyes sparkled beneath his hat. "Someone looks excited. I'm going to take a wild guess and say it's the snow that's got ya all fired up?"

I grinned widely and stared into his eyes dreamily. "You'd be correct. I love the snow!"

He grinned warmly. Brian almost always had a smile on his face. "Me too." He leaned down to ruffle Maggie's ears. "Have fun." He gave me a wink and headed to the back door, grocery bags in hand.

The neighborhood was quiet this evening. The familiar stillness from the falling snow was a comfort. The white blanket covered up the world, taking all the noise away with it. The night air held a magical enchantment, perhaps because the holiday season drew near. The cozy homes resembled a holiday card as they basked in the soft glow of Christmas lights. I wrapped my arms around myself in contentment, and watched as Maggie ran ahead of me, hopping from snow bank to snow bank, every once in awhile she would plant her face in the snow. *My silly girl.* Finally it was time to head home. Maggie and I did a final loop around the block and followed the snow covered trail until it took us to the end of the drive, neither of us in a particular hurry to end the evening. I looked at the old brown and white farmhouse. Home sweet home. It stood proudly tonight, showing off its own Christmas lighting. Yes, I felt good about this move. Something felt right, and it was high time my luck should change for the better.

⌘

My phone jingled, stirring me out of a very content slumber. I peeked my head out from the covers, blew the hair out of my eyes, and reached for the phone.

"I drank way too much last night."

"Uh oh. Are you still up for today?"

"I am hung over, but super excited to see your pretty face. I'll hop in the shower and head to you."

"See you soon!"

Forty minutes later Bryce pulled into the drive. Once I saw his truck, I went outside to meet him. He hopped out of the truck with a lopsided smile, clutching a cup of coffee against his chest for dear life. Although he looked tired, his brown eyes lit up when he spotted me. It sent my heart into another uneven beat.

I shot him a smirk. "Look at you. Don't you look fresh as a daisy."

His eyebrows rose and his brown eyes opened wide in surprise. "Oh, I bet. I feel like I'm going to fall over."

I stepped toward him laughing, and he wrapped his strong arms around me. I settled neatly against his chest and liked the way we fit together. For someone who was severely hung over, he still looked good and he smelled even better. *You are going to be trouble.*

"Morning," he smiled, looking down at me warmly.

I grinned back. "Morning, sunshine. Come on, hop in the truck. We have places to go and things to see!"

He looked intrigued and raised a single brow. "All right. I'm game."

We buckled up and I started the engine, rubbing my hands together. It was definitely crisp out. I loved it. I flicked on the radio and placed the truck in drive. Bryce leaned back into his seat and sighed in contentment. I glanced over at him and couldn't help but wonder just how badly his world spun at the moment.

"So," he looked curious, "where are we going?"

"I am giving you a walk down memory lane. I grew up out this way years ago. We'll swing by the house I used to live in since it's on the way, and then I thought we could take a walk around the lake I used to go to as a kid."

His eyes widened. "Oh! That's a neat idea."

"Good! I thought so." I looked at him with a sly grin. "The fresh air should do you good, walk off your liquor."

He groaned. "I know, I know. I'm sorry."

"Don't worry about it, things happen. I'm glad you came out to see me."

He smiled, a little shyly. "I wouldn't have missed it."

A warm feeling trickled into my heart and settled into my stomach, another good answer. I tried to play it somewhat cool and collected, but I couldn't contain my smile. I let it spread widely across my face.

"Oh, ow, my head." Bryce groaned, and held his hand against his forehead. "What is that sound?"

I furrowed my brows and listened intently. The radio was on low, other than that, I didn't hear anything out of the ordinary. "I don't hear anything. What does it sound like?"

"It's a steady squeal," he moaned.

My eyebrows shot up and I began to laugh. "Oh, I'm sorry. It's my heater, it has a bit of a squeal to it. I'm so used to it that I don't hear it anymore." I glanced his way quickly, his brown eyes processed what I had told him. "Sorry, buddy, but it's cold out and I need the heat or I will freeze! However, what I can do is turn the music up. It'll drown out the squeal for you. Deal?"

He laughed. "That'll work."

"Mmk." I leaned forward and turned the music up, chuckling. He watched me with somewhat of an entertained expression and settled deeper into the seat. A little while later, we turned down the old street where I grew up. The truck began to climb the snow covered hill at a steady pace.

We slid a little bit and I patted the dashboard humming to a song that played. "Come on, girl, you can do it." The tires caught and we once again had traction. I pulled next to the curb outside a light brown and white house. "Well," I began, "there it is. The house I grew up in."

I stared at the house silently, so many memories replayed through my head. I felt like I had stepped back in time, for I could see all of us kids running around the front lawn, screaming out in joy. This house was the last place, the only place, that held good memories of my father. Although he never did stick around long, in this house he had been somewhat of a father to us kids, even if it was only for a little while. The tender old ache appeared deep within my chest, it always hurt when I thought about him. Bryce leaned forward in his seat taking it in. "It's cute. Very nice."

I nodded. "Okay. Let's head to the lake shall we?"

"Sure," he was quiet for a moment. "Do you have a name for your truck?"

I glanced his way quickly. "I do, actually. It's nothing special. I call her my Beast."

He nodded. "All right. The Beast it is."

"How about you?" I asked curiously.

"I sure do. Guinevere."

My eyebrows rose up. "Jeez, that's quite the name."

He laughed. "Yeah, it is. It's the name of one of my favourite songs 'Guinevere' from the Eli Young Band. They're one of my favorites."

"Huh, I'll have to check out that song. I like them, but I haven't heard that one."

"You definitely should. It's a good one." He looked my way. So, you're a country music girl?"

I smiled. "You bet. I love it."

"Good, me too. I listen to music a lot, and in my truck…well, I sing pretty hard core. I don't care who's watching me."

I laughed brightly. "Oh, I love that! Do you dance too?"

"Of course," he said matter of factly.

It was a short drive from the old house to the small lake. It sure had changed over the years. As the population grew, so did the trail. The path now went around the entire lake, neatly taken care of. Every time I came here it was bittersweet. Memories of my childhood flashed like a film; this lake had been a major player. It was a different time back then, one where my parents were still together.

"We're here!" I announced.

We hopped out of the truck, and after a few slips and slides in the slushy parking lot, we came together shoulder to shoulder. Our safe, flat surface came to an end and it was time to make our way down the hill that would take us to the lake path. The decline was painted in slippery slush.

"I wonder who's going to fall first?" Bryce wondered out loud. He gave me a sly grin. "My boots don't have that much grip."

I lifted the corner of my mouth. "Well, if one of us is going to fall, I hope it's you." I let out a defeated sigh. "However, you are with me, so if one of us is going down, it's most likely me."

He laughed out loud. "Ah, you're a clumsy one are you?"

I turned my mouth downwards. "Oh, you have no idea. I am the Queen of accidents."

A half smile played on his mouth and he lowered his voice. "Good to know."

The temperature was much cooler by the water. I stuck my hands deep into my pockets. Bryce pulled out a pair of leather work gloves and pulled them onto his hands. "Hmm, these smell like horse. I haven't used them in awhile. The last time I wore them I was at the barn."

I looked back at him. "That's not a bad smell to have."

"Ha, I guess that depends on who your company is, but I guess not."

"Well, you're with a horse crazy girl so I certainly don't mind it what-so-ever. I miss it."

Conversation came easily today. Bryce would often reach down into the snow and form snowballs within his palms. I admired the way he threw them with a strong grace. I would not look that good. He formed another snowball as I strode ahead of him, continuing on with my conversation until I realized he was no longer in step with me. I stopped to turn when the impact of something cold and wet hit me in the shoulder. I looked down in surprise. A wad of snow started to melt downwards upon my jacket. My eyes settled on him and he looked mighty proud of himself.

He grinned broadly and held up his hands in a helpless gesture. "Sorry, I couldn't help myself."

I laughed. "Uh-huh. I don't know what it is about me, but people always pick on me. They don't have to know me for very long before it starts." I placed my hands on my hips and tilted my head to one side. "Case in point."

He laughed. "I don't know what to tell you. You're pretty cute, and I'm not going to lie, it was fun, for me at least."

I gave him a playful shove. "Jee, thanks." I looked at him quickly. "So, tell me about your little boy."

A warmth fell over his face. "He's one of the best things to ever happen to me. I swear, I could stare at him forever. Kids change you. I had to grow up really fast when he came along. It was no longer just myself I had to look out for. I was suddenly responsible for a new life."

"I can tell how much you love him. How old is he?"

"Thank you. He'll be five in January."

"That's a good age. They grow up so fast."

"They sure do, too fast for my liking," he paused. "So, are you close with your parents?"

"I am with my mom. Not so much with my dad. He hasn't been around much."

He nodded slowly. "I'm sorry to hear that."

I sighed. "Me, too. What about you?"

"I'm close with my mom and grandparents. My uncle is pretty much like a dad to me. I don't really speak to my father."

"I know how that goes. I'm sorry to hear that." I paused slightly. "I'm pretty close to my step-dad though. He's been more of a dad to my brother and me than our father ever has."

Bryce nodded and met my eyes. "Good. I'm glad you have him."

"Me too."

We walked in silence for awhile, enjoying the comfort of each other's company and then he spoke. "Are you close with your grandparents?"

My face fell slightly; he hit all the sore spots. "I was very close with my oma. We lost her very unexpectedly a few months ago. I'm not close to my dad's side of the family. When he left, they didn't make much of an effort to be there for us or help us out. We went through a pretty rough time, and my mom was a young mother. It was hard on her…on all of us, really."

His face softened as he gazed back at me. "Oh, that's too bad, I'm sorry." He was quiet for a moment and his voice lit up. "Well, you can borrow my grandparents, then." I laughed in surprise. "Well, thank you. What are they like?"

"They really love each other. Their morning routine is always the same. It starts with a hug and a kiss, and in their pyjamas they eat breakfast together, and read the morning paper. My grandma is really sweet and warm. My grandpa doesn't say too much, but when he does, it's blunt and the truth. He doesn't sugar coat anything." He paused and continued. "I once said to them, not too long ago, that I hope to be like them one day. Without missing a beat my grandpa said 'Well, then you better stick with one girl or you'll never find it.'" Bryce grinned a crooked smile and continued. "I told my grandpa I will when she's the right one. Why should I have to settle for someone who doesn't make me happy? That's not what love is about."

His brown eyes fell onto me and I nodded. "True enough. Love should never be about settling."

"Exactly my point."

We began our way up the hill leading to the parking lot. I glanced over at him. "How are you feeling?"

He looked upwards. "Actually, I'm feeling pretty good right now. I think the fresh air and moving around helps."

I smiled triumphantly. "Good! I figured it would help."

We climbed into my truck and Gord Bamford's '*When Your Lips are so Close*' came on the radio. I clapped my hands in excitement. "I love this song!"

A half smile played on his lips, one I was already growing so fond of. "Yeah? Me too. It's a good one."

I put the truck in reverse and pulled onto the main drag. "Do you smoke?"

He wrinkled his lip. "No. It's a gross and disgusting habit. I can't stand it." He looked at me with a slightly apologetic look. "I guess I should have asked if you do before I gave my opinion."

I laughed quietly. "No, no. I don't and I agree with you."

He relaxed. "Okay, good." He bit his lip quickly. "You don't have any kids, right?"

I shook my head. "Nope. Just my four legged critters."

He smiled. "Do you want kids?"

"I do, one day."

He nodded. "That's good." He paused, hesitating ever so slightly. "Have you ever been with someone who you wanted to start a family with?"

I thought about it for a moment. "No. Not really. I've been with some nice guys but none of them were exactly long term potentials."

"Gotcha."

A familiar tune started playing on the radio. "Oh! Jason Aldean!" I exclaimed.

He smiled again. "You're good at this."

I smiled. "Thanks! I'm very into my music."

"I like that. Me too. I'm glad we like the same stuff."

"It helps that's for sure. I went to his concert last summer. It was amazing! I had much fun." I glanced at him and he made an unpleasant face. "What's the face for? You don't like him?"

"No, I do. I was supposed to be at that concert. I had gotten my girlfriend and myself tickets. A week before the concert we had a huge fight and that was it. I couldn't do it anymore," he paused, "she kept the tickets and took some guy with her that she used to fool around with."

I winced in sympathy. "Aw, that's a crappy deal. I'm sorry to hear that."

He shrugged. "Yeah, it's alright."

I looked at him quickly. "Was it a serious relationship?"

He kept his eyes out the window. "We used to live together. After we broke up, I moved out, and for a little while we lived on the same street. Every morning on my way to work I'd pass her place and she would send me texts like *'It must suck for you to have to drive past me everyday'* and such. She'd post a lot of inappropriate things to my Facebook wall too..." he frowned slightly.

I was quiet for a moment. *This is awkward, what do I say?* "Ah, I see. One of those," was all I could manage.

He nodded. "Yeah, but that's in the past. Time to start new."

"That's a good way to look at it...a fresh, new chapter."

Once again, we were back at my place. I pulled into the snowy drive, stuck the truck into four-wheel, and began to reverse into the parking spot reserved for me. It was a tight squeeze as it was at a slightly awkward angle, right next to a tall evergreen tree and Cody's car was in the next spot over. I maneuvered myself carefully between the two and turned off the truck. I was aware of Bryce's eyes on me. I glanced up at him, he looked at me with a smile.

"What's up?" I asked carefully.

He smirked. "Not many girls can do that. I'm impressed."

I let out a light laugh. "Why, thank you."

We said our goodbyes and ended things with a quick embrace. I stood outside to watch him pull away and began to laugh. He was parked in a little snow bank and he did not have four-wheel drive. As he pressed down on the gas his truck slid back and forth before it finally caught traction. He grinned in the front seat and shook his head. I waved him goodbye and turned to head inside to the warmth of the house.

My phone jingled, a message from him. "I like spending time with you. You make me smile."

"I like spending time with you too. Drive safe."

⌘

"Oh, Ryleigh. My little china doll. How are you?"

"Morning handsome. I'm good. How are you?"

"I'm doing very well, thank you. I was wondering if you'd like to do something today? It's my weekend with Aiden, so I'm not sure how you feel about that…"

My head snapped up, and I bit my lip. Was I ready to meet his son? I think so. Nerves began to come to life from the idea. This was a huge part of Bryce's life, his entire world. I loved children and had worked with them for almost two years at one point in my life. But this…this was a whole new ballgame I would be stepping into. I held the phone carefully within my hands. *Jump in with both feet.*

"Sure! I would love to meet him. Looking forward to seeing you guys. Did you want to meet somewhere?"

"We'll pick you up in one hour."

"Okay. See you boys in a bit!"

I paced the kitchen aimlessly. I tried on three different outfits before settling on a pair of jeans and a button down red and white plaid shirt. I blew a piece of hair out of my eye impatiently. I hated waiting, the anticipation had time to fester and grow. I usually did pretty well if I was thrown into a situation and was left to sink or swim. It's the premeditated plans I had a harder time with. The waiting game was not my friend. I had an over active imagination, and it tended to taunt me with all the things that could go wrong. I decided to go fix my hair one last time and throw on some lip gloss.

A knock upon the door startled me. I opened it up and Bryce stood proudly next to an adorable little boy. His son's large, blue eyes stared at me curiously. Bryce smiled affectionately, holding on to his son's little hand.

"Hi," he turned to his son. "Aiden, this is Ryleigh. Ryleigh, this is Aiden."

I smiled warmly. "Hi, Aiden. How are you?"

Aiden looked up at me and gave a shy smile. He moved closer to his dad's muscular leg and answered in a quiet voice. "I'm good." He gave a timid grin and buried his head against his dad's jeans.

I smiled up at Bryce. He grinned right back. "Ready to go? I'm going to warn you, it's going to be a bit of a tight ride today. I only have a bench seat, and the car seat takes up a lot of room."

I waved my hand carelessly and locked the door behind me. "No worries."

I followed quietly to the vehicle and Bryce carefully hoisted his precious bundle into the car seat. I watched with a quiet appreciation as he buckled him in. "There you go, buddy." He looked at me and motioned for me to follow. "This way."

"Okay."

I followed him to the drivers side and he opened up the door. I glanced inside dubiously. Tight ride, he was not kidding. The car seat took up the entire passenger side and there wasn't much of a middle seat left. His truck was standard, and the gear shift sat where my feet were to go.

I looked back at him and he laughed. "Can you do it?"

I raised my eyebrows. "Are you kidding me? Of course I can." *I might have to do a few yoga moves to get there but I can do it. I hope.* I turned back to him. "This may not be graceful...umm, maybe you shouldn't watch."

He gave a bright laugh. "Oh, I have to now."

"Ah, lovely. Okay, here I go!"

With one foot placed inside I hopped in and began to scoot close to Aiden, who watched me with great interest. Once I had myself mostly in the right spot I realized there was nowhere to put my legs. I placed myself on an angle, lifted my feet over the stick shift, and placed them next to Aiden's. Bryce chuckled and got in. I leaned my back against his side and gave him a lopsided grin. "I'm in."

"You are," he smiled warmly, "and now it gives me a good excuse to be close to you." He reached for his seatbelt. "I don't mean to touch your butt, honestly. I'm just buckling up."

I laughed in surprise. "Sure, I believe you."

Bryce smirked. "Okay. There's a playground nearby, want to go?"

Aiden cheered and I smiled, looked like the idea was a winner. "Sounds like a plan."

It was a short ride to the park, merely across the street. We pulled in to the quiet parking lot and Bryce hopped out to unbuckle Aiden. I scrambled out Bryce's open door, and to my surprise Aiden crawled out behind me. He hopped out of the truck and smiled up at me. I grinned back.

I met Bryce's eyes and they danced with amusement. "I guess he chose to follow you."

I smiled. "He sure did."

Bryce pulled out a bottle of bubbles, and we stood next to each other talking quietly. Bryce dipped the large wand into the container and brought it to his lips, blowing softly. Bubbles of all shapes and sizes appeared, only to be taken by the breeze. The bubbles danced every which way, and in oversized gumboots Aiden chased after them, squealing in delight when he would catch one. I studied the child quietly, it was like looking at a much younger Bryce. They had the same dark hair and defined facial structure. The only difference I could see were their eyes. Bryce had warm, chocolate eyes whereas Aiden's were a deep blue. The little man was a real cutie.

"Come on, Dad! There's another playground!"

"Be right there, bud!" He glanced my way. "Shall we?"

"Let's go!"

Aiden took off running, as did Bryce. I followed behind at a slow jog. Aiden chose to play on the large playground castle, and Bryce jumped up to grab the monkey bars. With a strength and easy grace he pulled himself from bar to bar. Aiden clapped and watched with admiration. I kicked myself for not bringing my camera. These were the moments you want to remember in life, for it's the little things that add up to create such precious memories.

"Can you come up here with me?"

I looked down in surprise as Aiden stared up at me, big eyes hopeful. *How can you say no that face?* "Of course I will!"

His eyes lit up and he ran for the ladder. I followed and we stood at the top of the playground castle, over looking the soccer field. I let my mind wander. If Bryce and I were to get serious, I could do this. I could be a part of this world. I looked down at the little boy and found myself grinning.

"Hey bud, are you getting hungry yet?" Bryce called from down below.

"No!"

Bryce looked at me. "He's never hungry. It's like he forgets to eat."

"Don't you remember what it's like to be a kid? There's too much to do besides sit still and eat."

"True enough," Bryce stared up at the sky. "It looks like rain is coming."

The temperature shifted, and the air felt damp. "It does," I agreed.

Bryce looked at Aiden. "Hey, bud. Did you want to go to Chuckey Cheese?"

Aiden's eyes lit up like a Christmas tree, excitement pulsed through his little body. "Yes!!"

Bryce laughed and gave me a wink. "All right, let's go!"

⌘

The big mouse freaked me out. I stared at the big mascot waving to the kids and was baffled at how a giant mouse could comfort children. But then again, I was also terrified of clowns and they were a popular staple at children's parties. I stared back at the large gray mouse with the permanent smile, and couldn't help but wonder how badly it must smell in the costume. As it turns out, I wasn't the only one who was scared. As we neared the giant rodent, Aiden threw himself into his dad's leg and held on tight.

"It's okay, buddy," Bryce said quietly stroking his head, "you're okay."

Once we passed the threat of the lurking mouse, I looked around at my surroundings. It was like a carnival for kids. Children ran squealing every which way. You really had to watch where you went, for the kids certainly didn't. Uninterested, stressed parents followed closely behind the racing little ones. Bright, flashing lights lit up the place and music from the games played to no end.

Aiden and Bryce played a few rounds and I watched close by. Aiden looked at me and came closer. "Do you want to play a game with me?"

"Of course. Which one?"

"Umm, the water gun one." He looked over at his dad.

"Sure, buddy. Let's get you set up."

Bryce put in the tickets and we each grabbed a squirt gun. The object of the game was to aim the gun at the marked spot to fill up a water balloon, whoever filled it first won. I honestly tried to lose on purpose, but somehow I managed to win the game. To my surprise, Aiden took it well. He looked over at me. "You won!" he shouted in excitement. The next game he chose to play was a video type game with a *Pirates of the Caribbean* theme. Aiden started to play, but the images frightened him. His eyes widened in horror at the graphic characters on the screen, and he dropped the controller. "Daddy!"

he squealed. "Please finish it!"

Bryce hopped into action and took over. Aiden stood a good two feet behind his dad and watched as best he could, sometimes covering his eyes. I stood next to him as a silent comfort. After Bryce finished his turn, the little guy hurried off to choose a new game. Bryce and I stood closely next to one another. He leaned in closer to me. "I like your shirt."

I smiled, and glanced at him and then his shirt. "I like yours, too." He wore a light blue and white plaid shirt, it hugged his shoulders nicely and revealed his strong forearms. The man looked good.

"I'm getting hungry. I think it's time for food." Bryce announced. "I'm thinking Ricky's. Would you like to join us for dinner, Ryleigh?"

"I would. Very much so."

"Okay, good." He smiled.

"After dinner I can take you home. I have to drop Aiden off at his mom's. Can I come see you afterwards?"

I didn't have to think twice. "I'd like that."

We settled into the booth at the restaurant. Bryce and Aiden sat next to each other, I sat across the table. The waitress came to take our orders. I was in the mood for something warm and comforting, I chose tomato soup and tea.

Bryce studied the menu. "I'll have your farmer's breakfast special, and this little guy here will have the waffles." He looked at me. "We like our breakfast foods."

I grinned. "It's the best meal of the day."

The waitress wrote down the orders quickly and looked at me. "Does he want whipping cream with his waffles?"

I was taken aback by her comment. She watched me as if I should know the answer, almost as if he was a part of me. "I—" I began.

Bryce smiled. "He will."

I looked at him in relief. He shot me a wink. Our food came quite quickly as the restaurant was quiet. I slurped my soup, and Bryce cut Aiden's waffles as they giggled and chatted up a storm. I melted. Love was written on both their faces. Bryce's face was filled with such affection as he gazed down at his son, while Aiden's was filled with an admiration of a man he hoped to be.

⌘

Bryce pulled in my driveway and hopped out. I unbuckled my seatbelt and Aiden reached for my arm gently. He held an electronic game in his hands and he tilted the screen toward me. "Wait! You like horses right?"

I nodded. "I sure do."

He grinned. "Okay. I drew this for you." He held the game up higher and I looked down at the screen. He had chosen a pony with a long flowing mane and tail, and colored it purple, my favorite color.

Warmth spread throughout my heart. "Thank you so much, Aiden. I love it," I studied the little child. "It was really nice to meet you."

He grinned, and swung his rubber boots from side to side. "You're welcome."

I hopped out, and stood in front of Bryce. He looked tenderly from his son to me with an expression I couldn't quite read.

"Thank you for today," I began, "I had a lot of fun."

His eyes found mine. "So did I. I'll see you later?"

"Okay, I'll be here. Drive safe."

While Bryce dropped off his son, I did a quick tidy up of the place. The radio forever played in my house, and I found myself humming along to a song. My phone jingled.

"Aiden's out like a light. He didn't even last ten minutes. We tuckered him out."

"Glad I could help."

"I should be back in forty minutes or so."

"Okay. See you soon."

Forty minutes seemed like an eternity to wait. I had already cleaned the entire place from head to toe. What else was there to do? Maggie sauntered over to me and sat down. She placed her head in my lap, begging for an ear scratch. I smiled and rubbed her head. "Did you want to go for a walk girl?" I was answered by a high pitch whine as Maggie ran to the door, wiggling in an uncontainable excitement. "I guess that's a yes? Okay, okay, I'm coming."

Our timing was perfect. Maggie and I returned from our walk, and as I took off my coat and shoes, a knock sounded at the back door. I opened it up expectantly and there he stood. He gave a shy smile, I grinned back and gestured him inside. He stood tall, yet there was an uncertainty about him. When Bryce was with his son he had a different air about him, and although it was a quiet one, it was confident. When he was with Aiden, he knew his role and he filled it well. With me however, I sensed a slight uneasiness, almost as though he was unsure of what to do next.

"Do you want the grand tour?"

"Sure."

"Okay. Follow me." The tour was quick. Although my place wasn't teeny tiny, it was definitely no mansion. It was cute and functional. I noticed his eyes kept resting upon the acoustic guitar propped neatly against my bedroom wall.

"Do you play?" I asked, hopeful. I was in the process of attempting to teach myself to play guitar. I could only plunk out a few chords here and there.

"You don't mind?" he asked, his eyes lighting up.

"Not at all. I'd love to hear it actually sound good for once."

He grabbed the guitar eagerly and sat on the couch. I settled next to him and leaned back against the cushion. He ran one finger down the strings and he winced. "Oh boy, she's a bit out of tune."

I made a face. "Yeah, I thought it sounded off."

"Do you have a tuner?"

"Mm, I'm sorry I don't."

"No worries, I think I have an app for that on my phone."

I rolled my eyes. "That's good. They have an app for everything these days don't they?"

He laughed quietly. "Yes."

I watched as he concentrated, picking the strings one by one. A small smile grew on his lips. "There, I think I have it now." He strummed the strings in unison and closed his eyes. He smiled. "Got it."

He looked at me quietly. Studying me. My heart beat faster and I looked away. "So," I said lightly, "what are you going to play for me?"

"I have something in mind." He focused his attention to the guitar resting upon his lap, and began to play a beautiful tune.

"Why do I recognize this?" I muttered to myself.

He smiled. "Keep listening. You'll get it."

I closed my eyes and let the music surround me. It wrapped me up in a warm embrace. My eyes flew open, "Oh!" I smacked my hands happily onto my thighs. "Is it Tim Mcgraw and Faith Hill '*I Need Your Love?*'"

His half grin appeared. "Yup."

"That's such a pretty song."

"It is." He was about to start into another song when his head snapped up, and he turned his ear toward the radio. "Who's this?"

"Oh, it's Tim Mcgraw's new song. I think it's called '*That Girl*', or something along those lines."

He gave me a sidelong glance and smiled. "You know your songs."

I grinned right back. "That I do."

He played for a while more before gently placing the guitar against the wall. "Are you going to play for me now?"

I gave a short laugh. "I'm not quite there yet. One day. Promise."

"Okay. I'll help you out."

My voice grew excited. "Really? You don't mind?"

"Not at all. We can have weekly jam sessions."

I felt somewhat dreamy. "Now that sounds like fun."

We both smiled and talked for a little longer before we decided to pop in a movie. "Do you want a blanket?" I offered.

"No, I'm good thanks. I always run a little hot."

"Ah you're one of those, a walking heater. I'm the opposite, I'm always cold."

"Such a girl," he teased.

I snuggled in the blanket and leaned against the pillow, making myself cozy. He fell back into the cushion and stretched his legs in front of him, crossing one foot over the other lazily. The movie was action packed, and yet, I found it hard to focus on the film that lay before us. My eyes kept drifting to him. His body appeared stiff, like he was afraid to move, and his eyes intently focused on the screen ahead. Every once in awhile I would reposition myself, and he gave me a sidelong glance that lingered every so often. We kept a careful distance between us, our every move was carefully calculated. Once the movie was over it was 11:30 p.m. He lived in the next town over; a half an hour drive away.

He got up slowly. "Well, I guess I should get going. I'm getting pretty tired," his eyes looked me over quickly. "You look sleepy."

I stifled a yawn. I was. "Just a bit." I smiled sheepishly. "The couch is really comfy if you wanted to stay," I offered quietly.

He glanced quickly from the couch to myself. "No, I think I should head home. Thanks though."

"Okay, well have a safe drive."

He nodded and pulled his boots on. "Thanks, I will." He stood and looked slightly unsettled. I raised my gaze to his, but he couldn't meet my eyes for very long. As I watched him, a quiet hope formed in the back of my mind. *I wonder if he'll be brave enough to kiss me.* My thought was dismissed as quickly as it had come on as he leaned in to give me a swift hug. I returned the embrace warmly, though to be honest, I was disappointed.

Bryce fought back a yawn. "I had fun today. It was nice to see you again."

"It was. Have a good night." I leaned myself against the wall as he slipped by me.

His hand paused on the door handle. "Sweet dreams, Ryleigh."

"Sweet dreams, Bryce."

⌘

"Good morning, my little china doll. How are you today?"

I groaned as the phone lit up the dark bedroom. I clumsily reached out for the nightstand, my face buried in the pillow. My fingers clasped around the cold object and I slowly raised my head. The phone read 5:00 a.m. *So very early.* But the text was from Bryce, and my frown turned into a grin.

I let my fingers do the talking. "Morning. What are you doing up so early?"

"Sorry to wake you. I'm just heading to the gym. Did you want to go for sushi today? Are you up for it?"

"Absolutely. Sushi is one of my favorites."

"Mine too. I will pick you up at noon. Go back to sleep."

"Haha, okay. That shouldn't be too hard."

It wasn't. I placed my phone back onto the nightstand, and let my head fall heavily against the pillow. I drew the covers closer to my body and snuggled deeply into the mattress. *Ah bed. Sometimes this is such a nice place to be.* A little while later my alarm woke me. I groaned, but thoughts of what lay ahead put a quick pep into my sleepy step. I had my morning shower, applied some make up, and let my hair fall into a purposeful tousle. I threw on a pair of black pants and slipped on a dark jade green pullover. I glanced in the mirror and nodded in satisfaction, simple, yet cute. My kind of style. Tires pulled into the drive and I peeked out the window. He was here. I quickly pulled on a pair of converse sneakers, grabbed a light jacket, and ran out the door.

A little while later we hopped out of his truck and began to make our way to the restaurant entrance. I headed for the door briskly, my nose following the delectable aroma that seeped from the restaurant. Visions of salmon rolls danced through my head, taunting my empty stomach. Bryce slowed his pace a little. I stopped and looked at him questionably.

He began hesitantly. "My ex lives around this area. I hope we don't run into her here. She'd probably punch me in the face."

My eyebrows shot up. "Seriously?" *She sounds like a lovely girl.* My stomach grumbled quietly in protest. I looked at the restaurant with such hope, we were so close to the comfort of good food.

He shrugged his shoulders. "Probably. She's that kinda girl."

I felt a hint of disappointment. "I see. Did you want to go somewhere else?"

"No, it should be fine. Come on, let's eat. I'm starved."

Thank God. "Okay, good. So am I!"

He ran slightly ahead and opened the door for me, gesturing me inside. I stepped into the building and my eyes widened. Pictures were everywhere.

No space on the walls or the ceiling was left unturned. Snapshots of smiling customers filled every inch of the place.

"Wow. They sure like their pictures here."

He grinned. "It's part of the charm."

We followed as the waitress led us to our booth. We slid inside, facing each other and put in our orders. The food came quickly, and the waitress spread our meals into a visual delight in front of us. My eyes widened with a child-like giddiness.

"This looks amazing." I sighed happily.

"Enjoy." Bryce picked up his chopsticks and began expertly picking up his food.

I stared down at mine dubiously. There were no forks on the table, only a set of chopsticks. I picked them up carefully and said a silent prayer. The last time I had used these my food went flying to a neighboring table.

He noticed my doubtful look. "You okay?"

"Yes. I'm not particularly skilled with chopsticks, so don't judge me." I leaned forward out of the booth, scanning the room for our waitress. "I wonder if they'd give me a fork," I mused.

Bryce shook his head back and forth. "Oh no, you don't. That's cheating." He grinned. "Besides, I like dinner and a show."

My mouth opened in slight horror. "Ha. Fine, I shall do my best."

I hated chopsticks. I stabbed at what I could, and brought what little bits of morsels I could get to my mouth. No matter how hard I tried my fingers just didn't seem to be coordinated enough to make them come together in a functional manner. I was so hungry, but I couldn't get the food in my mouth fast enough. I let out a few frustrated mutters, Bryce seemed to be enjoying this a little too much. I watched him in envy eat his meal with ease. *I hate you right now. I'm starving here!* I gave up and picked up the rolls with my fingers. I smiled in satisfaction as the food pleased my taste buds.

Once the meal was paid for, we began to make our way out of the restaurant, when something caught my eye. My eyes widened as I saw a man using a fork at the table. A fork. I stopped in my tracks, jaw dropped and I lightly smacked Bryce in the shoulder. "See! They do let you use forks!" I exclaimed.

He barked out a laugh, grabbed me by the shoulders and kept me moving out the door. "That's cheating! I love sushi, we'll be doing this a lot. You'll get the hang of it."

We climbed into the truck, and Bryce started the engine. The wiper blades brushed against the windshield slowly. "What do you want to do now?" he asked.

"Hmm. Well," I began, "there's a really nice park with trails nearby. Did you want to go for a walk? It's only drizzling out."

"Sure. What's it called?"

"Campbell Valley."

His face lit up in recognition. "I know where that is."

"Okay," I settled back into my seat, and he flicked on the radio. "Who's this?" he asked.

"Luke Bryan."

He smiled and shook his head. "Very good." He put the truck in drive and we made our way to the park.

⌘

"I hope to have a property like this one day."

Bryce stood still, taking in the surroundings. We had chosen a trail that led to an old farmhouse that had been around since the 1920's. The old white farmhouse was well preserved, and sat in a large open field surrounded by a protective border of tall evergreen trees. The old wooden barn lay a few feet behind the house, next to an old schoolhouse that was painted in a cheery yellow. We peeked inside the windows of the old school. It was empty. I studied it closer, and my imagination filled the empty space. I could picture students sitting in old desks, wearing matching uniforms as they stared up at a teacher in a dark dress. I reached for the door handle and tried to open the door, but it was locked. A fog began to roll over the farmstead, sunbeams shone down and broke through what breaks they could find. Raindrops glistened on the dewy leaves from the old oak tree that stood tall next to the school house. There was no noise from the city here, the old farm lay perfectly still.

I sighed, it was beautiful. "I wish I brought my camera."

He turned to me. "You should have. It's so pretty." His grin grew sly. "Every time you come here, you're going to think of me and this moment. You're going to kick yourself for not capturing this memory."

I groaned. "You're not helping! How was I supposed to know we were going to come here? For all I knew, we were just going out for sushi."

He smiled. "I'm sorry. I like bugging you."

We followed the bark mulch trail and walked in comfortable silence, each taking in the quiet beauty we were in the midst of. The ground was slightly squishy from the recent rainfall, and we hopped around near lying puddles that entered our path.

Bryce cleared his throat. "There's an old racetrack around here somewhere. I went there as a kid once."

"A horse track?"

"No, for car racing."

"Oh? Well, let's see if we can find it. That's something I would like to see." A frown appeared on my face again. "I really should have brought my camera. Dammit." He laughed. "Yes, you should have."

We found a map of the park and began to figure out a route that would take us to the track. "What do you think?" he said, "which way should we go?"

Hesitation filled my voice. "I'm not good with directions, or maps for that matter."

He raised an eyebrow. "Oh? Well then, I think I should leave you in charge."

I looked at him suspiciously. "Okay…if you're sure. You can't say I didn't warn you though."

"I like adventures. And this way if we get lost, I can blame you." He grinned. I studied the map closely, and carefully. "I think we should go this way." I gestured to the left. "I know the trail we need to get on, and it's on the opposite end of the park."

"All right," he looked around. "It would be faster if we crossed through those bushes." He stepped forward to investigate and frowned. "Hmm. Those puddles look deep."

I chuckled. "Aw, you're such a princess."

His eyes widened and he let out a good, loud laugh. "Princess? No one's ever called me that before." We matched our steps and he muttered under his breath. "Princess."

I laughed. "Sorry, I was just stating a fact."

"Did you want to cut across?" He gestured his arm openly.

I studied the path ahead, and glanced down at my converse sneakers. The water resembled more of a small pond than a puddle. A sheepish grin appeared. "My feet will get soaked."

He laughed again. "Ah-ha! Who's the Princess now?"

The track held an eerie quality to it. It was so quiet, a far cry from back in the day when crowds of people would gather around to watch the fast cars speed around. It now stood silent and still. The cement was cracked and bits of grass broke through the cold surface. Trees encircled the track acting as a barrier from the outside world, holding it's secrets.

"It's amazing," I said under my breath, strangely enchanted by it's broken beauty.

"It sure is. I don't really remember this place. I'm glad I got to see it again." He leaned against an old railing. "So, were you popular in high school?"

I smiled. "I wouldn't call myself popular. I knew everybody, and they knew me. We were all friendly enough to each other and would make conversation...I guess I was kind of in the middle group. I never had any desire to be the center of attention. How about you?"

He shook his head. "No. I've always been quiet. I feel a little uncomfortable in large groups. I was the kid who would eat lunch by himself."

I looked at him with sympathy. "I'm sorry. That's kind of sad. If it makes you feel any better, I would've talked to you."

He smiled. "It's all right, didn't bother me. Things changed once I joined the football team. I loved it and I was really good. But even then I wouldn't call myself popular."

I nodded. "High school. That feels like so long ago now. I don't know where the time has gone."

"I know. I'm becoming an old man."

I laughed. "Hardly. Twenty-six is not old."

For the most part we walked in silence. As much as I enjoyed spending time with him, he left me unsettled. I didn't quite know why. He was hard to read at times, he seemed to be stuck inside his head; trying to find the words. It was also the way he looked at me. No one had ever quite looked at me the way he did. He made me feel beautiful, desirable, even. We shared a lot of the same hopes in life; children, owning acreage, horses, trucks, and most of all, music. Perhaps that was one of the most terrifying things for me. He was the first man I had been with where I could see a glimpse of a life with someone, a future. We had only known each other for a short time, but he was quickly becoming one of my best friends.

Bryce cleared his throat. "Have you ever been to Saskatchewan?"

"No. I'd like to go there one day though. I love the prairies, it feels like home. I think I'll end up settling out there eventually, and get my ranch….one can only hope. Why? Have you?"

"I go almost every summer. My uncle has a cattle ranch out that way. I love it out there, the lifestyle, the freedom. My uncle lives in a small town and everyone knows each other. It's pretty neat." He paused and his face took on a faraway look. "In the summertime everyone gets together and throws a barn dance. It's so much fun."

My eyes widened with wonder. I looked at him, eager for more. He did not disappoint. "We often park the trucks in the fields, lay in the back with the music going and watch the stars. I've seen the Northern lights in those fields."

A hand flew to my chest. "You are so lucky. I've never seen the northern lights, but I've always wanted too."

He looked down at me and nodded. "You will. I will make sure of it."

I smiled brightly and felt hopeful. I looked back at him and believed his words. They sounded like a promise, one that he would keep. "I'll hold you to that."

He grinned. "I've been out there for winter as well. We hitch the horses to the sleigh and go for a ride in the snow." He looked thoughtful for a moment. "I should have moved there after high school. Life would be so different."

I shook my head, taking in the images his words painted. "That sounds amazing, almost like a country song."

He looked at me, suddenly serious. "It kind of is. I'll take you there this summer. We'll make a road trip out of it. Hit the Calgary Stampede first then head out to my uncles."

Has anyone ever told you that you're perfect? I tucked a piece of hair behind my ear casually. "I would love that. I don't think you know how happy that would make me."

He smiled warmly. "It's a deal then."

CHAPTER 4

The holiday season was upon us, my favorite time of the year. This year however was going to be a bit empty for my family. My oma took her last breath on Mother's Day. A massive heart attack took her away, and just like that, she was gone, leaving behind a huge void in all of our lives. Christmas had been our holiday, the music, decorations, family gatherings, food, and the love. I would call her with the countdown to Christmas starting in November. Over the years, it had become our ritual. Sadness washed over me. There would be no Christmas baking together, no wrapping the gifts, no oma.

I went home for the holidays. My horse, Tess was still living at my mom's as I wouldn't be starting work as of yet, and couldn't afford the cost of horse board. So that was another ache in my life. Being temporarily horseless. A good majority of my life revolved around the barn. It was one of the few places I felt content and free; I could tell my horse all of my worries, fears, and moments of happiness. She would never judge, she would never say a word, she would just listen quietly until I got everything off my chest. And when the world got to be too much, she was always there, willing to take me away from it all.

"Tess!" I called and waited for my horse to find me. The ground shook beneath my feet and I smiled. She was on her way. I peeked underneath my arm and saw her trot toward me. I focused my gaze on my boots. A hot breath blew against my neck, causing me to shiver slightly. Tess began to check my pockets, and nudged me with her nose roughly.

I laughed. "Okay, okay. You get a Christmas treat too." I reached into my pocket and pulled out a peppermint snack. I extended my palm flat and lifted the snack to her mouth. She extended her neck and lipped the treat off my palm. As she chewed, she lightly tossed her head up and down in quick jerks, surprised by the new taste.

With hands on my hips I giggled. "Is that good, pretty girl?" I took her silence as a 'yes.'

I stepped closer to her. "Head down."

I waited for her to lower her head before slipping the halter on securely. I clipped on her lead rope and clucked for her to walk on. We strode to the main gate and I pulled back the bolt, letting the gate swing open. Tess stopped, raised her head, and made herself stand to her full height. I looked up at my horse, she towered over me. I could not see over her large back. Her nostrils quivered in excitement, her body shook with anticipation.

"You excited, big girl? I think we should go for a walk, come on." I didn't have to coax her, she was right behind me.

⌘

"I'm so full it hurts!" I moaned as I sprawled myself onto the couch with my legs outstretched. We had just finished Christmas dinner, and I was certain I would be full well into the New Year.

"Me, too," Sky groaned. "But it was so good, I just couldn't stop."

My mom beamed. "Good! I'm glad you kids enjoyed it."

It was a quiet Christmas this year, for it was just the three of us. My step-dad had flown to Alberta to spend the holidays with his family and children. We exchanged our presents early in the morning so this evening would be a nice quiet one. Sky, my mom, and I were flaked on the couch, admiring the glow of the Christmas tree, sipping on sparkling apple juice. The dogs lay at our feet, all chewing happily on their Christmas bones. I sighed heavily, today had been a good day, the only thing missing was snow. The hours escaped me and soon, it was time for bed. I said goodnight to my family, and with Maggie wearily trailing after me, we made our way to the bedroom. I had left my phone in the room and noticed the blue light blinking. I sat down on the edge of the bed and checked my missed message, it was from Bryce. I smiled warmly and found I missed him.

"Merry Christmas, my little china doll! I hope Santa was good to you."

"Santa was very good to me. Merry Christmas to you as well. How was your day?"

He must have still been awake for he responded quickly. "Mine was very good, thank you. So much food, I'm so full!"

"Good, me too! So, so much food. I'm off to bed now, it's been a long day. Sweet dreams, talk to you soon."

"Thanks, you too. Goodnight."

It was good to be home again, to be with family. The holiday season passed in a blur, like it usually does. And just like that, it was time to head back to the place that I now called home. I snuggled into the front seat of my truck and snuck a peek at Maggie. She was flopped in the backseat fast asleep. We knew this drill all too well, the long ferry ride home. I covered myself with a blanket I had brought along, and read the message on my phone.

"Hello, beautiful. Are you coming back down this way soon?"

"As a matter of fact, I am. I am on the ferry heading home now."

"Good! Do you want to spend New Years Eve together?"

"I would love too!"

"I look forward to it! Oh, and Luke Bryan, 'Your Mama Should've Named You Whiskey.'"

I smiled. He always sent me songs he thought I would like, and so far, he had been bang on. He was my own personal music mixer, my play list had grown immensely since I had met him. If it wasn't songs, he knew I had a thing for the older muscle cars, especially the Mustangs. He would often send me photos of them, or beautiful scenery to brighten my day. He knew how to make me smile.

I got home in the late afternoon. I was pleased that the rain held off as I unloaded my Christmas haul. My place suddenly seemed very lonely. After spending the last two weeks in a bustling house, the silence was overwhelming. I needed a night out with one of my best friends, Jane. We had grown up across the street from each other and had known each other since before Kindergarten. Life had taken us far away at some points in time, but we always kept in touch. We were more like sisters than friends. Through thick and thin, we'd always have each other's backs, no matter what life tossed our way. I dialed Jane's number and we made plans to see each other immediately.

I strode into the coffee shop and spotted her. "Jane!"

"Ryleigh!" Jane jumped out of her seat and her brown eyes filled with excitement. We gave each other a warm hug.

"I'm going to grab a Chai Tea, I'll be right back." I said as I made my way through the holiday crowd to put in my order.

"Okay," Jane tucked her brown hair behind her ear. "I'll save us a seat."

A moment later I plopped down in the seat across from Jane. She smiled. "Sooo," she began. "How's Bryce?"

I laughed. "Jee, way to cut to the chase."

She giggled. "I know." She waved her hand carelessly. "I'm dying to hear all about him. You look so happy."

My heart fluttered. *I am. I really am.* It had been a very, very long time since I had felt this content. "I am really happy. He's so different from the others."

Jane blew on her hot drink. "Oh, how so?"

"Well, when I talk, he actually looks at me. Really looks at me. I don't know...we seem to have so much in common. He gives me hope for a future." I smiled a little. "What can I say? He's my country boy."

Jane laughed. "Oh, well then I'm sure he's perfect for you. You always seem to get stuck with assholes so I've got my fingers crossed for you." Her eyes glowed. "So...is he a good kisser?"

I placed my coffee cup on the table and ran my hands through my hair in slight frustration. "I wouldn't know. He hasn't kissed me yet. We hug a lot, but that's as far as it's gone and it is driving me a little nuts," I bit my lip, "I will not be the first one to make the move, no matter how old school that might make me."

Jane's eyes widened. "He hasn't tried? He hasn't tried to make a move?"

I shook my head. "Nada."

Jane leaned back in her chair. "Wow. How long have you guys been going out for now?"

"Almost two months."

"Well, holy crap. Are you seeing him for New Years Eve?"

I nodded. "We are."

She smiled. "You should get a New Year's kiss then."

I rested my chin against my hand. "I hope so. He's definitely a shy one. But let me tell you, Jane the anticipation is driving me bonkers. At the end of each date as we say goodbye I never know what to do with myself. I feel like I'm in high school again. I'm all for moving slow and getting to know each other but I don't want to get stuck in a rut and let the moment slip away."

Jane nodded. "Don't worry, your kiss will happen soon."

⌘

"Oh. my Ryleigh, how are you?"

It was 5:00 a.m. There was only one person I knew who would take the risk of texting me so early, and I would let him, happily.

"Good morning. I am sleepy but good. You?"

"I'm great! Just heading to the gym now. I'm looking forward to tonight."

"Me too!"

"Good. Go back to sleep. You'll need your energy to stay up late."

I had every intention of going back to sleep but excitement got the better of me. I was up and dressed by 6:30. Around 8:00 a.m. there was a knock at my door. I glanced curiously outside the window and didn't see any new vehicles in the drive. I answered the door and Brian stood outside with a smirk on his face.

"Good morning," he said brightly. "I just wanted to let you know I love doing laundry after you."

This sounded like a trap. My face pulled together in a confused expression. "Oh?

How so?"

He grinned again and pulled his hands out from behind his back. "You forgot these. I think you would miss them. They're pretty cute."

Heat poured into my cheeks and I knew I had gone beet red. I covered my face in my hands briefly, and grabbed the pair of lace panties he held. "Brian!"

I squealed. "I'm so embarrassed." I began to giggle nervously.

He hunched over, hands across his knees laughing. "I like the bow."

My eyes grew wide. "Hardy har, har. Aren't you a funny one." I glanced down at the panties and looked up at him once more. "You are right, they are one of my favorites, but I will be shutting the door on you now."

Brian leaned in the doorway quickly. "Happy New Years!" I shut the door and began to fan my face, hoping the redness would soon disappear.

Bryce arrived shortly after 1:00 p.m. Today was the first day he seemed light and carefree around me. He bounced through the door. "Happy New Years!"

I smiled. "Happy New Years to you as well." I gave him a quizzical look. "Whatcha got planned?"

"Come on. Let's go. I have an idea."

"Mmk. Be right there."

I locked the door behind me and followed him out to the truck. He slid in quickly and leaned over to unlock my door. I hopped in, glanced at his secretive face and wondered where he would be taking us. I settled happily against the seat, I didn't care where we were going as long as I was with him. Today was going to be a great day. Bryce muttered under his breath awhile later. "Darn. It looks closed."

I leaned over the dashboard of his truck, looking at the museum. "It does. We should check the doors while we're here at least."

"Good idea." He hopped out of the truck, and with a bounce in his step he made his way over to the large glass doors. "Oh," he muttered, "it's closed for renovations until February 11, next year. I've been wanting to go here for quite awhile."

I looked up at the giant building, disappointed myself. "I'm sorry. Well, on the bright side, at least now you know when you can come back."

"True enough. Hmm…" he looked around, "do you want to grab a drink? The old bar I used to go to is just around the corner."

I looked across the street eagerly, I was in a festive mood. "I could go for a drink."

"All right, let's head out then."

We made the short drive to the pub and found a vacant seat. We sat across from each other in a corner booth near the pool tables. The bar wasn't too full as of yet. Christmas stockings still hung by the fireplace, and cheery red and green garland swept over the mantle. Bryce held a cold beer between his hands while I sipped on a cooler. I studied the quaint little bar around me; Bryce's old stomping grounds. The place was cute, it had a western feel which suited Bryce very well.

"So," I began, "were you a bit of a wild man back in the day?"

A mixture of emotions ran through his face. "A bit. I regret it, looking back. I had a lot of growing up to do. I had to change my life completely, especially when my son was born. I, uh, I drank way more than I ever should have."

I looked up at the quiet man who sat before me. I couldn't picture a party animal within him. He was polite, careful and warm. I had always felt safe with him. For being as reserved as he could be, there was a protective quality that hovered the surface. He would step up if need be, no questions asked, but he was also a little broken. Every once in awhile a flicker of quiet conflict would run behind his eyes. I only recognized the look for I too had seen it within my own eyes.

"Is it okay we're drinking?" I asked softly.

He laughed then. "Oh, yeah. I can control myself."

"Okay. I'll hold you to that. You're my ride home and I'd like to get there safely," I said lightly.

"Of course. I'll only have one."

I nodded. "Okay. Me too. I'm not the world's biggest drinker to begin with, I'm kind of a light weight." I pressed my hands against my cheeks. "My cheeks always go red when I have alcohol. I hate it."

He chuckled. "I don't. I think it's cute." His hand grabbed at something quickly. "Here, I have a present for you."

"Oh?" I looked down at 'my gift' with an amused expression. "Wow. Thank you. I've always wanted one of these," I said rather dryly. Bryce slid a teeny salt shaker in front of me.

"Do you like it?" He grinned.

"I love it. I don't know how I've made it this far in life without one."

Bryce took a long sip of his beer. He stared into his glass looking deep in thought. "Can I ask you something?"

"Fire away."

"What made you choose me?" His voice grew quiet, and he looked away as my eyes met his.

"Hmm," I said softly, looking at him. He was clearly uncomfortable. "I can't honestly tell you that. It was just a gut feeling. Even through your words you felt right. I liked the way you wrote; there was a certain depth behind it. And then when we finally met in person, you were who I hoped you would be." I shrugged. "What made you choose me?"

"I was drawn to you. I thought you were beautiful, and you're a country girl. You had the whole package. The more we spoke and began to get to know each other you just fit. Plus," he grinned, "you look like a famous person, so that's a bonus."

I leaned back and laughed then. "I don't see it. At all."

He pulled out his phone and studied it for a moment before turning the screen toward me. I found myself staring at a picture of Amy Adams. I thought she was beautiful, so, naturally I was flattered. It wasn't the first time I had been compared to her, still, I didn't see the resemblance.

Bryce's eyes widened and he looked from me to his phone. "How could you not see it? The nose is a dead giveaway."

I shrugged my shoulders. "I'll take your word for it."

I smiled as I remembered the first time he had compared me to her. It was after our first meeting and he sent a text a few days later.

"Has anyone ever told you that you look like Amy Adams?"

"Actually, yes. But I do not see it."

"It was driving me nuts, you reminded me of someone, but I couldn't place it. I've been trying to figure it out for days. I was watching Leap Year and it hit me. That's it! That's her. You look like Amy Adams!"

I smiled at the memory and gazed back at Bryce. He looked at me with an eager expression. Bryce finished his beer and looked around the room quietly. His eyes fell back to me. I looked up at him, and this time he didn't look away. His gaze softened. "You make me nervous," he said softly.

I sat back and felt a whoosh of breath escape my lips and then I smiled, ever so slowly. "Good, I'm glad." His eyes widened, he looked taken aback. I cleared my throat and continued on. "Because you make me nervous too. I'm glad we're on the same page."

His shoulders and face relaxed. He nodded slowly. "Shall we go?"

"Yes. I'm getting kind of hungry though. There's a grocery store in the complex, do you mind if we stop there? I can make us dinner."

"Works for me!"

I wandered the grocery store aisles aimlessly. "Are you picky with food?" I asked.

"I'm a guy. Nope."

I laughed. "Good. How does a chicken stir fry sound?"

"Delicious."

I marched purposefully to the aisles where I would find my ingredients. I noticed he lagged behind. I turned around to ask him if he had a preference to noodles when I caught him checking me out from behind. His eyes widened a little bit, he looked like a deer caught in headlights. *I could have so much fun with this right now.* However, I chose to let it slide, this time. I grabbed the noodles and tossed them in my nearly full grocery basket when Bryce offered to take it for me. I let him. We made our way to the tills and I remembered I was dangerously low on a very important bathroom necessity: toilet paper.

"Oh!" I snapped my fingers. "I need to get toilet paper." I chose what was on sale and hugged the parcel to my chest.

He chuckled next to me. "How cute are you."

I looked surprised. "Well, thank you. But how so?"

He nodded at me. "I like the way you're hugging that thing."

I looked down as a warm heat rushed across my cheeks. "Ah. I didn't notice."

"I did. I like it."

⌘

"Do you need any help in the kitchen?" Bryce was on his hands and knees in the living room wrestling with Maggie. I couldn't help but linger on his strong forearms that were exposed.

"No, I'm okay right now. Dinner should be ready in about ten minutes or so."

"Okay. It smells really good."

I finished sautéing the vegetables and grilling the chicken. I mixed it with the steam fried noodles and tossed the mound of food in a Sesame Ginger Thai dressing. For the finishing touch, I sprinkled shaved almonds on top. I looked down at the meal and nodded in satisfaction.

"K, it's ready!" I called in a sing song voice. I liked the picture that played out before me; Bryce wrestling happily with my dog, a full kitchen table, and music softly played in the background. The house felt warm, and happy. *I* felt happy.

"This is really good. Do you mind if I have some more?"

"Go for it! I made plenty."

"Great, thanks," he eagerly helped himself to another serving. Bryce leaned back in his seat and patted his stomach. "That was really good. I'm so full." He glanced at the clock. "Hmm, it's seven o'clock. Since it's New Years, do you want to go to the pub for a few drinks?"

"Sure, there's one just across the street. We could walk there." I offered.

He grinned. "Sounds like a plan."

It was a brisk night. We walked shoulder to shoulder at a quick pace, our breath floated in a cloud of white smoke amongst the chill air.

"We should have taken my truck," Bryce began. "My knee is still sore from our walk the other day."

I giggled. "You're such an old man."

He raised one eyebrow. "I've got bad knees. I was rough on them back in the day." He looked at me with a sly expression. "Plus you made me walk for five hours the other day."

I burst out laughing. "Five hours? Hardly, maybe an hour and a half tops."

He muttered under his breath and I kept walking, a smile upon my face. Such a delicate flower he was. Up ahead in the distance, the pub shone brightly under the streetlights. I glanced at Bryce and his face looked relieved. His pace quickened and he had a sudden hop in his step. He cut in front of me and held the door open. "After you," he gestured with his arm. I smiled and slid past him.

The pub was quiet. Besides ourselves, there was only a handful of people scattered about. We slid into a nearby booth and the waitress met us quickly.

"What can I get for you two?" she seemed distracted.

"I'll have a beer."

I glanced over the drink menu. "I'll have a long island iced tea, please."

She placed our drinks in front of us and I sipped it eagerly. "Oh yum," I leaned toward my drink and took another sip. "Did you know," I began, looking at him, eyes shining, "that there is no iced tea whatsoever in a long island? There's about five different alcohol's in this sucker."

He smiled, looking rather amused. "No, I didn't know that."

I nodded matter of factly. "It's true. It would definitely explain why I got so drunk on my birthday." I smiled at the memory, now that was a good night. The next day, however, well, not so much.

A smile lit up his eyes. "I'd like to see you drunk. What are you like?"

I grinned. "I'm a very happy drunk. I talk a lot, I'm sure most of it is pure nonsense. I get very giggly, and if the mood strikes me I really like to dance."

"Hmm," he said slowly, "I think we're getting you drunk tonight."

I smiled and took another sip. "Works for me. It is New Years Eve after all."

Bryce leaned forward. "Hold out your hands, palms facing me."

I looked down at my hands slightly confused. "Okay." I did as asked and watched him curiously.

He studied my hands closely. He then raised his and held them against mine. My hands looked very small. Bryce had hard working hands, I felt the calluses run roughly against the smoothness of my own. Our eyes found each other and we held on to each others gaze.

The waitress came back to our table suddenly. "Do you guys want to order something for last call?"

Bryce and I stared at each other, eyes wide. "What time is it?" I whispered.

He glanced at his watch, and a somewhat amused yet disappointed look ran across his face. "Just after eight o'clock."

He raised an eyebrow and my mouth opened slightly in surprise. *Talk about an early night.* We burst out laughing at each others expressions and ordered another drink.

"Well, that was short and sweet," Bryce looked at his watch one more time before he zipped up his jacket, trying to keep the cold out. He glanced around the parking lot. "Ah, how about we have our own party? There's a liquor store right there."

I nodded. "That's convenient, sounds like a plan."

Warm air brushed my cool skin as we stepped inside the heated store. Bryce made his way to the beer section. I reached for a pair of peach ciders, and held the cold cans a careful distance from my skin.

"Whatcha getting?" I sidled up beside him.

"Something good and cheap." His eyes studied the selection in front of him. "Oh, this works." He reached for a brand Black's Label. "It's only $10. Can't beat that." He paused and reached for a single can to add to his armload, a Bacardi rum and coke mix.

I looked at the haul he held easily. "Do ya got everything you need?" I said somewhat sarcastically.

A half grin played on his face. "You bet."

We shared a good laugh when we entered my driveway. My eyes fell to a familiar black car parked in front of my truck. "Oh, my brother's here!" I said brightly.

Bryce slowed his steps. "Oh?"

I stopped and turned to him. "Yeah, don't worry, he's a really nice guy. Super laid back and he is hilarious."

Bryce nodded unsurely. "Okay. I'll take your word for it. I've had issues in the past with brothers."

I waved my hand and brushed off his comment. "Yeah, well you haven't met mine yet. You'll be fine." I looked back at him. "I don't think I told you, but he's moving in with me next month. The basement has two bedrooms and this way we'll save on rent."

He nodded. "Smart."

"Yup. Follow me. I promise, he won't bite."

We found my brother, Skyler in the kitchen snooping through my fridge. He looked up, a sheepish grin appearing on his chiseled features. "Hey, Ry. I was just looking to see what goods you had," his big blue eyes landed on Bryce. "Hey," he said with an easiness and strode over, hand extended. "You must be Bryce. Nice to meet you."

Bryce stepped forward and shook his hand with a firm grip. "Nice to meet you."

Sky looked back at me with hopeful eyes. "Whatever is in your fridge smells amazing. Can I have some?"

I laughed, my brother could eat all the time. It really irked me, he looked like a fitness model. For the most part, we would make great roommates, we had always gotten along, and we shared many of the same interests; fitness, cooking, adventures, and overall we enjoyed the same types of music. However country did not fall into that category. For while it was my favorite genre, Sky loathed it. I chuckled as country music played from the radio this very evening. I could tell Sky noticed, but tonight he had to be on his very best behavior, and after all, he was not officially my roommate as of yet so I ruled the roost…for now at least.

"Sure," I responded to Sky's pleads. "Eat away."

"Beautiful, thanks!"

Bryce put our drinks in the fridge. I leaned back against the counter top and took a quick scan around the place. I didn't see many of Sky's boxes. "How much did you bring over?"

"Mm," Sky chewed eagerly, "not much, just some bedroom stuff. I can only fit so much in my car. I was hoping you could help me bring some things over with your truck."

"Yeah, for sure."

A large grin appeared on Sky's scruffy face. "Fantastic."

Bryce cracked open a beer and leaned against the radio. He and Sky made small talk and I smiled at him warmly, knowing how nerve wracking this was for him. If I hadn't known earlier that he was nervous, I'd never be able to tell by looking at him now. Conversation flowed easily between the two men. Bryce looked relaxed and he chuckled. He offered Sky a beer, at which he took gladly. *Look at my boys. They fit.*

Bryce looked my way, nodding towards the radio. "Who's this?"

I listened for a moment. "Eli Young Band. '*Drunk last night.*'"

Bryce shook his head in disbelief. "How do you do this? It's throwing me off." He looked at Sky. "She's good at this. I've never met anyone who could do that."

Sky knew nothing about country music and shrugged. "She likes this type of music."

A few moments later, a new song on the radio, Bryce looked at me again. "Who's this? This one is a bit tougher."

"Hmm," I bit my lip. "High Valley, '*Have I Told You I Loved You Lately?*'"

"Dammit," Bryce muttered. "Yep."

Bryce continued quizzing me, and I managed to get them all correct. I must admit, I felt pretty cheeky. I could tell he was getting a kick out of it, yet at the same time it drove him nuts.

Sky's eyebrows rose. "Wow, that is kinda cool."

Half an hour later, Sky gathered up his things to leave. "It was nice meeting you," he said to Bryce and turned to both of us with a wave. "Happy New Years."

Bryce and I smiled at Sky and we said our goodbyes. I turned to Bryce. "So, I told you, didn't I? He's a really nice guy."

Bryce smiled sheepishly. "Yeah, yeah, he is. Super laid back, I'm not used to that."

"Yup," I nodded. "That's my brother. Just never, ever try to take food away from him. He will snap you in half."

Bryce's eyes widened with amusement. "That's funny." His eyes glanced around the room. "Do you mind if I play some guitar?"

My heart skipped a beat in excitement. "Please do."

His face lit up. "Great, thank you."

He plucked up the guitar and sat on the couch. He placed the guitar in his lap carefully and adjusted his position. I watched dumbfounded. He made it look so easy. Beautiful music soon filled the room. I settled next to him and watched, wonder filled my features. His fingertips moved from fret to fret, string to string with a grace I envied, and also desired.

He put the guitar down and sat back, taking a sip of his cool beer. He chewed on his lip thoughtfully. "What are you like when you're angry?" He stopped then and looked at me carefully. "Actually, I can't really picture you angry."

I laughed. "Oh, believe me, I can get angry. Overall though, I'm generally a fairly happy person. I don't like to get into arguments. Life is hard enough, why make more trouble then necessary?"

"I agree completely."

"Good!" I began. "I suppose when I do get extremely angry I sort of shut down. I get very quiet and will often just get up and leave, put some distance between myself and the situation until I cool down."

He looked amused. "Huh. That's sort of what I do. I get really quiet. I don't like to argue." He looked at me again. "We'd be terrible in a fight. Both of us walking the other way."

I laughed then. "I suppose so."

"Yeah." He looked thoughtful, reminiscing on some old memory. "My ex hated that. She liked to argue and get in my face, she always wanted me to yell back but that's just not me. I get real quiet and leave the room. She'd often follow behind, bickering." *She sounds like a real doll.* "Well, you won't get that from me. I don't have that in me…at all."

"Good. I'm glad." He smirked a little. "Show me your mad face."

I laughed. "But I'm not mad!" He held his stare, waiting. "Oh, fine." I pressed my features into what felt like an angry face.

He burst out laughing and I joined in. "That was terrible! You didn't look angry at all."

I shrugged. "I don't know what to tell ya, I don't feel anything close to anger tonight."

He stood, brushing his hands on his jeans. "Come here." He extended his hand, and pulled me off the couch in a swift, quick motion and nestled me into his arms. He looked down at me with a grin, giving me a quick squeeze.

With his left hand he interlocked our fingers. His right hand slid down my arm until he found my hand, and placed it neatly on top of his shoulder. I held on with a firm grasp. His free hand traced down my lower back as he pulled me in tightly. As our bodies drew close, I wondered if he could feel my heart pounding in my chest. I felt his muscles ripple beneath his skin, and in the moment I truly felt like a little china doll. I felt delicate and fragile as I was pressed against a pillar of strength, but it also felt safe. We fit together well.

His voice grew soft. "Do you dance?"

"Not very well."

He smiled softly. "Hold on tight, I'll lead."

We danced across my living room floor. I held on as he carefully maneuvered me left to right, front to back. He watched me closely, tenderly. His hands clasped around me tighter, and I returned the silent gesture. *I've never felt this before.* This was a perfect moment. I closed my eyes and wished I could always hold on to this memory, this feeling. One day as I sift through the endless events in my life, this snapshot would take me back to here and now, bringing with it a warmth that would run through my heart.

We danced for awhile, I barely heard the songs on the radio. We ended up back on the couch, talking for hours, picking at each others thoughts, discussing the future, our favorite memories, and our hopes and dreams. Each time we'd crack open a new can we'd clink them together and with a quick "cheers!" take a sip. His eyes drifted to the camera charging on my kitchen table for tomorrow's event; the annual New Years Polar Bear Swim. It was a local event held on a beach not too far away. It was an open invitation, whoever wanted to participate could sign up. The partakers would line up on a beach in their bathing suits, and when the big horn blew, everyone would run into the ocean and take a quick dip. It was madness if you asked me. Bryce and his uncle were participating tomorrow morning and I had agreed to tag along, as a photographer only.

"Nice camera." He picked it up and held it carefully.

I stretched out on the couch and looked toward him with a sleepy smile. He held the camera close to his eye, looked through the viewfinder and snapped a few shots my way. He glanced at the display screen, smiled, and placed it back down. Bryce turned on his heel and took six long strides until he sat next to me. I pushed myself in an upright position, facing him.

"What time is it?" he asked.

I leaned forward to steal a glance at the clock. "It's almost midnight."

He nodded slowly and leaned closer. "Good."

This is it, it's actually going to happen! I forced my gaze to his. He searched my face carefully, looking for permission. His brown eyes found mine once more. He leaned in and our lips met. We kissed, slowly, softly. I pressed myself into him, and he placed an arm around my waist drawing me closer. Our lips parted and we pulled away slightly, our noses touching. We smiled and both let out the same breath of relief. Our eyes met briefly and our lips found each other's once again.

⌘

"Ryleigh? Are you awake?" I opened my eyes in slight confusion. The music played softly and the room was bright. I blinked a few times and pressed my lips together. A small smile appeared. *My lips. His lips.* I pressed a finger to them and looked up. Bryce sat next to me, his hand resting on my hip. He stared down softly.

"You fell asleep on me."

"Oh," I said groggily. "I'm sorry. I didn't realize."

He laughed quietly. "It's okay. It's 4 a.m., I think we should go to sleep. We have an early morning tomorrow. The swim starts at ten."

4 a.m.? How did that happen? Where did the time go? "Right. Okay."

I got up clumsily and made my way to the bathroom to brush my teeth. I lightly bounced off the wall. *Ooooh boy. I'm a wee bit tipsy.* After I freshened up, I began to shut down the house. I stepped into the living room and Bryce was stretched on the floor, eyes closed.

"You can't be serious," I stated, hands on my hips. "You are not sleeping on the floor." Bryce mumbled something inaudible. "Come on, let's go to bed." I reached down to help him up. His hands clasped mine and he rose to his feet.

"Bed?" he said sleepily.

"Yes, that thing with a mattress where people generally sleep. Silly boy."

He grinned at me then and led me to the room. He looked around and his face lit up. "You have a fan."

"Yes, I can't sleep without the noise."

"Me either." He flicked it on and positioned it strategically. I climbed onto my side of the bed and flopped down, exhausted. Bryce pulled off his shirt and climbed next to me. *Holy Jesus.* I suddenly felt wide awake as I admired his fit form. As he slipped next to me, I noticed the tattoo of a bull on his right shoulder. I smiled to myself, I liked tattoos and he wore it well.

"Mmm," he muttered. "Come here. I'll keep you warm."

I scooted closer to rest my head against his chest, listening to the steady beat of his heart. His arms pulled me in, and I wrapped my free arm around his waist. He was so warm. I snuggled in and let his body heat spread to my cool skin. He lifted his head slightly and pulled the extra blanket over top of me to ensure I stayed warm. "Goodnight, my little china doll. Happy New Years," he kissed my forehead softly.

"Happy New Years, my Bryce," I mumbled quietly.

I never wanted this day to end, but I could not fight the heaviness that burned my eyes. This was a battle I would not win. My eyes fell closed, and I welcomed the darkness. I fell into a quiet slumber; the sound of Bryce's heart beat softly in my ear like a lullaby.

⌘

Dear God, someone turn out the light. And the noise, make it stop! The light was the sun. The awful, repetitive noise was the alarm clock. I opened my heavy eyes and blinked a few times until my vision became clear. I sat up slowly, the room still slightly spun around me. I held my palm up to my forehead. *Ouch. My poor, poor head.* I wiggled my toes slowly and bent one of my legs. It felt heavy and slow. I looked around the room impatiently for the source of the awful noise that carried on with a steady rhythm. It was so loud to my tender head. I leaned forward on my stomach and looked for the sound. I found it. It came from Bryce's phone, he had set the alarm before going to bed. It was now 8:30 a.m. We had gotten a whopping, satisfying four and a half hours of sleep. *This is gonna hurt.*

Bryce slept soundly. I watched him for a moment. He looked so cozy, so peaceful. This wasn't going to do. If I was up, he should be too. I leaned closer. "Bryce?" Nothing. "Bryce? It's time to get up sleepy head." Still nothing. I looked around and my eyes landed on a pillow. That would do. I picked it up and swatted his shoulder. "Wake up, sleepy head."

His eyes flew open and he sat up quickly. He groaned loudly, hands flying up to his face as he plopped back down. "Ow, ow, ow. Why did you make me drink so much?"

I laughed and crawled over him to get out of the bed. "Morning, sunshine. And I did no such thing."

He opened one eye and managed a small smile as I rifled through my closet. "Morning. Um, I didn't try anything last night, did I?"

I turned to him, caught off guard. "No, not at all. You were a perfect gentleman."

He seemed relieved. "Good. I don't want you running off on me."

I smiled. "My feet are firmly planted."

He grinned. "I like that."

The cold air helped wake me up. I sucked in a deep breath, tasting the salt in the wind. The gentle *whoosh whoosh* of the waves from the nearby beach ran steady in my ears. Bryce and I leaned against the tailgate of his truck and waited for his uncle to arrive. Bryce tilted his head back, testing the air sleepily. He pulled the hood of his sweater over his head and groaned. He looked done for.

"Well, I'm sure the cold ocean will wake you up," I teased.

He gave a light snort. "Oh, I'm sure it will. I don't know what I've gotten myself in too." He gave me a sidelong glance. "Are you sure you don't want to join us?"

"Hell no."

He laughed. "All right. Oh," he straightened, "there's my uncle."

Butterflies rippled through my stomach. This was a very important moment for me. Bryce often spoke of his uncle, and he had nothing but good things to say about the man. He considered him more of a father figure than an uncle. His uncle sounded like the type of guy who would give you the shirt off his back, and although he was a little scatterbrained, his heart was always in the right place. *And here I am about to meet a very important person in Bryce's life and I am severely lacking sleep and nursing a hangover. Good job, Ryleigh.*

A tall man with graying hair and matching facial scruff strode over to us. His brown eyes lit up when he saw Bryce. "You look like hell. Did you have a good night?" he smirked.

Bryce smiled and pointed at me as I stood next to him, holding my camera. "It's her fault. She made me drink."

Traitor. My jaw dropped. "I did no such thing. If I recall, it was all your idea and you popped open those cans by yourself."

Bryce laughed then and gestured to his uncle. "Uncle Mike, this is Ryleigh. Ryleigh, Mike."

Mike's face lit up and he eagerly extended his hand toward mine. "Ah, Ryleigh. It's nice to finally meet you. I hear you have a horse?"

I glanced at Bryce and he smiled a little shyly. I looked back at Mike. "Yes, I sure do."

We walked in step together, Mike and I chatted about horses for the most part. An easy banter arose between Bryce and Mike. I smiled warmly, I liked his uncle already. He had a laid back and happy nature. It was very natural to feel at ease in his presence. It was nice to see Bryce in this light, one he was perfectly content in the comfort of those surrounding him. Despite being severely sleep deprived and hung over, he looked light and satisfied. We all made our way to the beach, and Mike dug out a blanket he had brought along. We laid it on top of a washed up beach log and sat. There was nothing left to do but wait for the event to begin.

Bryce groaned and curled up into a ball on the cool pebbles beneath our feet. He tightened his hood and mumbled. "I just need to rest my eyes for a bit."

I chuckled and popped off the lens cap of my camera and snapped my shot. This would be a fun memory to look back on one day, evidence of a good night. Mike sat beside me and pulled out a bag of snacks. "Are you hungry?" He offered the bag to me.

Bryce sat up. "Food?"

I laughed. "Such a boy."

He plopped next to me and hit his shoulder against mine. He took the bag and placed it in his lap. "Want some?"

"Yup." I reached into the bag and munched on the salty snack.

Mike stood. "I'm going to wander around and check out the stands." With that he left, already finding someone else to chat with. I laughed quietly, some people had the gift of gab and he was clearly one of those people.

"I have a present for you."

I looked down at Bryce's hand and held mine open, waiting for my surprise. He placed a heart shaped rock into my palm. My lips twisted into a grin, and I turned to meet his eyes. "Thank you. I like this one."

He smiled. "You're welcome."

I slipped the rock into my pocket and looked around. The sky was bright blue with hints of pink scattered throughout. The pier shone in the distance and the ocean glinted like blue diamonds. It was too pretty to not take a picture. I pulled out my camera, and began capturing my memories. The beach began to fill as groups of people milled about, trying to find spots of their own. It was clear just by looking who would be the spectators, as they were bundled up heavily, myself included, and those who would take the plunge, for they seemed to wear clothes that would tear off easily. There were a few hardcore contestants who were already strutting around in their suits. I shook my head in disbelief and shivered at the very sight.

Next to where we sat, stood a very large white rock, which gave the beach its name. Someone had propped a sturdy beach log against it, allowing it to act as a makeshift ladder. Kids and adults alike tried to climb to the top. Bryce was no exception. He stood at the bottom of the log and judged the route he would take. He put one foot in front of the other and began to make his way to the top. The rock looked slick. He launched off the top of the log and grabbed tightly onto the large rock formation. One leg was bent upwards, the other dangled. This looked like a bad idea, he wore cowboy boots, and they weren't exactly meant for rock climbing. I could see it now. Bryce tumbling helplessly down to the ground and breaking something. Yet, I picked up my camera and began snapping my shots. He made it safely to the top and stood proudly. I called to him and I captured some nice portraits. I tipped my head in a silent thank you.

A small sound caught Bryce's attention. A young boy was stuck at the top of the log. He looked helpless as he stared desperately toward the top of the rock. Bryce smiled sympathetically, and held out his hand. The little boy clasped on as Bryce pulled him up next to him. *Dammit. Why did he have to be so sweet?* My thought must have been written across my face for his eyes met mine and he grinned a big movie star smile. Once he was ready to get down, he helped the little boy first and then he carefully slid down the log until his feet were firmly planted on the ground. He strode over to me looking rather triumphant.

"I thought you were going to fall."

"Ha, so did I."

Mike appeared. "It's time!"

I shivered at the thought of what was about to happen. It was not a warm day, the breeze carried with it a bitter cold and I could not imagine the ocean feeling anything close to welcoming. I snuggled deeper into my winter jacket. "Y'all are crazy."

Bryce grinned and tore off his shirt. His jeans and boots were next until he stood in nothing but his swimming shorts. My gaze took him in appreciatively. The contestants all lined up near the shoreline. I watched in disbelief, there were hundreds of people. They were insane. The horn blew, cheers broke out and everyone took off running into the cold water. I adjusted my lens and snapped a few more shots. A few moments later Bryce and Mike ran toward me, glistening in salt water, smiling brightly.

"That was amazing!"

"Super refreshing. Not as bad as I thought."

Madness. The men looked at each other. "Want to go in again?"

"Yup!"

And they did. They ran into the water like a happy dog fetching his prize. I was dumbfounded. Once again they ran to me, but unlike last time, they looked cold this round. They bent down, reaching for their towels to wrap up their shivering bodies. The men shook from head to toe and I heard their teeth chatter uncontrollably.

I stood enthusiastically. "Picture time, boys!"

They posed, side by side and I forever captured their happy, proud smiles.

"I have a p-p-present for you," Bryce chattered.

I held my steady hand under his trembling one. I opened my palm and he placed a white seashell in my grasp, perfectly in tact. I looked up at him in slight wonder.

He smiled. "I dove in, and found it. I thought you'd like it."

I love you. "Thank you. I love it!"

He smiled a chattering smile. "Good, I'm glad."

The men dried off as best they could and threw on their clothes. We dodged through the crowd of freezing people and made our way back to the parking lot. Mike paused in front of his truck door. "It was nice to meet you, Ryleigh. I'm sure I'll be seeing you soon." He winked and hopped inside his truck.

With a raised eyebrow, I turned to Bryce. He smirked and nodded his head to the truck. "Let's go. I need some heat."

A little while later we stood in my living room, my head rested on his shoulder as he looked through the photos I had taken of our day. I was done for. My stomach felt ill, and tiredness weighed heavy over every inch of my body. I fought to keep my eyes open, but the world around me started to blur, I was going down, fast.

"I'm so tired," I yawned.

He tilted his head against mine. "Me too. I need sleep. I think I should go home. When I'm hung over I can be a baby and you don't need to see that side of me so soon."

I laughed quietly and nestled against his chest. "I had fun. Drive safe."

"I will."

As I lay in bed, I let my body grow heavy. I felt myself sink deeper into the comforter. My phone suddenly jingled causing me to jump in surprise. *No. No. No. Leave me alone, world.*

I swiped my screen and a message appeared. "I'm home. Goodnight, dear."

I smiled and let the heaviness take me under.

CHAPTER 5

"So let me get this straight. He spent the night, alcohol was involved and you two slept next to each other, and nothing else happened?" Jane rose an eyebrow as she took a sip out of her coffee mug.

I laughed. "Yes. It was an amazing night." The memory of us dancing across the living room floor swept me away momentarily, a smitten smile took over my lips.

Jane set her cup down. "I think you have a good one here. It's about time, you've had such terrible luck in the past."

I sighed heavily, my past experiences didn't leave much of a smile on my face. "He's something special. I feel like I'm in uncharted waters here. He's open about a future. He wants the same things out of life that I do." I chewed my lip nervously. "I may be in trouble here."

A heavy tug gripped at my heart and I wished it would go away. I knew this feeling all too well. I was waiting for the hammer to drop, for all of this to be taken away from me. I wanted so desperately to just enjoy the moment, to let the happiness and the warmth take over like a security blanket. However, I felt just the opposite. I somehow managed to feel like an uninvited guest. My past tended to be cruel, I was able to see glimpses of happiness only to have them ripped away from me. *I walk a careful line, my face a carefully composed mask. Don't look too closely, for I won't let you in. I will keep you at a safe distance where you can't hurt me.* I shook my head sadly.

Jane leaned forward. "Let yourself be happy, Ry. He seems to really like you. Let him in."

I forced a smile. "I know, I'm trying. These things are not easy for me." I looked upward and a lopsided smirk appeared on my face. "I'm glad we're taking things slow but, Jane," I leaned forward. "It's exhausting waiting for it to happen. I want it to be special, but it's so much work to you know," I circled my hand in the air, hoping the right words would come to me. "Be ready all the time. The anticipation is killing me! There's a lot of upkeep in being a woman."

We both let out a hearty laugh then. "Don't worry," Jane said, "when it does happen it will all be worth it. And Valentines is next month. If it doesn't happen before then, that'll be the day!"

I wrinkled my nose. That was next month. A whole month away. I could be dead by then.

⌘

"To the left. Left! No, Sky, to the left!" I yelled out, slightly impatiently as I held a death grip on the couch. I was helping my brother move some of his larger items out of his apartment and the truck was nearly full. Sky adjusted to the left and we heaved the couch in the back of my truck. We wiggled it against the side, and as luck would have it the couch settled perfectly along the corner.

Sky hopped off the tailgate and looked relieved. He dusted his hands together. "That's it. I think we're done."

"Good," I stretched out my arms slowly, wincing slightly. I was sore. I looked at Sky teasingly. "Aren't you glad I own a waste of metal for a vehicle?"

He rolled his eyes. "Yeah, yeah, whatever."

I grinned. "You love it."

It was an inside joke between Sky and me. He was forever harping on me that my truck was a waste of metal, for he simply didn't have the need for such a large vehicle. Whenever he actually needed my truck, I liked to point out that my truck was indeed useful.

I looked at the back of the pickup. "All right, I'll strap the load down and you can follow me."

Sky nodded. "Sounds good. I'm going to get my keys. I'll be back."

I began to tie down the load when a strange male voice sounded behind me. "Are you moving in or out?"

I turned in slight surprise to face a tall man leaning against the side of my truck. He casually smoked a cigarette. *Get off my truck please.* The man had a mop of dark hair and his face was unkept. His eyes looked seedy, and they took me in carefully. A smile spread to his face. I looked down at him in slight disgust and eagerly glanced back to the apartment doors, hoping my brother would appear.

"Moving out," I said curtly and focused on tightening the straps.

"Aw, well that's too bad," he grabbed at one of the red straps and began to twirl it through his fingers, watching me.

I raised an eyebrow and yanked the strap from his hand. "Sorry, but I'll be needing this, thanks."

Apprehension settled over me. I did not get a good feeling from this man at all. I fixated my gaze back to work and the man did not move, he remained silent and the smile did not leave his face. *If he so much as tries to touch me, I will knock him to the ground. He doesn't know who he's dealing with.* Although I am a sweet and polite girl, I knew how to handle myself if things were to come down to it. Life had thrown a lot of unexpected lessons my way, and you tend to pick up things along the ride. Thankfully, the apartment doors squeaked open and Sky appeared, making his way to me.

I smiled in relief and looked down at the man. "Please, get off my truck now."

He glanced from myself to Sky and he stood up tall. With a nod, he strode away without looking back. *Good riddance.*

"Who was that?" Sky asked.

"No one. Ready to get out of here?"

"Almost. I just have to return a quick call, but I can do that in my car. Give me five minutes?"

I nodded. "Sure, no problem. I'll warm the truck up."

I hopped into the driver seat, started the engine and looked at my clock. 7:00 p.m. Not bad. I held a hand over my stomach as it growled hungrily. The plan was to race home, unload and then treat ourselves to a sushi dinner.

I calculated the drive home, and the time it would take for us to unload the latest haul. I guessed we could have it all done by 8:30 if we really hustled.

My phone jingled and a message appeared. "What are you doing tonight?" Bryce.

"I'm just helping my brother move some stuff to our place. Afterwards I have no plans. You?"

"I'm out in Chilliwack for Aiden's birthday dinner. I'm not sure how long I'll be but did you want to get together afterwards?"

"Yes! I'll text you when we're just about done. I'm guessing we'll be finished by 8:30ish"

"Okay. Things will probably wrap up here by then. I will see you soon!"

Sky and I hustled home. We unloaded as quickly as we could manage, we were both starving. Afterwards, we walked across the street to the quiet restaurant and found an empty table. Sky's face lit up like the sun as his meal was placed upon the table. My plate shortly followed, and I felt the same excitement flit across my own face that my brother still wore upon his features.

"This looks amazing!" I proclaimed. "Oh yum, I am so hungry."

My brother and I ate heartily. I noticed he maneuvered his chopsticks with an easy grace. I picked mine up and began to mimic his motion. It was nothing to be proud of, but it was a slight improvement from my last attempt. I leaned back happily in the booth as I felt myself getting full.

"What are you up too?"

I cleaned my hands with a napkin and reached for my phone. "Just eating sushi."

"I'm jealous. Are you getting any better with the chopsticks?"

"A bit actually!"

"I don't know if I believe that. I better see some improvement the next time we go out."

"Ha. Oh boy, the pressure is on now!"

"Yup. I'm getting ready to leave, I should be there in 45 minutes. Do you mind if I use your shower? I didn't have time to shower after work, I went straight to see Aiden."

"Not at all. See you later."

Bryce was a welder. He often said he always needed a shower after work, as his job wasn't tidy. Excitement surged through me followed by the ache that this could all end. I closed my eyes briefly and willed it to go away. *Be happy. You deserve this.* And I did. I was a good person, yet sometimes I couldn't help but feel cursed. Bad things always seemed to happen to me. It's as though the universe kept a running tally of my happy/easy vs. sad/struggle ratio. From my past, I would say it heavily favored the sad/struggle ratio. When things finally go well for me, someone decides, meh, this won't do. It's been a smooth ride for her too long, let's throw an obstacle in there, let's really make her work for it. And I was exhausted. I have had to pick myself up off the ground far too many times. I did not want to have to sort through the scattered pieces only to put myself back together once more. After so many hardships, I didn't fit together like I used too, some of the pieces were missing. *Please, no more.*

Sky and I paid for our meals, and we went our separate ways. I gave the house a quick tidy and picked out a clean outfit. I hesitated. I really should shave my legs, just in case, you never know. Murphy's law, the day I don't will be the day we would go down that road. I was in mid shave when my phone jingled. I rinsed the shaving cream off my hands. *His timing is impeccable.*

"So, we can go to the bar and listen to music that we don't like, or we can drink at your place and listen to country?"

"No brainer. My place."

"Good. Oh, it looks like I might be late. I just got pulled over."

"What? Oh no."

"Yup. Speeding and driving while texting. Damn."

"Put down your phone and behave!"

Half an hour later bright headlights lit up the living room. I pulled on my boots and ran out the door. He was already waiting for me on the back deck. "Hi," he said brightly.

"Hey you." His arms encircled me before we walked eagerly to his truck. There was an excitable energy between us tonight, it felt easy, natural. I climbed in while moving children's toys off to the side.

"So," I began cautiously, "how bad was the damage?"

He laughed. "Not that bad. He was nice and gave me a bit of a break. I only got charged for speeding. He appreciated the fact that I was cooperative."

"Good. Oh," my voice rose. "I love this song."

He smiled and turned it up. "And I didn't even plan that. It's a good one."

"Luke Bryan. Your Mama Should've Named You Whiskey," I said under my breath. He looked over and smiled my way.

"Just a little taste won't hurt at all, but once I get a sip I know I'm gonna wanna drink it gone, all gone. 90 proof is an understatement I get around you and I'm way past wasted I can't think at all," we looked toward each other quickly and sang the chorus. *"Your mama should've named you whiskey. I never should've let you kiss me. And every time you leave it hits me. Your mama should've named you whiskey"*

"Good song indeed," he said under his breath. The liquor store was our first stop. I treated myself to Malibu and pineapple juice. He went with his Black's. I looked at him dubiously. "You sure you want to go with that one again?"

He grinned. "Yup."

We paid for our drinks and I slid inside the truck. "So," I said, "there's a drug store across the street. I need to stop there. I should buy some Advil just in case. If tonight is going to be anything like New Years I want to be prepared."

His eyes widened and he laughed. "Done."

I found the Advil and grabbed a pack of Gravol as well, just in case, better safe then sorry. I found Bryce picking out a toothbrush and deodorant. I didn't comment, but I'm pretty sure my smile said it all. *He's planning to stay the night.*

We waited in line to pay for our items when he spoke. "Look, it's you."

I looked at him slightly confused. "What?"

He leaned around me and picked up an InStyle magazine. Amy Adams was on the cover, her hair flowed and she wore a gorgeous red dress. I rolled my eyes and laughed. "I don't see it!"

He looked from the magazine to me and held it in front of his face, peeking out from behind. "How can you not see it? The resemblance is crazy."

I rolled my eyes and put the magazine back on the rack. "I'm flattered, thank you."

When we arrived back at my house, Bryce hopped into the shower. He came out grinning, fresh and clean. "Thank you. I feel so much better now."

I smiled. "You're welcome."

⌘

"Okay. The object of the game is drinking." I looked at him teasingly as he sat across from me at the kitchen table. An empty mug sat between us and he passed a quarter through his fingers. He continued on. "Whoever bounces the quarter into the cup wins that round so to speak, as the other person has to take a drink."

"Mmk. That sounds easy enough."

We took turns, waiting for the clink of the quarter to land in the mug. I wore a smug grin, I wasn't half bad at this game. I smiled happily as my quarter once again landed in the mark. His jaw dropped slightly in disbelief as he had to take another swig.

"Are you sure you've never played this before?" his eyes narrowed. "You're good at this."

I smiled innocently. "This is my first time. Like I told you before, I really don't drink that much. Only with you it seems."

"I'm a bad influence on you."

"Not really. It's Friday night, a night to kick back and have some fun."

His grin broadened. "It is. So," he clinked the quarter into the mug and continued, "I don't know why, but you still make me nervous. I still feel shy around you."

I looked up at him quickly. "Oh. I-I'm sorry. I don't mean to make you nervous," I bit my lip. "Am I doing something in particular?"

He leaned back in the chair, smiling. "No. I really like you," his eyes looked serious. "I'm not always going to be this way. I promise."

I met his eyes. "I like you too. Don't worry, I think you're doing fine. Besides, you're not the only one who's unsure."

"Okay."

We wrapped up our game and stretched out on the couch and listened to music. He sang lightly to a song, one of our favorites, Gord Bamford's, '*When Your Lips Are So Close.*' This boy was trouble. It wasn't the first time I had thought it, and I doubt it would be the last. Trouble with a capital 'T'. I was falling hard. Damn him. Damn his charms. I studied his strong jaw line as the glare of the lamp cast a soft glow against his skin. My gaze lingered over his body. That was good too. Contentment fell heavy over me. In this moment, I felt like one of the luckiest girls in the world. Bryce stood and took my hand, gently lifting me to him. I fell into his arms, and once again we began to dance across the living room floor. *Time, you can stand still right now. You have my permission.*

"Do you know how to waltz?" he asked.

I shook my head. "I do not."

"I'll teach you."

I watched our feet move together and listened closely as he gave me directions. Left. Feet together. *Check.* Front to back. *Check and check.* Right. *Check. This is easy.* Front, and lift. *Whoops. What? I missed that.*

"Oops, sorry," I muttered.

"No worries. You'll get it."

He took me through the steps once more and I found my rhythm. My confidence grew and I was able to lift my gaze from our feet to his face. He looked very amused.

I smiled uncertainly. "What is it?"

He chuckled. "Instead of a gentle lift, you kinda pop up. You're very bouncy."

"Ohh," I groaned and buried my face in his chest quickly. "Sorry. I thought I was rocking it."

He laughed. "It's cute. You are very cute."

I smiled, suddenly feeling shy. "Why, thank you."

We danced to a few more songs before we settled next to each other on the couch. "Can I ask you something?" he said cautiously.

"Anything."

"Have you ever been engaged?"

"No. You?"

"Yes. I was to Aiden's mom."

Makes sense. As long as it wasn't to the other one. "How come it didn't work out?"

Bryce shrugged. "We were always better off as friends. It wasn't meant to be." He looked at me. "Have you ever been pregnant?"

Jeez he's just firing them away here. "No."

He nodded. "You haven't the found right guy to start a family with?"

"Not even close."

"Okay. I'm sorry, I was just curious."

"Fair enough."

He studied me. "You want kids, right?"

"I do. One day."

He nodded. "They change your whole world, your entire being. It's a love like never before." He looked deep in thought. "Aiden is my world. I'd do anything for him." He bit his lip. "But I do know when the time comes, it'll be him who has to walk into a new family."

I sat closer, sensing this was hard for him. "I've seen the two of you together, there is no denying the love you have for him, and his for you. You boys have a very strong connection. Nothing can come between something like that."

He looked at me with thoughtful eyes. "Thank you."

"I'm just stating the truth."

He blew out a breath. "Please don't ever cheat on me."

I sat back in surprise. "What?" *Where is this coming from?*

He looked at me sadly. "I'm a nice guy, so I'd probably forgive you and stay. I'd find a way to look passed it. But please, don't do that to me."

This was a man who spoke from experience. I looked at him, his guard down. He sat next to me, completely vulnerable. In this moment, we were polar opposites. Bryce wore his heart on his sleeve, while I remained closed off. I could never let myself be so exposed; the thought alone was enough to terrify me. My walls went up and I hated myself for it.

"I would never do that to you, or to anyone else for that matter. I am not that type of girl."

He looked at me, smiling softly. "I know. But you're a pretty girl. Pretty girls can have whoever they want."

"Bryce, I'm looking at who I want." *I will never hurt you.*

He looked at me softly, sadness brimming amongst his eyes. "Come here," he pulled me in and I snuggled against his chest, his arms held me tightly. "I thought I lost you awhile ago."

I looked up at his quiet voice, confused. "Oh? How so?"

"Do you remember that day when you took me for that five hour walk?"

I laughed and swatted him lightly. "It was not five hours."

He smiled. "My head drove me insane. I kept thinking *"I really like this girl. She's quiet, so am I. That's cool. But you need to say something. Anything. Don't walk into the fence. Don't fall. Watch where you're going. Say something!"*

I straightened and looked at him fondly. "We're more alike than I thought." I smiled brightly.

"Oh yeah?" He shook his head. "I have never met anyone quite like you before. I think that's what scares me. I'm definitely used to girls who don't stop talking."

I shrugged. "I'm comfortable with silence. If I have something to say, I'll say it. If not, then I'm fine enjoying the company around me. If you're looking for a real chatty girl, I can tell you right now that it won't be me."

He shook his head quickly. "No, I like that you're quiet."

"Good."

His head snapped toward the radio. "He's my favorite artist!"

I listened. "Paul Brandt? He's good. I like him too."

Bryce looked thoughtful. I could tell he was sifting through an old memory. "I got to see him live once. We waited after the concert and I got to meet him," he smiled, "I got my picture taken with him, I was so excited. I couldn't help but think 'holy crap, I'm touching Paul Brandt." He laughed. "I couldn't stop smiling."

I looked at him closely and a smile pulled at my lips. "How cute are you?"

We stayed up for hours just talking. It was quite simple really, and yet, I

96

couldn't remember the last time I'd had so much fun. The yawns eventually began to take over. I peeked at the clock shining bright, it read 3:00 a.m. I began to wonder if we'd ever get to sleep at a decent hour while we were together.

"I'm so tired," I said groggily.

"Me too. Bed time?"

I nodded, he would get no argument from me. We brushed our teeth, got into our PJ's and made our way to the bed. Bryce set up the fan in his favorite spot. I lay on my side, head propped against the pillow. He placed his body next to mine, and wrapped his arms around me.

"Mmm," I let out. "You are so warm. I love it." I moved in closer. "My heater."His arms tightened around me. I let my eyes close, enjoying the moment; the darkness of the room, our warm bodies pressed into each other, and the soothing sound of the fan in the background, it was perfect. Bryce shifted his body and placed his hands on either side of me. I was gently placed on my back, and found myself staring up at him. I smiled softly and wrapped one arm around his neck, the other traced slowly down his back.

He smiled, shaking his head slowly from side to side. "Hmm. I'm still nervous."

I said nothing. My fingers ran through his hair in a quiet manner. I held his gaze and tried to focus on my own breathing. My heart raced a mile a minute and I worried it would be too much. This felt right. It felt safe, even though my body was going into overdrive. I had never cared about someone the way I was beginning to care for him. No one ever looked at me the way he did. His eyes took me in so softly, like he was looking at something very special. My mind began to waken. *It's actually going to happen. This is happening! Just remember to breathe.* He leaned in and our lips found each other's in the dark. With one arm cradled around my side, he gently lifted me into a sitting position and my arms brought him closer. His fingertips traced down my sides and they paused at the bottom of my shirt. I lifted my arms overhead. His eyes met mine and he nodded, a tender smile growing. With one hand he cupped my face and pressed his lips to mine. With his free hand, he ran his fingers up the small of my back, and with a quick motion unhooked my bra.

I pulled my face away from his with sudden surprise. "Smooth move."

He smiled. "I'm glad it worked out that way."

We laughed quietly and I lied back as his warm torso pressed against mine. I ran my fingers through his hair once more, and traced a fingertip down his back, admiring the smoothness of his muscles. He pulled away slightly and met my eyes. "Are you okay?"

I smiled slowly. "Yes." I studied him closely and let my fingertips trace his face, and our two bodies became one.

CHAPTER 6

I wiggled my toes happily. I was perfectly content wrapped up in the arms of someone I was getting dangerously close too. *I didn't expect to find you. I don't want to need you. But you are becoming my light and it's starting to feel safe. Loving you, that's what scares me the most.*

Bryce let out a content sigh and pulled me closer. "Morning, you."

I turned over to face him. "Good morning."

He leaned in to kiss me. "I didn't expect that to happen," he smiled, "but I'm glad it did."

I grinned. "Me too."

His phone alarm went off and he groaned. "No." He wrinkled his nose. "I have to help my mom's friends move today." He looked at me with a mischievous look. "Why'd you make me drink so much?"

"Ha. You're a funny guy." I gave him a quick kiss. "Have fun today, I'm so done with moving."

He grinned. "So what you're saying is that you don't want to help?"

I grimaced. "Not particularly."

"I wouldn't let you help anyways. You've done too much already." He groaned and got out of bed. "I don't want to go."

I couldn't help but laugh at his pout. He looked downright miserable until his eyes twinkled slightly. "Come here, you."

I met him in the center of my bedroom where he wrapped me in a long, tight hug. I let my head rest against him, I could have stayed there all day. Moments later we stood at the back door where I watched Bryce slowly pull on his boots.

He straightened and reached for his jacket. "I'll see you soon. I wish I didn't have to go." He stepped forward and we shared a kiss.

"Have fun moving," I teased.

"Yeah, yeah. I'll do my best."

⌘

"Settle down Maggie."

My black dog bounced excitedly from left to right as I struggled to clip on her leash. Jane and I were at the lake, taking the dogs for a walk. It was a beautiful day, but cold. The sky was bright blue and white puffy clouds floated lazily overhead. I sucked in a deep breath, and felt the cool winter air burn into my lungs. The icy breeze hit me, and it stung my ears. I quickly pulled the toque lower against my head.

"She's a cold one," I stated.

Jane zipped up her jacket higher. "You're not kidding."

"How have things been going for you?" I asked.

"Pretty good. Aaron and I are going away this weekend, so that'll be a nice change of pace."

"Aw, sounds like fun. Sometimes it's nice to get away. Change of scenery."

Jane nodded. "Yes, it is," she looked at me with a raised eyebrow. "How are you and Bryce?"

A warm heat flushed my cheeks. "Really good."

Jane stopped and grabbed my forearm. "Oh my God! It happened, didn't it?"

I leaned my head back and stared at the bright sky. "Yes, it sure did." I smiled fondly at the memory.

Jane studied my face quizzically. "So, I take it things went well?"

"Oh, Jane, you have no idea. It was amazing. A perfect night."

She smirked. "That's all you're going to give me isn't it?"

I nodded. "Yup!" *My lips are sealed.*

After the walk, I drove home and settled onto the couch. Today felt like a writing day. The weather had turned gray and wet, and I had no desire to go outside unless need be. With a mug of steaming tea and pyjamas on, I grabbed my notebook and mindlessly wiggled the pen in my hand. When I found the words I placed the pen to the paper and let my wrist do the rest.

She will call and you will run.

Her words paint such a pretty picture.

Her eyes will pull you in.

At her touch you will tremble and beg for more.

She isn't me.

Three's a crowd and I drew the short end of the straw

Yet you won't walk away,

And I can't run.

Your love is such a lonely place to be.

She will point at you. You will play her part.

Her beauty isn't for all to see.

Yet you can't look away.

Why couldn't it be me?

I'll never compare.

Three's a crowd and I drew the short end of the straw

Yet you won't walk away,

And I can't run.

Your love is such a lonely place to be.

I read it over a few times and nodded in satisfaction. I wrote for a little longer, plucked a few chords on the guitar, and an odd feeling washed over me. It settled over and held on tight, and I did not like it. I realized I missed him. *I don't like this. I don't like it one bit.*

I was used to being on my own, it's what I had come to accept from life's experiences. There were very few people who would stand by your side through the darkness and the light, share your laughter and help to wipe away your tears. I was aware I had trust issues, but when you see time and time again, the same words on a different face, the dances all begin to look alike. The same lines get recycled over and over, but the outcome always remained the same; I was alone in the end.

It's not just romantic relationships that had left a mark. It started when I was so very young. A man who should have been there, his words should have meant something, but they didn't. And he never stayed to tell me it would all be okay. He'd still make his rare appearances every so often, but they had always been short lived and they would come at a price. I'd be left standing alone, looking at the hurt in my brother's eyes. It had taken a toll on us as a family and I couldn't do it anymore. So, I built my wall, and I built it strong. It would take a very special, strong and patient man to break it down. Still, with all that said, I really didn't try to be bitter. I always yearn to find the light amongst the shadows. Bad things don't last forever, at some point they must end and the light will break free. Like Gary Allen's song states, *"Every storm runs out of rain. Every dark night turns into day. Every heartache will fade away."* I hold on to that hope. I would always hold on to that hope. I would always wish for happiness, and hopefully, it would find me and never let go, for I'd been waiting so long, and so patiently.

I stared at my phone. It shouldn't be this hard to pick it up and send a text. I chewed my lip, what the hell. I'll do it. "Hey. How are you today? Are you up for doing something?"

"Hello, my little china doll. Yes, I am. Do you want to meet me at KMS tools? It's across from the mall. I need to grab some supplies for work."

I smiled, *my little china doll.* I loved it when he called me that. "Okay, sounds like a plan. What time?"

"I'll be there around eleven"

"Okay, see you in a bit."

I was proud of myself for finding the place, and I didn't even use my GPS. Directions and maps were not my friends, but today luck was on my side. I pulled into the parking lot and didn't see his truck yet. I found an empty space and backed in. I hopped out and headed for the entrance when his blue truck pulled into the lot.

Bryce hopped out with a bounce and opened his arms to wrap me up. "Hey. It's nice to see you." His arms encircled me and he tossed me lightly from side to side. I pulled back and glanced up at him curiously. "Hi, you seem like you're in a good mood today."

He grinned. "I am." His eyes went to the store. "This is one of my favorite places. I could spend so much money in here, it's crazy."

I smiled. I could relate. "That's how I feel about tack stores."

We walked into the store, and he was immediately drawn to an item. He held a large metal clip shaped like a D. He studied it carefully and checked it for strength. I had no idea what the thing was.

"Umm," I began, "what is that?"

"It's a Bessey clamp."

My eyebrows rose. "A Bessey clamp?" I chuckled. "It sounds like the name of a cow. Here, ol' Bessey."

His eyes went big in surprise and he laughed. "Great, now every time I use one of these I'm going to think of a cow."

I shrugged. "Sorry."

He took me through the aisles, and pointed out tools he would love to have one day. He was like a kid in a candy store, bouncing from aisle to aisle with an eager hunger. I listened quietly, feeling slightly out of my element, but enjoying the lesson. His eyes expertly searched for the quality in the products. He would nod in approval, or his top lip would curl ever so slightly from disappointment. I smiled to myself, noticing he couldn't hide much; his face was rather animated, it told many stories.

He stopped in front of a particular welding machine and sighed heavily. "Now this is a beauty. I would love to have this one day."

I looked down toward the yellow piece of machinery, and snuck a peek at the price tag. "Ouch. That's a pretty penny."

"It is. I'm going to need one in the future."

"Oh?"

He nodded and looked at me, a hopeful look crossed his face. "I want to have my own mobile welding business one day." He pressed his lips closed and the thought took him away. "One day," he said quietly.

I stepped closer. "It will happen. If you want something bad enough, there's always a way to make it happen."

He smiled then and nodded. "You're right." He purchased some of his goodies, and we found ourselves sitting in his truck, talking. He looked at me with a bit of an unsure expression on his face. "I had a terrible sleep last night. Did you get the picture I sent you?"

"I did, of an owl."

He shuddered. "Yes. That thing freaked me out. It hung out in front of my bedroom window all night."

"Hmm, I can't quite remember the old wives tale about owls, but apparently it's a bad omen if they look you in the eye. I don't remember the exact reason for it though," I looked at him quickly. "Did it look you in the eye?"

His eyes bulged. "Yes! Didn't you see the picture? It looked right at me!"

I laughed loudly. "You look terrified! Why are you so scared of them anyways?"

"I watched a terrifying movie about aliens last night, and an owl was in it," he mumbled.

"Ohh, I see now. So, you're a chicken?"

"Oh yeah."

"What was the movie called?"

"The fourth kind," he shuddered. "I will never, ever watch it again." He then went on to describe, in great detail I might add, the events of the movie. I enjoyed every minute of it. Once he was done his tale, he let out a breath and looked at me.

I smiled and grinned playfully. "Hoot hoot."

He shuddered. "No! Don't you dare."

I held up my hands in a truce. "Okay, okay. I won't."

"Good. So, what do you want to do now?"

"Hmm, coffee?"

"Sure. There's a Starbucks across the street and we can browse at Chapters after?"

"Sounds good to me."

He ordered himself a coffee, and I ended up getting my usual Chai Tea Latte. I ignored the smirk he gave me. He liked to razz me about drinking tea. Apparently it made me an 'old lady.'

"You don't know what you're missing," I joked.

We found a table outside, under the space heater. The gray clouds began to dissipate as dusk was near. Shades of burnt orange and a rich red splashed across the sky. It was turning into a lovely night.

Bryce's phone went off and he glanced at it, darkness clouded his handsome features. "My ex has been texting me lately."

My back went up. Of course she was. "I see," was all I said.

He shook his head. "She can't leave some things alone…" he trailed off. "My mom still keeps in touch with her. It bothers me. I've told her to stop, that it's not fair to me. I wasn't happy with her and I deserve to be happy."

I traced the top of my cup, feeling rather uncomfortable. "Yeah, that doesn't sound like a good situation."

He frowned. "No." Bryce glanced at the space where his truck was parked. "Aw, my truck looks so tiny."

I looked behind me and smiled. A large lifted dually had parked beside his. I giggled, he was right, his looked small. "That things a beast. It can make anyone's truck look small," I offered.

He grimaced. "Sure, sure. I really need a new truck one day. Something with more room, and one that I can start my business up with. Can't afford that yet."

"Yeah, unfortunately trucks are not cheap; I'd like to get myself a newer one soon, something with less kilometres on it. One day it will happen. For now though, your truck's fine. I like it."

"Yeah, I do too. My ex actually helped me buy it. She made more money at the time then me." He frowned. "She liked to hang that over my head."

She sounds like a peach. "I'm sorry to hear that. No one should talk to someone they care about like that, it's not fair."

"No, no it's not."

We finished our drinks and the conversation flowed in a happier direction. We soon wandered over to Chapters and began to browse the seemingly endless rows of books. I flipped through a travel book and glanced out of the corner of my eye. Bryce was one row over, watching me.

I raised a brow. "Whatcha doing?"

He seemed to think for a split second. "So this is who you really are then?"

"What?" I put the book down.

"You're perfectly content looking at books, you know your music, you love your animals, and you're so…so nice. This is who you really are?"

I was slightly puzzled. "Yes, this is me. This is who I am and who I'll always be."

He seemed happy with the answer. "I like that."

I made my way next to him. "Where is this coming from?"

"I'm just not used to this. I'm used to girls pulling a fast one. I think they're one person and before I know it, they turn into someone else completely."

I nodded, I got it, to some extent. "Well I can assure you what you see is what you get."

"I'm glad."

We finished up in the bookstore and were once again in the front seat of his truck. An idea seemed to strike him. "There's a horse boarding place near here. I know you're not bringing out your horse yet, but did you want to see it?"

Horses. I perked right up and looked at Bryce, eyes wide with excitement. He laughed. "I'll take that as a yes."

"Yes!" I said with a bounce.

He plugged his Ipod into the stereo and began quizzing me. He managed to stump me on a few songs. He looked thrilled, and I pretended to pout.

"Here it is." He pulled over to the side of the road and I leaned forward to look out his window, nearly crawling on his lap. He looked up with a very amused expression on his face. I glanced at him quickly, smiled and went back to studying the property.

"It looks cute," I sighed. Horses. Barns. Heaven.

"It is. It's a pretty decent place."

"I'll have to check it out in the daylight. Would you be up for helping me look at boarding stables when the time is right?"

He grinned. "I would love too."

"Good." I settled into the seat with a smile on my face.

Once I was home, I drew myself a bubble bath. I turned the music on and soaked in the warmth for quite some time, enjoying the high from the day. Afterwards I did laundry and stretched out across my bed. My phone jingled and I had a picture message from Bryce. I waited for it to download before glancing down at the screen once more. As I did, butterflies appeared in my stomach. He sent me a picture of a couple sitting at a large table covered in a white cloth. Amongst the table were guests dressed in formal clothing. The picture was taken from behind and the focus of the photo was of a woman in a white wedding gown, leaning her head lovingly against her newly wed husband.

It was an outdoor wedding with white twinkling lights strung up under a pink sky. He had written a simple message underneath. "I want a wedding like this one day."

My heart began to thump unevenly as I stared down at the beautiful image before me. I couldn't pull my eyes away; it scared me a little, but it also set a fire of excitement. I cleared my throat and typed a simple response.

"It's beautiful."

"Dean Brody's crop circles just popped into my head. Beam you up, they're going to beam you up! Ahh."

"Haha that's funny. It's a catchy song."

"No! Not anymore. What are you up too?"

"Nothing much, just winding down for the night. You?"

"I'm watching a scary movie."

"Why do you do this to yourself?"

"I don't know. Do you want to come over and protect me tonight?"

"Protect you eh? Yes, I could. Will you protect me if I get scared?"

"Of course."

I looked at the clock, it was 7:00 p.m. Not too bad. I'd never been to his house before, but I was up for an adventure. "Okay. Text me your address. I'm coming in my pj's."

Thank god for GPS. I would have been lost without it. It was one of those dark and gloomy nights where you really don't want to leave the house, but I found myself dancing to my truck as butterflies of excitement fled through me. I hopped in, turned on some good tunes and plugged his address into the GPS. Thirty-four minutes away. Not too bad. As I neared my destination I passed his house the first time. It was hard to see the addresses in the dark. I cursed under my breath and after repeating the loop, I found it. I had to park a few houses away as parking was limited.

"I'm here."

"Okay. Go to the right, through the gate. I will meet you there."

I followed his directions and he met me halfway. He was in a blue T-shirt that made his arms look good, and his tattoo peaked through ever so slightly. His outfit was completed with plaid pyjama pants and a broad grin.

"I found you!" I said, rather happily.

"You did." He looked at my pj's. "Cute."

He led me inside. "It's not much," he said rather apologetically.

I looked around briefly, trying to find my bearings. The first room was the kitchen, it was rather small, but it seemed functional and held modern appliances. Bryce's bedroom door was slightly behind where the fridge stood, and to the right of the kitchen lay the bathroom and Mike's bedroom. Next to Mike's room was the living room. It held two loveseats, a TV, and a book case. A few pictures hung on the walls here and there, but other than that the place only seemed to hold the bare essentials. Mike was going through a divorce and had recently moved in with Bryce.

I looked around, nodding. "It's not a bad place, I like the flooring."

He smiled wryly. "Yeah, that part is nice."

I followed Bryce into the living room where his uncle stretched on the couch, feet propped up. We greeted each other warmly and I found a seat next to Bryce. Mike leaned forward and began to give a quick recap on the movie. I turned my attention to the TV and watched the movie tentatively. Horror wasn't my genre, I had a weak stomach for these things. As I focused my eyes on the big screen ahead, someone got decapitated. I cringed and looked away as the head bounced down the stairs, the eyes still wide in surprise. I covered my eyes quickly. Bryce placed his hand on my leg and patted it comfortingly, chuckling. Thank goodness I had come near the ending of the movie, it was shortly after 10 p.m. when Bryce rose stiffly from the couch.

"I should get to bed. I have to be up early for work tomorrow," he groaned slightly and held his hand open for me to follow.

I said my goodnight to Mike and followed Bryce to his bedroom. His room was small. It had just enough space for a dresser, night table and bed. His clothes were folded up in the corner, and tiny little slippers were placed neatly below the dresser. I smiled, those must belong to Aiden.

I walked to the cartoon slipper collection and knelt down to admire them. "How cute are these?" I murmured to myself.

Bryce smiled. "You think those are cute? Wait for this." He rifled through his closet and pulled out a set of tiny work pants and a matching shirt.

My hand grazed my chest. "Those are adorable!" I stepped closer and traced a finger over the stitching. "Kids clothes are so cute, they're just so little!"

His face lit up, all the while looking at me. "They sure are," he took my hand and led me to the bed.

I settled beside him and rested my head against his shoulder. "I've missed my heater," I sighed.

He laughed brightly. "Oh yea?"

"Mm-hmm."

"I'll always be warm for you."

I smiled. "That works for me, I can always use the extra heat."

He flopped down against the pillow and pulled me down with him. "Have you ever tried those overnight oats people are talking about?" he asked.

My eyes lit up, it was one of my favorite go to breakfasts. "Oh yes, I have. You need to try it, they're a game changer."

He barked out a laugh. "A game changer, eh?"

I grinned and nodded. "You're missing out on life. I'll email you the basic recipe and you can add in whatever you want."

"Huh, I'm kind of excited to try it out now, thank you." He squeezed me tighter and let out a slightly disappointed sigh. "I think we should try to sleep, mornings come quick. I can leave you the spare key if you wanted to sleep in tomorrow. Just lock up before you go and hide the key under the mat."

I gazed up at him. He smiled down at me with an almost adoring look, his brown eyes bright and happy. My stomach twisted into knots; it was one of the many looks he had given me which made me feel I belonged to someone in a very good way. For the first time in my life, I felt like I didn't have to be alone anymore, that I was holding onto something very special.

I laid my head against his chest. "Thank you, that's very sweet, but I think I'll get up with you and head home so Maggie won't be left alone for too long."

His eyes took on a sly look. "You mean I get to see Ryleigh in the early hours of the morning?"

I laughed and lightly smacked him. "Haha, you're a funny guy."

We settled against each other neatly. My body relaxed and grew heavy next to his when all of a sudden he sat up.

"Oh," he said, "I'll be right back, I have something for you."

"Oh?" I propped up on an elbow and waited for him to return, my curiosity growing.

Bryce strode in with a fleece blanket hanging over his elbow. He looked at me and smiled. "This is for you to use, I know you get cold easily and this is a cozy one." He straightened the blanket out for me to see, his head peeked over the edge. "And it's got horses. It's a win, win."

I shook my head in wonder, he really had been paying attention over time to the things I had said. It was small, thoughtful gestures like this one that made such an impact. He was beginning to feel like home, my safe place.

"Here you go," he leaned forward and draped the blanket over me. With a smile, he crawled into bed. He sat up for a moment to flick on the fan and turn out the light.

He chuckled and kissed the top of my head. "Goodnight, my Ryleigh, I'm glad you're here."

I sighed heavily with contentment, there was nowhere else I would rather be. I stole a glance at the clock, it was quarter to eleven. "We did it," I whispered softly.

"We did what?"

"We're going to bed at a decent hour together."

He laughed in surprise. "So we are. Sweet dreams."

"You too. Watch out for owls."

He groaned. "Don't start!"

I laughed. "Goodnight, Bryce." *My Bryce.*

Five-thirty came early. I awoke to the sound of Bryce groaning and hitting the alarm. My eyes blinked open slightly, and for a moment I felt disorientated, unsure of where I was. Something very soft and warm brushed against my cheek. I peeked down; it was the fleece blanket, my extra insurance for a warm night. A smile broke out onto my sleepy face.

"Watch your eyeballs," he warned.

I pulled the cover over my eyes and I was glad that I did. Even through the comforter, the light shone brightly. I heard Bryce get dressed and then the bright light went out. I sat up sleepily and followed him out into the kitchen, stretching my arms slowly over my head. He turned on the coffee maker and leaned against the counter, yawning. He looked at me and smirked. I knew he was laughing at my appearance but he didn't say a word, although he didn't have to. The glint in his eyes and smirk on his face said it all. I excused myself to the washroom and hesitantly peeked into the mirror and let out a groan. My long auburn hair was slightly askew. I quickly ran my fingers through the strands to tame them. My eyes weren't quite all the way open, and pillow lines marked my cheek. I turned on the tap, let the water run warm, and splashed my face, hoping it would make me look alive. I stepped out of the washroom and entered the kitchen where Bryce poured coffee into a traveler mug. He wore a long sleeve shirt, a pair of black work pants and work boots. My gaze lingered, he was a nice sight to see first thing in the morning, I could get used to this.

He peeked under his elbow and smiled warmly. "Are you sure you don't want some coffee?"

I wrinkled my nose. "No thanks."

He screwed on the lid to the mug and looked at the time, his face falling ever so slightly. "It's time to head out."

I followed him to the door, and quickly pulled on my jacket and boots. We walked side by side in comfortable silence into the street together. It was an eerie morning, a light drizzle fell and a thick fog blanketed the earth hiding everything that was once familiar.

"Creepy," I mumbled.

"It is."

I stopped at the end of his driveway and looked down the street, left to right. "Huh, I don't remember where I parked." The fog certainly didn't help the matter.

He laughed. "What?"

I shooed him away. "Go to work. I'll find it."

He looked at me, with a dubious expression. "You sure?"

"Yes." I walked into his arms and gave him a quick hug. "Have a good day."

I chose to go left and walked slowly, scanning the street. The quietness of the morning was broken when Bryce fired up his engine. His truck tires pulled out, and away he went. I continued walking a bit further but nothing looked right. I decided to head the other way, and sure enough there was my truck. Success! I let my engine run for a moment before testing out my heater. I flicked on the radio to fill the silence.

My phone jingled. "Did you find your truck?"

"Yes! In it now."

"Good. You're so cute. All confused and lost because you forgot where you parked, haha."

I smiled, placed the truck in drive and headed for home feeling perfectly content.

CHAPTER 7

"What does your dream property look like?"

That was an easy question. I had always dreamt of owning hundreds of acres of rolling hills where I could sit outside and watch my horses run. A rustic, western looking barn had always completed my fantasy, with the looming mountains in the distance. My dream home had never been large, I had always wanted something simple; a cute and cozy farmhouse with a wrap around porch. I envisioned a large oak tree by a pond, with a tire swing hanging from one of it's gnarled limbs. My own piece of paradise. I wanted to live in a place where the seasons change, and snow comes to settle for the winter. I rested my face against the palm of my hand and got lost in the vision. I could see myself being very happy on my farm, looking after the animals and raising a family. I tore myself out of the daydream and picked up my phone.

"Have you ever seen the show Heartland? That's it."

"Yes! I'll buy it for you. All you have to do is make me babies."

"Done deal."

"Haha, okay! Can we get a donkey after I build you a horse barn?"

"I love donkeys. Of course! A miniature one?"

"Yes! Well, my break's over, back to work I go. I'll talk to you later."

As I set my phone down, it jingled. It was my friend, Ben. "Hey. Did you want to do something today?"

"Sure! I'll be over in ten."

"K! See ya soon. Jared is here too."

I frowned slightly, Jared and Ben were roommates, and I had known Jared first. We had been close briefly, but Jared and I never seemed to be on the same page, not entirely. The guys lived close to me, a short ten minute drive down the back roads. Jared's place was where everyone went to gather. Summertime was a good season at Jared's. We would often get together for BBQ's in the backyard or bonfires. Jared usually kept a stash of marshmallows set aside for me after all this time. One of our first real trips together had been a camping trip. The memory still brought a smile to my face. We had a marshmallow roasting competition together, and Jared had cooked a gourmet chicken dinner with roasted potatoes over the campfire. When darkness settled over the campsite, we decided to go for a walk to explore the site. It was pitch black and neither of us had brought the flashlight along. We had wandered hand in hand for well over an hour, trying to find our way back. His truck had an automatic start, and he repeatedly pressed the button on his keychain to start his vehicle. We each held our breath and stood perfectly still, listening for the sound of his engine. When we heard his engine rumble to life, we ran toward the sound. Eventually, we found our way back. Although they were short lived, they had been good times.

I pulled into Jared's drive and hopped out of the truck. My stomach still formed knots as I walked up the familiar steps to the front door. I had shared many laughs here, as well as tears he would never know about. I knocked on the door loudly and a male's voice called from inside. "Come in!"

I stepped inside the warm house, and found Ben and Jared at the kitchen table drinking a beer.

"Hey, Ryleigh!" Ben called brightly. "How are ya?"

I unraveled my scarf and pulled the toque off my head. "Good!"

Jared came to greet me and took my jacket. I looked up at his tall frame, his blue eyes looked uncertain. I often noticed he never felt at ease in my presence. We kept a safe distance from each other. A lot went unsaid between us, but neither of us wanted to face it. We pushed it further into the closet, and kept the door shut tightly.

I smiled hesitantly at Jared. "Hi." I said quietly.

He smiled slowly. "Hey." He studied me. "Come on in."

"Okay."

He tried to smile brightly, but it did not reach his eyes. "Ben's in the kitchen."

I followed him quietly and sat next to Ben. He looked at me eagerly, excitement lit his eyes. "I'm trying out a new recipe. You're staying for dinner."

I laughed. "You don't have to twist my arm."

Ben dealt out a deck of cards while Jared got one of my favorite fruit drinks from the fridge. A delicious aroma slowly began to fill the room, and my stomach rumbled in anticipation. I looked at the guys before me, and smiled as I picked up my hand of cards. A good meal was coming up, with good company. Today was turning out to be a very good day, the only thing to make it perfect was Bryce. I spent the majority of the early evening with the guys before it was time for me to head home. I managed to beat the darkness, and had time to take Maggie for a quick walk. I came home, kicked off my shoes, and slipped into my pj's. I knew my nightly Bryce text would be coming soon. Like a reliable clock, my phone jingled.

"My Ryleigh. How are you?"

"I'm doing very well. And you?"

"I'm doing good too. What did you do today?"

"The usual, cleaned, errands, got my security clearance started for work. Then I went to see some buddies of mine."

"Oh? Do you have many guy friends?"

"I do."

"I see."

Although they were just words on a screen, I could sense his displeasure. "It's nothing for you to worry about. I promise."

"I trust you, it's just I know how guys think. Can I meet them one day?"

"Of course."

"Okay. I don't mean to sound jealous, but the fact that it bothers me shows I care about you, as odd as that sounds."

"I get it. A little jealousy is only natural. Do you have any girl friends?"

"No. I don't have that many friends. I have two buddies I'm close too, but we don't see each other that much. And then there's the guys from the football team, but I only see them when the season is on."

"Ah I gotcha. Well, you don't have to worry about me. Promise."

"Okay. I trust you. Can I say something?"

"You may."

"I don't want to scare you off and have you run away on me."

"Shoot."

"I hope you're the one I end up marrying."

My eyes flew open in surprise and the phone slipped out of my grasp. *He said what now?* A flutter grew deep within my stomach. This boy played with my feelings. Feelings that I wasn't sure what to do with. *Don't break me, please. Handle me with care, us china dolls, we break.* I stared back at the screen. It wasn't a proposal; it was a hope. But the fact he brought it up meant he thought about it, I was on his mind. Bryce wore his heart on his sleeve, and I never could. I did not like to be vulnerable. I grew frustrated with myself. My wall went up once again. How I wanted to let that wall shatter for him, for the truth was, I thought about him quite often. He had found a way into my head, into my heart, and he stood strong. I wanted him next to me. I was ready to share my life with a good man by my side, and yet I remained a closed book on the matter. For unless you could read my thoughts, you would never know my secret hope.

The length of time grew between his sent message. I knew he would be holding his breath. I had no doubt in my mind, in my heart, that I could see forever with him. And I wanted too. He was becoming my best friend. He felt right with every fiber of my being, two paths that were meant to cross. The question was, would I ever be brave enough to say those words when the time came for it? Three words, eight letters. I had never said those words. Ever. If I said it, if I took that leap, I hoped he would be there to catch me.

I picked up the phone once more. "I can see a future with you as well." I hoped those words were satisfactory enough for him. My finger hovered over the send button. I tapped it quickly and watched as the message was delivered.

"I'm glad. I have to go to sleep. Goodnight, my dear. Sweet dreams."

"You too." *Oh Bryce, please be patient with me.*

⌘

I awoke with a start in the middle of the night. I didn't have nightmares very often but when I did, they sat with me. I stared at the dark ceiling and words ran through my head. *I'll be watching you leave. The distance will grow in between, you've been the better half of me. Take me by the hand and let's pretend this will all be okay; I'm sorry I wasn't strong enough to let you walk away.*

I picked up the pad of paper and pen that I left lying on my nightstand for times like these. I scribbled down the passage and flopped back down. I had a hard time getting comfortable. I turned onto my side, and stared through the dark at the empty bed. *I wish he was here, I miss him.* It had been a long week. Work was busy and Bryce had long hours. He was exhausted, so I let him be. I kept busy with daily activities and caught up with friends. It had now been just over a week since we had last seen each other. We spoke everyday, but the loneliness had begun to grow, and I did not like that. I hated feeling tied to someone. I felt perfectly content before he had come along, and perhaps that was what had been bothering me all along; for I didn't know how lonely I was until I had someone standing beside me.

I drummed my fingers impatiently against my quilt. This was not good. I knew who I was as a person, I liked the woman I had become. I didn't need someone to feel complete. I was perfectly capable. They say before you can truly let someone else into your world, one must first learn to accept themselves and be content with their own company, and I could honestly say I was. But my mindset was now changing. I couldn't help but think how nice it would be to fall asleep every night next to the one you truly cared about, and to wake up to that same face, to have someone standing beside you when things got tough, and to laugh at the joy's that would be sure to follow.

Gravel crunched on the driveway outside and I looked up. I magically hoped to see a dark blue pickup. It was not. Instead, a familiar white van had parked near my truck. It was James, my step-dad. I knew what this meant. My bed from home, my mattress was here! I had moved in a bit of a hurry, and my mattress did not fit in the already full load I carried. James offered to drop it off along the way in an upcoming business trip, and today was my lucky day. The temporary bed I had been using was not comfortable at all; I hated it with somewhat of a passion.

"It's here Maggie, it's here!" I danced with joy and quickly pulled on my shoes. I met James outside with a big grin. "Hi, is that my mattress?"

He smiled. "Yup. Come on, let's get it unloaded. I have to head out to Kelowna and I'd like to get there before it's dark."

"Sure, no worries, thank you so, so, so much!"

James grinned. "You're welcome."

James helped me take apart the other bed and we placed my mattress against the wall of the bedroom. He didn't stay long and we quickly exchanged goodbyes. I got busy putting my bed frame together when Sky came home. I grew frustrated as the bolts didn't line up properly through the frame.

"Stupid thing!" I yelled. "Ouch!" I pulled my finger back quickly as the bed frame bit me.

Sky poked his head in the door, one eyebrow raised. "Whatcha doing?"

I looked back at him once, and focused my attention back to the frame. "Trying to put this stubborn thing together."

"Ah, I see. Did you want some help?"

I looked at my brother in relief. "Please!"

"Sure." He strode in and knelt beside me, checking out my progress. "Okay, here, hand me the bolt."

I dropped the tiny piece into his palm and held the frame steady as he began to screw the bolts into place. "So," Sky began, "how tight am I putting these things in? What's his thrusting power like?"

I dropped my jaw in absolute horror, and smacked him across the back of the head. "Sky!" I nearly shouted. I looked at him with wide eyes and we began to laugh. "We are way to comfortable with each other," I mumbled.

Sky snickered, shoulders rising up and down in a quick motion. His blue eyes stared back at me with mischief. "Well, it's a legit question."

I rolled my eyes. "Never you mind. Just put them in tight."

Sky smirked. "Ah-ha. Okay."

Once the frame was securely put together, Sky helped me flip the mattress onto the empty frame. I pushed the bed to where I wanted it, just under the windows, and began to put fresh sheets and pillow cases on. I stood back, and brushed my hands together. My bed was complete. I looked at it with a frown, realizing one of my throw pillows was missing. I glanced around the room and saw the corner of the pillow peeking from behind my door. I pushed the door back and opened it wider. Something hard and heavy cracked against the top of my head. My teeth clacked together, and a sharp pain tore through my skull. My eyes began to water immediately. Sky stared back at me with wide eyes. Concern and guilt crossed his features.

My hand flew to the top of my head to assess the damage. I touched it gingerly, and felt a goose egg forming. "Son of a bitch! That hurt! What was that?"

I looked down at my feet, a large metal object lay lifelessly on the floor. Sky quickly bent over to pick it up. "Ah crap, that must've hurt. Are you okay?"

I touched my head carefully once more and winced. "I think so, but holy hell does it ever hurt!"

The corner of Sky's lip went up. "Uhh yeah, sorry. I forgot to take my chin up bar out of your door way."

I glared at him. "If I fall asleep and don't wake up tomorrow, this is all your fault."

⌘

"Ryleigh?"

"Bryce?"

"I'm dying."

"What?"

"I'm so sick. I tried to go to work today. I was almost there when I got really dizzy. Then I threw up, so I went home. I don't know what's wrong."

"Do you want me to take you to the doctor?"

"No. I took some flu medicine. It helps a bit, I think."

"Aw, poor guy. Are you okay?"

"I think so, just dizzy and tired. I hope I didn't overdose on the medication."

"How much did you take?"

"Uhh about two good glugs worth. I was just researching on the internet on how much is too much, and I think I've scared myself now. Do you think I over did it?"

"I think you're all right, you shall live to see another day."

"You can come over if you like. I just hope I don't get you sick. I already feel better than I did this morning. I've only thrown up once."

"Are you sure you want me there?"

"Yes. Come over. I haven't seen you in forever."

"Okay. Do you want me to bring you anything?"

"Just you."

"That I can do. I'll see you in a bit."

I knocked on his back door a short while later, and a very sleepy looking Bryce greeted me. His skin was paler than normal, his cheeks slightly flushed with fever. Yet, when he saw me, a smile lit his eyes.

"Aw, how are you feeling?" I asked as I gave him a careful hug.

"I'm okay, a lot better than I was earlier. I'm afraid I'll be no fun today, but I wanted to see you. Do you want to watch a movie?"

"I'd like that."

We each grabbed cozy blankets and snuggled on the couch. We enjoyed a movie and some light banter until his uncle Mike came home. He looked surprised to see Bryce home already. Bryce quickly filled his uncle in on his unfortunate start to the day.

"Huh, that's no fun. Make sure you get a good sleep tonight." Mike stretched his back and patted his stomach. "Well I'm starving," he looked at me. "Ryleigh, would you like some dinner? I was thinking of pasta and salad."

"That sounds delicious! Thank you."

Mike disappeared in the kitchen. I settled back against the couch and a sense of familiarity washed over me, I felt like I was home among family. Bryce chose another movie and I did not enjoy his choice. It was gory, it fell into the same category as 'The Saw' films. Most of the time I either had my hands over my face, or hidden behind the blanket. Bryce watched with amusement, I honestly think he spent more time watching my reactions than the movie.

"You're such a girl," he teased, lightly poking me. "It's not real, it's just make up."

"I don't care, it looks real! This is gross." I shivered.

Mike came in and offered me a plate of pasta, which swam in tomato sauce. On any given day, I preferred tomato based sauces over creamed ones. However, my stomach felt unsettled from the movie and the sauce bore a close resemblance to blood. Still, I was a little hungry and I didn't want to be rude. Mike sat down, joining us. He had no problem eating his meal.

Bryce noticed my hesitation. "Looks a bit like blood, eh?"

I glared at him "Shush."

I did my best to eat the pasta, I got through at least half. Bryce laughed and leaned toward me. "Do you want me to finish that for you?"

"Could you?"

He chuckled. "Yes."

After dinner the three of us stayed up for awhile visiting before it was time for bed. "Did you want me to stay?" I asked Bryce quietly.

His eyes grew soft. "Of course."

My face lit up. "Okay. I will."

I climbed into the familiar bed and pulled the covers close to my body. I placed my head gently against the pillow and winced. My head was still tender from the beating it had unexpectedly received; washing my hair had been excruciating.

Bryce noticed and he looked concerned. "You okay?" he asked quietly.

"Yes, my head is still sore from Sky's stupid chin up bar."

He shook his head. "You really are a clumsy one, aren't you? Here, let me see."

His fingers carefully ran through my hair, gently touching the sore spot. I winced and shied away.

"My poor girl," he muttered. "What am I going to do with you?"

I gave him a lopsided grin. "My aunt says I should be bubble wrapped."

He laughed loudly and studied me. "You know, that's not such a bad idea." We held each other through the night, our torso's pressed into one another. It was such a simple act, yet filled with such delicate kindness and affection, no words were needed. I fell asleep easily. Morning came fast. I awoke on my stomach with an arm resting along my back, legs intertwined with Bryce's. A smile spread to my face, I could wake up to this every day.

Bryce groaned. "I should go to work today."

I turned over. "Do you feel okay?"

"Much better than yesterday. Come on, help me get up."

Bryce and I stood in the dim kitchen. He pulled on his work boots and I attempted to put on my jacket. My extended arm hit the dangling light fixture above the kitchen table, sending it swinging back and forth roughly. I quickly grabbed it in an attempt to steady the fixture. Bryce's eyes went wide and his mouth gaped open with a slight grin.

"Oops!" I gave a sheepish look. "I'm going to take this whole place down."

He laughed. "Cute, cute girl."

We walked outside together and went our separate ways. Once again, as I started up the vehicle, my phone jingled.

"I wanted to kiss you but I didn't want to get you sick."

"You'd be worth the risk."

"I'll keep that in mind for next time."

⌘

"Did you want to come cuddle me while I sleep tonight?"

I read the message with a fond smile, yes, of course. "Most definitely."

"Okay. Can you come around seven?"

"Will do."

"See you soon."

The day passed quickly. I filled out work forms for the majority of my day. I was able to squeeze in a walk with Maggie, and a visit with Jane in the late afternoon. As of lately, I felt light, carefree, and blissfully happy. But most of all, I felt hopeful and free; like there was light at the end of my long dark tunnel. I packed my overnight bag, and hummed a happy tune. I said a quick goodnight to Maggie who was flopped lazily on the floor, and left her in my brother's care. Sky was now officially my roommate.

I gathered up the rest of my things when my phone jingled.

"Mike came home with some beers. Do you have something to drink?"

I scanned the kitchen and my eyes fell on the Malibu. "Yup. I don't have juice though. Do you have some?"

"Yes, orange juice."

"Okay, that'll do. I'm coming in my pj's again and I didn't want to have to stop somewhere."

"Haha, okay. Hurry up!"

"On my way!"

I made good time, the roads were fairly quiet. I turned the music up higher and sang along at the top of my lungs, while dancing happily in my seat as I let the tune carry me away. I felt mighty proud of myself, I had nearly memorized the route to his house. I found a spot to park along the roadside, grabbed my bag and jogged to his back door. I barely finished the first knock when he swung the door open, a big grin on his face.

"Hey! Come on in! I was playing guitar."

"Excellent!" I leaned around the corner, and waved to Mike who watched TV in the next room.

"Let's get you a drink first. I made you some orange juice."

He reached in the cupboard and pulled out a cup. The fridge door swung open and he grabbed the juice jug. I mixed my drink to taste and followed Bryce to his room, taking my spot on the bed. I leaned back against the wall and stretched out my legs, happily swinging my feet from side to side.

I smiled at him. "Play me something pretty."

He laughed. "Okay." And he did just that.

In the stillness of the room, with the guitar being the loudest thing amongst us, the nerves set in. I'm not sure why they kept teasing me, but tonight, they were back. I noticed he felt it too. It was clear from the way he carried himself this evening, I hadn't seen that insecurity in him for awhile now. Our eyes met, and we each gave each other a small, shy smile.

He shook his head. "I can't sing in front of you yet."

"Oh?"

He looked up, slightly frustrated. "I'm still a little shy around you."

"Still?" Who was I to judge, he had the same effect on me.

He shook his head. "I really like you."

"I'm glad, because I like you too."

He placed the guitar against the wall and stood. "Do you want another drink?"

"Sure." *Liquid courage, seems I'm not the only one who needs it.* I finished the last sip and handed him the cup with a smile. "Thank you."

I stretched onto my stomach and waved my feet up and down. He walked in, his eyes took me in. I glanced his way with a smirk. He smiled. "Nice bum."

I burst out laughing. "Why thank you. I kinda like it too."

He raised one eyebrow. "It's very nice." He gave me an appreciative look. "Here," he extended the cup to me.

I pushed myself up, and reached for it carefully. "Thanks."

Bryce settled next to me and grabbed his laptop. He brought up the YouTube home page and began to play some of his favorite songs. I sighed contentedly. I took a sip of my drink and let out a small cough, it was a lot stronger than the one I had made.

He watched nervously. "Sorry. I make them strong."

I nodded. "That you do. Are you trying to get me drunk?" I raised an eyebrow playfully.

"Maybe," he grinned.

"Well, give me two of these and I might be two sheets to the wind."

"Good to know!"

"No, I don't want to embarrass myself."

He was quiet for a moment. "I don't think there's much you could do that would make me think any less of you."

I smiled warmly. "Thank you." I leaned into him, finding comfort in the music and his welcoming shoulder. I was on my third drink, and I had to pee like a racehorse. I got up and found myself wobbling a little bit. "Whoops!" I exclaimed.

He jumped out of bed, eyes dancing, and held out his hand. "Here," he took me firmly, "lean into me, I've got you."

I took his hand and wrapped my free arm around his neck. My feet stepped onto the solid floor. I looked up at him with a half smile. "Thanks."

"No worries."

I slipped past Mike, who was fast asleep on the couch with the TV still on. I followed the music into Bryce's room a moment later. He stretched out on the bed. I climbed in next to him, and placed my head against his chest. He sighed and held me tightly. I breathed deeply, taking in the scent of fresh laundry and his tantalizing cologne. He always smelled so good.

"You know how most people link certain smells to memories?" he said quietly.

"Yes."

"I've never been that way. Mine has always been music. I can lie for hours and do what we're doing right now."

I sighed. "Me too."

"I think you're my favorite. I love that you know your music. I've never met anyone besides myself who was like that."

I smiled. "What can I say? It's a gift."

He blew out a breath. "I'm looking for a nice girl to settle down with and have babies. Someone who doesn't make me angry on a daily basis." He stopped, and continued, "I don't know how you look at things but the way I see it is this. You really need to like the person you're going to be with. You'll spend a lot of time together, and you want to look forward to being with that person, not dread them."

I lifted my head and found his eyes. I searched his face softly. "I completely agree. You should never be forced to settle. The person you choose to be with should be your best friend. Build a solid foundation first and foremost. If you're friends first, I truly believe you're more likely to stand by each other." I chewed my lip, "I really like you."

He closed his hand around mine. "I really like you too." He relaxed his features, and continued, his voice lifting, "I know what we should do soon."

"Oh, and what's that?"

"Park in the middle of nowhere, and lie in the back of the truck listening to music. We can make a bed in the back and watch the stars."

Take me out of the city lights, away from it all. He's a live version of a country song. I peeked back at him, and a smile grew that hurt my cheeks. "I would love that, it sounds perfect."

"I think so too. I still have to take you to the States. There's a tack store there that I know you'll love. I know I sure do."

I squeezed him tightly. "That sounds like a very good day. I will feel like a kid in a candy store." I let out a quiet breath. "I hope I get my ranch one day…the acreage, the peace and quiet, somewhere to let the horses run. My mom always teases me that I should have been born in a different era."

He laughed. "That's what my family says about me, too. Tell me about your dream home."

"Hmm," I began slowly. "I like a house with character that holds a certain country charm. A wrap around deck, nothing too big, but big enough for a family. Definitely a wood burning stove. They are such life savers. The heat and the smell just can't be beat."

He smiled. "I like that. You forgot a garage with a man cave above it. Oh, and a gym."

I giggled. "We can add that to the list."

He looked down and kissed the top of my head. "Done deal."

⌘

My eyes blinked open slowly. A thought entered my mind, and I cleared my throat to voice it out loud. I stopped talking and a puzzled expression spread across my face. Bryce had one eyebrow raised, and wore a crooked grin.

"What? Did I say something wrong?"

Both eyebrows shot up and his mouth opened into an "O" shape. He laughed brightly. "You fell asleep. I was talking to you, and you didn't answer, you just went out." His smile grew, "but you woke up finishing where ya left off."

I covered my face with my hands. "I did not do that!"

"You so did. Silly, cute girl." He glanced at the time. "It's just after two a.m. I think we should sleep before you pass out on me again."

I smiled sheepishly. "Okay."

I lied next to his warm body, perfectly at ease. My eyes felt heavy, and I let them close without a fight, but sleep was not yet to be. His fingertips traced over my shoulder and lingered along the collarbone. I shivered as his touch sent goose bumps across my delicate skin.

I heard him sigh softly. "So pretty," he murmured.

I smiled slowly and his lips found mine in the dark. I pressed myself into him and wrapped him up tightly, bringing him closer. I could never seem to get him close enough. His fingertips slowly traced down my stomach, sending another course of shivers. He lifted the shirt above my head and tossed it aside. I wrapped my arms around his neck, and gently kissed along the top of his shoulder. He tilted my head softly to one side as he pressed his lips against my neck. He pulled back slowly, lifting my chin so our eyes would meet. We both smiled and his lips met mine hungrily. My hands found his, our fingers interlocked and he gently raised them over head. Our eyes burned into each other and I knew that our night was only just beginning.

⌘

I shifted carefully on the hard seat beneath me. Jane grinned. "You a little sore girl?"

I laughed quickly. "Perhaps." I blew on my hot tea and took a careful sip.

Jane arched an eyebrow. "You look exhausted," her eyes ran over my face. "But that smile seems to be a permanent fixture."

I grinned warmly. "I know, my cheeks hurt." I leaned back into the chair dreamily with thoughts of him running through my mind. The pieces were beginning to come together.

Jane's voice pulled me out of my daydream. "Valentines is in two weeks, do you guys have any plans?"

I pursed my lips. "Not really, but that's kind of how we are. Nothing is ever planned out in advance. It's always a last minute kind of thing. How about you and Aaron?"

Jane nodded. "I'm sure Bryce has something up his sleeve for you. I think Aaron and I are doing dinner together. Nothing super fancy."

"Dinner's always good. I'm sure you two will have a good night." I smiled, and rubbed my hands together in anticipation. "I hope he has something planned, it doesn't have to be anything fancy, but I won't lie, I've got my heart set on sunflowers."

Jane laughed. "I'm sure he'll deliver. You guys seem to fit really well together. I can't wait to meet him."

I nodded. "Yes. We should all plan for a double date very soon."

Jane's face lit up. "It's a deal!"

⌘

"Hello, beautiful."

"Hi, handsome. What are you up too?"

"Aiden and I are watching Enchanted again. It makes me miss you."

"That's cute. I miss you too."

"We'll see each other soon. Then everything will be perfect."

"Sounds like a plan."

On Bryce's weekends with Aiden, I didn't like to intrude on their father/son time, so I usually used those weekends to get caught up on housework, errands, and see friends. Today in particular had been a fantastic day. I spent the day in Vancouver with Jane and Aaron. They knew that being temporarily horseless was very hard on me. A huge part of my world was missing. Jane and Aaron surprised me by arranging a tour through the Patrol Horse stables. For me, it was heaven on earth. The smell of sweet hay, horse sweat, and leather had wrapped me in a warm embrace, I never wanted to let it go. I took in every piece of information I could and listened intently as the officer's shared their stories. I approached each and every horse in the stable and rejoiced as they greeted me with a hearty nuzzle, their warm breath blowing in my face. I had to be dragged out of the barn, for I would, could not, leave under my own free will. Before we left, I took a handful of stickers and a police car fridge magnet for Aiden, I thought he would get a kick out of them.

After Jane and Aaron dropped me off, I decided to make myself a quick snack. To my dismay, my fridge was nearly empty. This would not do, I liked my food. A trip to the grocery store was next on my list. The store was chaotic, people were in a frenzy as they grabbed items from the shelves left and right with a sense of urgency. I chuckled under my breath, a new excitement brewed within me. In our part of the world, we didn't get blessed much with snow during the winter. Our winter usually consisted of rain, and a lot of it. For the past week, the radio had been calling for a snowfall warning. For many, it would seem it caused stress and panic. It had a slightly different effect on me. Snow brought great joy and a giddiness that took me back to childhood. Today was the "big" day, snow was expected to start falling in the early evening. I grabbed what I needed from the store and stepped out into the bitter air. I looked up to the sky in somewhat of an impatient anticipation; gray clouds were beginning to take over the bright blue. I let out a deliberate, heavy breath and watched with satisfaction as it danced among the breeze. *Let it snow!*

Once I got home I decided to take Maggie for an evening walk, eagerly awaiting the arrival of the coming snow. The pink gray sky teased me as it spit out a few flakes here and there. It couldn't come fast enough. After the walk, I kicked off my boots and threw my toque against the floor in semi disappointment. From across the room, I saw my phone blink. I had a message. I swiped the screen, revealing a text from Ben.

"Hey. What are you doing tonight?"

"Just finished taking Maggie for a walk. I want my snow!"

"Me too! I can't wait for it!"

I smiled, Ben was just as snow crazy as I was. "Yup, let's hope it starts soon!"

"I sure hope so. We should build a snowman."

"Haha, done deal!"

"Do you want to come over tonight? Jared and I were going to watch a movie."

"Sure! I'll be over in a few."

I once again pulled on my toque, winter boots, and jacket. I found my keys, said a quick see ya later to my brother, ruffled Maggie's ears and walked out the door. I climbed into the frigid truck, my breath floated in white puffs next to the steering wheel. I started the engine quickly and eagerly waited for the heater to blow warm air. I placed the truck in drive and took off into the night. The roads were icy, so I took it slow. I pulled in next to Jared's beast of a truck and hopped out. With two knocks on the door, Ben greeted me. "Hey, Ry. Come on in."

"It's so nice and warm in here." I rubbed my hands together, trying to bring the feeling back into my fingers.

I followed Ben to the living room, plopped down on the couch, and placed my feet up on the stool in front of me. Jared sat on the couch, bath robe on, drink in his hand.

"Hey," he nodded my way, "how are you?"

"Great. Just waiting for the snow." I beamed.

Jared smiled. "Yeah, that's right. You're a snow girl."

"You betcha."

After the movie, we talked and joked around, laughter filling the room. I kept stealing glances out the window in hopes the glow of the streetlights would reveal the magic of falling snow. I looked at the time, it was now 9:30 p.m. and the white flakes had yet to make an appearance. I pouted, slightly. I shifted positions and winced quietly. My stomach had been bothering me lately. A wave of nausea came over me, and just as quickly as it had come, it was gone. *Don't you pull anything on me stomach. We are not doing that again.*

Half an hour later, my phone jingled, it was from Bryce. "It's snowing!"

I jumped off the couch with a hopeful cry, and ran past a startled looking Ben and Jared. I pressed myself into the window and squealed. "It's snowing!"

I wrote back eagerly. "Yay! I'm SO excited, you have no idea. It's snowing here too."

"What are you doing tonight?"

"Visiting with some friends now but I think I'll head out soon. Why, what's up?"

"I dropped Aiden off and stopped in at a buddies for a bit. I'm leaving now, do you want to get together?"

"That would be really nice. My place or yours?"

"Let's do yours. I'm not that far from you."

"Okay. I will see you in a bit."

"All right, boys, I should head out of here." I stood up carefully as to not jostle my uneasy stomach anymore.

"Okay. Enjoy the snow." Ben grinned back at me.

"Oh I will."

Jared got up slowly and made his way beside me. "Snow, huh?" he looked outside unsurely.

I rolled my eyes and zipped up my coat. "Come on, Jared. Look at it! Be happy." He grinned back and followed me into the frosty night air. We stood on his front deck, quietly looking up at the sky. White flakes danced from the great gray clouds up above. I felt his gaze upon me and looked at him slowly.

Jared gave a melancholy smile. "Enjoy your night."

I nodded slowly. "You too."

Ben suddenly stepped next to Jared, grinning. "Snow! Damn, it's cold out here."

I stepped down the stairs and pulled open the truck door. I threw my hands in the air and twirled. "Enjoy the snow, boys!"

I rushed into the basement suite in a hurry. "It's snowing!" I yelled to Sky, who worked away at his computer station. He raised an eyebrow and looked out the window. "Damn," he muttered.

I shook my head in disbelief. "It's the weekend. Lighten up, you don't have to drive in it."

"Mmhm," he mumbled and focused his attention back to his work.

Maggie bounded forward, wiggling in excitement. I crouched down to her, and placed her face between my hands. "You're a snow dog. You love it, don't you, girl?" She sat and gave me her paw. I laughed. "Good job."

I stood, and stretched my back. "Bryce is coming over tonight."

Sky looked at me quickly. "What? I see."

His tone did not sound pleased. "Is that okay with you?"

Sky sighed, and his eyes never left the screen before him. "I have a ton of work to do tonight."

"Hmm, we can go to his place then if you don't mind watching Maggie."

"Not at all. Thanks."

"Yep." I reached for my phone. "Can we do your place instead? My brother has a lot of work to do."

"Yeah no worries. I'll head home then."

"Okay, I will gather some things and I will head out shortly."

As I pulled onto the main highway, the snow began to fall heavy. I flicked my wipers up another notch. A light coat of white blanketed the world, making the once familiar landscape look foreign. I loved it. The roads were quiet. I took my time and let the four tires beneath me create a fresh set of tracks in the white powder. I swayed back and forth to the music that poured through the speakers. My fingers tapped lightly against the steering wheel and matched the beat. I found my exit, and took the turn. It wouldn't be long now before I pulled up in front of his house.

My phone jingled. "I swear, I hit every red light on the way here."

I smiled, I didn't. "You're home now though, right?"

"Yup."

"Good, I just parked, see ya in a few."

I stepped out of the truck carefully. My stomach churned slightly. *No. No you don't! Behave yourself.* I picked my way carefully down the snow covered sidewalk. *Don't fall. Do not fall.* I placed one foot in front of the other slowly and felt rather smug by the time I knocked on his door. He opened it with a grin, country music filled the kitchen.

"It's snowing!" He said happily.

I turned to look back at the white landscape behind me, bouncing in uncontrollable excitement. "It's so pretty."

I stepped inside and the tip of my boot caught on the doorstep. I stumbled inside in an ungraceful manner. *Damn! Out of all the places to take a misstep it had to be here?* I stood up quickly and looked at him, eyes wide.

He studied me from head to toe, grinning. "You really are a clumsy one."

"Unfortunately. It's a gift, really."

He chuckled. "Poor girl. Come here." He gave me a warm hug.

"Hello, Ryleigh!" A happy voice called from inside the living room. I peeked around the corner and Mike sat with a buddy. He wore his usual happy grin.

"Hey, Mike! Hi," I nodded to his friend. "How are you?"

"I'm doing great. You?"

"Wonderful." I noticed Bryce's guitar rested across the living room table, he had been playing earlier.

Bryce placed his hand on the small of my back and whispered in my ear. "This way."

I followed as he led the way and a picture caught my eye. I planted my feet and stopped short. "This is pretty." I admired a picture of sunflowers in an old silver bucket. "They're my favorites," I whispered under my breath.

Bryce leaned around, looking at me. "I'll have to remember that."

I smiled brightly. *Next Friday, buddy. Valentines!* I followed Bryce into his room. His laptop was set up on the bed. I knew what would be coming next. He left the room and came back, carrying his guitar. He sat on the edge of the bed, and I sat next to him, hands in my lap.

"I found the best online music tutorial. I haven't stopped playing since."

I raised a brow. "Oh yeah?"

"Yes!" he studied me. "I think we should go to guitar lessons together. It'll be fun, and you'll learn so much." He looked at me, suddenly serious. "I'm going to buy you some things for your guitar, a tuner and clamp."

My jaw dropped in surprise. *Marry me.* "Really? Are you serious?"

He laughed. "Yes. Anything for a guitar buddy."

I smiled broadly. "You've got yourself a deal."

Bryce studied the computer screen and his eyes lit up. "Ah. This one. See if you can guess it."

"Mmk." I shut my eyes and listened as the music filled the room. I began to hum the familiar tune, and a smile grew on my face. "Cop car. Keith Urban." I opened my eyes and Bryce shook his head, smiling.

"Yes."

Bryce played for close to forty minutes. I settled into a comfortable position and enjoyed my free show. He looked relaxed tonight, happy. His hands moved quickly across the frets, picking at the strings. His foot bounced in rhythm to the music he created. I couldn't look away, he drew me in like a moth to a flame. To my surprise, I welcomed the pull and let it take hold. He put his guitar away and turned on the music. I climbed out of bed, and studied the photographs that hung from the wall. They were all of Bryce and Aiden. *So precious.*

His low laughter caught my attention. I turned, an eyebrow arched in question. He grinned again. "You're dancing."

I furrowed my brows and realized he was right. My shoulder lightly bopped to the music, and my hips swayed from side to side. "It's a reflex. I can't help it."

He stood next to me and placed his arms around my waist. "I like it," his eyes fell to the pictures on his wall. "Do you want to look at some photos?"

"I would love too."

"Okay."

He rifled through his drawers and pulled out a tiny album. He sat on the bed and gestured for me to sit beside him. I did and began to eagerly look through his memories. Most of the photos were of Aiden; from a tiny baby, to the little man he was becoming. I stole a glance at Bryce's face, his eyes filled with reminiscent thoughts.

"He looks like you," I offered.

He smiled warmly. "He does. He's a mini me." His eyes widened slightly, an idea had come to him. "Do you want to take a look at my past?"

"Sure," I said, curious as to what that was.

"Okay." He pulled out a disc and placed it in the laptop. "It's from my football days."

"Oh," I said curious and focused my eyes to the screen. As the video played, I couldn't help but smirk. The man wore the uniform well, no denying that. I looked up at him with a sly smile. And he was fast, his feet and legs moved in a blur as he expertly dodged the opponents. He smiled with pride next to me.

"I could never throw a football. I always found it to be so tricky. You guys make it look so easy," I mused.

"I'll teach you." He smiled.

"Okay. You will have your work cut out for you."

He looked at me, grinning. "Oh, I bet."

My eyes opened wide. "Hey, now!" I lightly shoved him away from me.

He popped out the disc and carefully put it away. He leaned forward and typed in a song and pressed play. He gave me a tender look and smiled. "If you give me a little girl, I will sing this song for you."

My heart fluttered, and I forced myself to swallow. Kip Moore's *'Hey Pretty Girl'* filled the room. A hand flew up to my chest. *Oh Jesus, he was going to kill me.* The loving lyrics filled the room.

"Life's a long and winding ride better have the right one by your side. Happiness don't drag its feet and time moves faster than you think. Hey pretty girl, you did so good. Our baby's got your eyes and a fighter's heart like I knew she would. Hey pretty girl, you did so good."

A wave of emotion took over, and I was surprised as I began to blink away tears. I looked away quickly and pulled myself together. He leaned over the computer and chose another song. Eric Church's *'My hometown'* was next. I smiled; this was a good one. His new album would be coming out in two days and Bryce had been counting down the days until he could hold it in his hands.

"So," he began, "when are you up for parking by the river and having our truck date?"

My face lit up, and I grabbed his forearm in excitement. "Anytime!"

"Anytime, eh? Okay," he glanced my way. "I want to take you dancing somewhere. Maybe a weekend away?"

I squeezed him tighter. "I am so in!"

The song came to an end, and he leaned over the keyboard, deep in thought. He studied me and slowly smiled. He typed something in and soon Hunter Hayes *'Wanted'* came through the speakers. And then he looked at me. My blood froze, my heart nearly stopped. I felt completely exposed. *Ah crap.* I took a deep breath and met his gracious gaze. I offered him a small smile.

He reached out with certainty and drew me against his chest. "Come here," he said quietly.

I wrapped my arms around his torso and settled against him. I let out a breath, and felt safe, loved. His arms squeezed tighter and he gently rocked back and forth to the tune. The music was still going strong as we stretched ourselves out on the bed. My head fell to his chest, our fingers intertwined. We talked and laughed for hours, like we usually did.

He propped himself on to one arm and brushed a lock of hair out of my eyes. "Stop it," he said quietly.

I smiled innocently. "Stop what?"

"Looking the way you do."

A puzzled expression crossed my face and he continued. "You're beautiful," his fingertip lightly tapped my nose and he smiled. "I think this is one of my favorite things about you. You have the cutest nose."

I laughed. "That doesn't sound very flattering."

"It is, and your eyes, they are dangerous."

He looked at me once more, and studied my features. "You really are a good girl, inside and out. This is who you are?" he bit his lip. "You're a pretty girl, pretty girls usually have boyfriends. You can have anyone."

My hands found his face. "Yes. I am who I've always been," I met his eyes and held his gaze. "I'm not like those other girls. I only need one good man in my life."

A smile played on his mouth. "My uncle from Saskatchewan is coming here in a few weeks. He's a musician. I think you should meet him. He'd love to play something for us."

"I would love to meet him!"

"Good," he chuckled.

He settled back down, head on the pillow. The music filled the quiet room and our feet bopped in rhythm to the tune. I placed a hand over my stomach as it had begun to jump uneasily once again. *Please, not tonight.* I pushed my worry to the side and struggled to stay awake.

"Ryleigh?"

A soft whisper in my ear woke me. "Mmm." I mumbled, clumsily opening my eyes.

Bryce leaned down, smiling softly. "You did it again. You fell asleep on me."

I forced my eyes to open completely. "No, I didn't."

He laughed loudly. "You did!" He leaned over top of me. "Have I told you how cute you are?"

I smiled. "I think I've heard that a time or two, but it never gets old."

He chuckled and tapped my nose. "Well, you are."

"What time is it?" I whispered.

"Four a.m."

"Sweet Jesus." I sighed.

He laughed once more. "Time for bed?"

"I think so."

"Okay, I'll shut things down."

And he did. Before he climbed back into bed, he left the room and came back with the spare blanket he reserved for me. He placed the quilt on top of me and quietly climbed in next to me. His lips pressed against my shoulder and a smile crept upon my face. I knew where this was going and I suddenly felt wide awake. I turned to face him. We both smiled, and I knew we would be seeing the sunrise together.

CHAPTER 8

We slept until noon. I was the first to open my eyes and I stared up at a white ceiling. *White. What was it about white? Oh! Snow!* I sat up quickly and looked out the window eagerly. "Dammit!" I sat down, severely disappointed.

Bryce woke up, confused. "What is it? What happened?"

"The snow is gone. It's raining," I mumbled heartbroken.

Bryce stared at me through half sleepy eyes. "Aw. I'm sorry." His head hit the pillow heavily and then he started to laugh. "Poor girl."

Damn weather. I was up now. Sleep would not be coming back to me so easily. I stared down at him, it looked like he could sleep the day away. *What to do?* I tapped my fingers restlessly against the comforter with the hope a brilliant idea would welcome me, or sleep would wrap me up and take me down. I glanced at Bryce once more and through one eye, he watched my restless fingers. I noticed and my face fell. "Sorry."

He smiled. "No, it's okay." He glanced at the clock. "It's after noon. Do you want breakfast…or lunch at this point?"

"I could eat."

"Okay. Time to get up!"

I sat at the kitchen table and watched Bryce fry eggs. He still looked half asleep. A song must have been in his head, for he swayed to a tune only he could hear. The dinging from the coffee maker lit up his face. He poured himself a cup and held on to it tightly.

"Good?" I asked.

"Yes. It's a shame you don't like coffee."

I wrinkled my nose. "No, no. You enjoy it." He carried the full plates and gently placed them on the table. He sat across from me and looked famished. He grabbed something from the fridge and slathered it over his eggs.

"Do you want some?" He extended the bottle near me to smell. I did and it burned my eyes, causing them to tear up. My stomach turned.

"Oh!" I exclaimed and moved away quickly, wafting my hand in front of my nose.

He laughed. "It's the good hot sauce!"

I wrinkled my nose. "That's potent. Whew, you enjoy."

After the night we had, neither of us was very energetic. I felt sick, every inch of my body screamed from pure exhaustion. My stomach turned quickly and I hoped my breakfast would stay down. Bryce was a mirror image of how I felt. We exchanged small, sleepy smiles throughout the day before we ended up crashing on the couch.

"Are you still alive?" he whispered in my ear, playfully poking me.

"No," I mumbled.

"Aw, poor girl. I'm sorry."

I reached out blindly, patting him. "It's okay. It was a good night," I smiled. "A very good night."

A smile lit his voice. "Yes, yes it was."

I passed out on the couch and woke from a nap feeling worse than ever. I decided it was time for me to head home. I was certain I was going to be sick, and he did not need to be apart of that. I pulled my hood over my head and pouted as I watched the rain come down. I wobbled with tiredness. Bryce stood across from me not looking much better himself.

"Drive safe, okay?" he said sternly.

I nodded. "I will. My bed is calling my name."

"Mine too." He stretched out his arms and wrapped me up. He released his grasp slowly and smiled. "We'll see each other soon, okay?"

I smiled a sleepy smile. "Okay, sounds like a plan."

I never would have guessed that would have been the last time I would hold him. I didn't know that would be our goodbye. If I had known, I would have never let him go.

⌘

"Today's the day!!!"

I laughed as I read Bryce's text, I knew what today was, February 11, Eric Church's new CD, *The Outsiders* was released.

"It is! Yay! I'm sure it will be amazing."

"I'm so excited! I'm heading to work, talk to you later."

"Have a good day."

"I will thanks, you too."

For the past few days, I felt like I had been dragged behind a bus; well make that the past two weeks. I was utterly exhausted, and found it hard to concentrate on anything. Headaches became a frequent visitor and my stomach was all over the place. It was now February 12th and Valentines was almost here. Despite feeling like death warmed up, I grew excited for the big day. *All he has to do is show up with sunflowers and a smile. Simple and perfect.*

I hunched over slightly, and wrapped my arms tenderly around my stomach. *Go away.* Concern had begun to nag me as I was awoken at four a.m. by some very strange pains in my stomach. I searched my closet in a tired daze, and found the item I desperately sought; my heating pad. I plugged it in quickly and pressed the comforting heat to my sore stomach, and tried to go back to sleep. The pain made me nervous, anything odd with my stomach always left me feeling uneasy. I never wanted to have to revisit those days that had taken so much from me. The only one I had confided in was Jane.

"How are you feeling?" Jane asked.

"I'm in pain today. I think I'm going to need to see a doctor."

"Stay put, you're not driving. I'll take you."

"It's okay, I can drive myself. You don't have to drive all this way."

"No. The last thing I need is for you to pass out while you're driving. Stay. I'll be there soon."

"Okay. Thank you."

I watched out the living room window until I saw Jane pull into the driveway. I gathered my things, and slowly made my way to her car. Her eyes grew wide as I got near and slid into the passenger side. I gave her a small grin. I noticed she didn't wear a stitch of makeup, and her hair was slightly askew, she must have bounced right out of bed to be here with me.

"Oh, Ry. You look terrible. Really pale."

My lips pulled down in a frown. "Jee, thanks."

"Oh, no. I'm sorry. I'm just glad I'm the one driving you."

It was early in the morning and we found a clinic that was open. The wait wasn't long. My name was called and I followed the nurse.

"Here," she handed me a clear cup, "we're going to need a urine sample."

A wave of anxiety flowed through me. *Please God, don't let this be bad. I can't do this again.* I said my prayer and gave the nurse what she needed. I was then escorted to a private room and there I sat, waiting for the doctor. I bounced my feet nervously, waiting. Why is it time seems to stand still in the doctor's office? I read every poster on the wall, twice. Finally, the door opened up.

"Hello. I'm Doctor Ladner. What can I do for you today?"

"I'm not too sure. I feel like I'm getting the flu or something. I'm exhausted and I've been getting weird stomach pains."

"Are you having any nausea?"

"A bit. It comes and goes."

"Can you explain you're stomach pain to me?"

I did. She listened intently and made notes into her computer. "When was your last period?"

"January 2nd." A cold chill fell down my spine and I straightened my back. My eyes grew wide and my jaw dropped slightly. *Oh. Oh boy.*

The doctor's head turned toward me swiftly, and her voice rose. "You're late."

And there it was. Two words that could change someone's world forever. A million thoughts ran through my head at once, one screamed at me louder than the rest. *He's going to leave you now.* I shook it out as quickly as it had come in. This was a game changer.

"I'll be right back." The doctor got up and left the room.

She left me alone with my heart pounding in my ears, and the fear building within threatening to break out. This wasn't how it was supposed to happen. I had always wanted to be a mother, and I'd make a good one. But not yet. It was too soon. *What the hell is he going to think?*

The doctor came entered the room once more. "You're urine test showed that you're not pregnant." I looked at her, slightly hopeful. "However," she began, "I think it's still too early to tell. Your Hcg levels may not be high enough yet. I'd suggest testing again in a week or two. So, no alcohol. Take care of yourself. If you start bleeding, or the pain intensifies, you go to the emergency immediately."

I nodded slowly and left the room. I walked down the hall to the waiting room feeling dazed. *Is this really happening? I have never been here before.* My feet stopped short, my body momentarily shut down and refused to cooperate. I placed a hand over my stomach and let it sit there for a moment. I glanced down, could I have a little life growing inside me? I continued walking and knew I looked terrified. As soon as she saw me, Jane stood, eyes wide, mouth gaped open.

"Oh my God! What's wrong?"

I shook my head from side to side and felt the tears coming. People in the waiting room glanced at me with a sudden curiosity. I needed to get out of this place and quickly. "Not here." I set off at a brisk pace and set my sights on her car. She followed and unlocked the doors. We slid inside and I focused my gaze blindly outside. "There's a chance I may be pregnant."

"Holy shit."

"That about covers it," I said blankly.

"Are you going to tell him? Whoa, what are you going to say?"

I thought about that. Hell if I knew. "Well, he's been here before. I may need to lean on him a bit."

And there it was. I may have to lean on *him.* I didn't know how I felt about that. But then again, this was Bryce…my Bryce. He was different. If I had to let down my guard, my stone wall, it would be for him.

"Ry? Are you okay?" Jane's voice cut me out of my trance.

"I think so," I bit my lip. "I can't tell him this over the phone. It has to be in person." I smiled wryly. "Nice Valentines, huh?"

Jane blew out a breath. "Wow. Wow, wow, wow," she looked at me softly. "No matter what happens I'll be here for you."

I turned to her as the tears began to fill my eyes. "Thank you."

⌘

"How did your day go?"

I stared blankly at Bryce's text. *Terrifying as hell. You might be a Daddy, round 2.*

"Okay. Yours?"

"Just okay? What's wrong?"

"My friend took me to the doctor's. I haven't been feeling too well lately. My stomachs been bothering me." Amongst other things.

"Uh-oh. That doesn't sound good. Is it from drinking?"

"No. I'm just feeling under the weather. If it gets any worse I may have to go to the hospital and I have no desire to go there."

"Maybe you're pregnant?"

I sat up like a rocket. No, not like this. I would not bring this up over a text. "No…"

"I wonder what it is then? I hope you don't die."

"Oh, jee, thank you. That is so reassuring."

"Haha sorry."

"I hope an owl beams you up. I'm going to sleep now, goodnight. Sweet dreams."

"You too. Feel better."

I did not sleep. I could not sleep. As tired as I was there was no turning off my head. I pulled out my Ipod and turned the music up, hoping it would drown out my thoughts. I sang along quietly and willed the fear to go away, it did not. So, I began to make a list of all the things I would need to do. First and foremost would be to buy a pregnancy test, and that was it. That was all I could decide on with some sort of a certainty. I bit my lip and chewed it mindlessly. Do I tell Bryce? It wasn't a sure thing yet. Do I scare the crap out of him for no reason? It might be best only to tell him if I had too. What a dilemma I was left with. I didn't want to lose him, for he was one of the best things to have happened to me in a long time. A very long time.

I must have fallen asleep for the jingle of my phone startled me. It was now morning. I blinked sleepily and reached for the phone, it was a message from Bryce. "How are you feeling?"

"I'm okay. My stomach is feeling better, just a little sleepy."

"Okay. What's your favorite song on The Outsider's CD?"

"Number 3, 5, and 7. I don't know their names yet."

"I'll have to listen to them after work. Have a good day."

"You too."

I sat up ever so slowly and looked around the bedroom with foggy eyes. Was yesterday a dream? Did that really happen? I sighed heavily, for I knew it was no dream, this was a new reality I had been thrown in too. The weight of the world settled on my shoulders in an instant. My life could change forever, in so many ways. I let out a heavy sigh. What was I going to do today? Get out of the house for a start. I could not be left alone with my thoughts. I needed to keep my mind, myself busy. And so, I showered, pulled myself together and called Jane.

"Do you want to do something today?"

"Of course. Do you want me to come out your way?"

"No, I'll meet you at your place. Be there in half an hour."

"Okay. See you soon."

I drove down the familiar road and parked in front of Jane's house. I sat inside the truck for a little while before I finally got out. I felt weird, like I was having an out of body experience. I stood in front of the wooden door and raised my hand to knock. I froze. I stepped back for a moment and buried my face in my hands. I took a few slow, controlled breaths and tapped the door loudly.

Jane answered, smiling sympathetically. "How are you doing?"

"Okay, I suppose."

She nodded. "What do you want to do?"

I lowered my voice. "I need to buy a test. Can you come with me?"

"Of course. I'll drive."

There I stood in the drugstore aisle, eyes wide, staring at a wide variety of pregnancy tests. I glanced at the write ups, different brands, and the cheery colors they used to market them. *Holy Hell.* I grabbed at what looked to be a decent brand, and noted the package held two tests inside. I made a face as I read the back of the box one last time. This tiny, insignificant package and its contents held my fate in its hands.

"You okay?" Jane's voice was soft.

"Yup."

I marched toward the checkout and laid my purchase on the counter. I felt like a spotlight shone down on me, letting the world know my fear. I avoided the eyes of the worker who stood before me, and handed her my debit card. She placed the test in a bag, I grabbed it quickly and walked out, Jane right by my side.

"Do you want to grab a warm drink?" Jane asked.

"Yes. I don't feel like going home yet."

"Of course. I have all day."

We sat outside in the fresh air. I held the warm drink firmly in my hands and watched the world go by. Everyone looked so free, like they didn't have a care in the world. I watched their chests rise up and down, breathing in an easy fashion. I wished I could do that. My breaths were choppy and difficult; I had so much weighing me down. I rubbed my temples absently, trying to chase the worries away. But they did not move. They stood tall and unflappable, demanding my attention.

"Are you going to see him tomorrow?"

I looked at Jane, concern on her face. "I believe so. It's Friday, so it'll be in the evening. You and Aaron have plans right?"

"We do, around dinnertime though. Do you want to take a day trip to the Hot Springs tomorrow? We can get away for the day and grab some lunch?"

"You are the best, Jane. Yes, I am in."

"Good. Be at my house by 10:30."

"Will do."

I turned my phone off for the night. I needed the quiet. I needed to think. I needed to breathe. I pulled out the contents of the pregnancy test and read the instructions, paying very close attention to the words intended to deliver wonderful news. I read through the pamphlet twice, folded it back up and slid it into the box. I laid the pretty package on my bed, and stared at it in silence. I reached over, picked up the box, and threw it across the room. I placed my hands in my hair, hugged my knees to my chest and gently rocked myself back and forth until tiredness pulled me into her heavy arms. I rested my head on the pillow quietly and let my mind wander freely into the dark. I wished he was here with me now. His arms held the safety I needed more than ever. I listened to the silence as it echoed around me. What I wouldn't give to hear his quiet, reassuring words in my ear. If this were to happen, a part of me was glad it was with him, we would find a way to make this work. I had faith he would stand by my side.

Sunlight peered through the blinds, telling me that another day was here. I lay in bed for a few more moments before I convinced myself to get out of bed. *Oh!* Right, I had to be at Jane's by 10:30. I turned on my phone, wondering if she had tried to contact me at some point. Nothing from her, but I had a message from him.

"Morning. How are you feeling today?"

Scared. "Much better, thank you."

"Good, I'm glad to hear it. I'm just pulling into work now. I'll talk to you later. Happy Valentines!"

"Happy Valentines to you too! Have a good day."

Driving felt good. I loved road trips, they provided a temporary freedom of escape, a new possibility. Despite everything, this was a moment to hold on too. I relaxed as Jane and I made our way to our destination. Jane turned the volume up loudly as we danced and sang along to the music that pumped out of the car speakers. Jane had bought Eric Church's new album, and every song made me think of Bryce. I could picture him singing along with a happy grin plastered to his face. I already knew which ones would be his favorites. As the day went on, I began to feel lighter, happier, almost worry free. I was excited to see him. Despite what I would need to tell him tonight, I knew he would wrap me up and tell me that everything would be okay. And I needed that, so very much. I didn't want to be left standing all alone in this.

It was almost three in the afternoon by the time we pulled into Jane's driveway. "Thank you for today, I had so much fun!" I said, with a genuine smile on my face.

Jane gave me a quick hug. "Me too. You needed a fun day. Good luck tonight."

My stomach twisted slightly. "Thank you. Happy Valentines."

"You too!"

I drove home, singing a happy tune. The butterflies began to grow. He would be off work soon, I would hear from him within the hour. I rushed home and ran to my door. I needed to freshen up and choose something pretty for tonight. Sky was going to his girlfriends for the night, so we would have the place to ourselves. I scrubbed my face, applied some mascara, and eye shadow strategically, making my green eyes shine. I shook my hair loose from the topknot I had been wearing earlier. My long auburn hair cascaded down my back. Next item on the list was to find an outfit. I stared into my closet blankly. What should I wear? I tried on at least five different combinations before finally settling on a pair of black pants, a jade green lace tank with a black pullover. I gave myself a final inspection and nodded in approval. I was ready. I paced the house at least five times before my phone jingled. My heart jumped in my chest. I looked down at the phone and read the message.

"Hey, Ryleigh. There is no easy way of doing this... and I feel like a total ass telling you on Valentines day, but I've begun seeing someone and I'm afraid that we can no longer talk or hangout. I'm really sorry that I'm telling you over a text, but I thought you should know. Take care and I really hope you find someone special. You're a great girl, and any guy would be lucky to have you."

For a moment, I felt nothing. Absolutely, fucking nothing. And then it came, and it came hard. An invisible force punched me in the gut swiftly, I couldn't breathe. A vice like grip took over where my heart was supposed to be. I placed my phone on the counter and cried. I cried until I couldn't breathe. My knees grew weak and I let them give way, sinking to the floor. How could he do this to me? Today of all days, and now? Fucking now? His timing was stellar. I suddenly felt cold, so very cold. An emptiness settled over me and it hurt, it physically hurt.

I was so confused. It was only four days ago I had spent the night, and it was a good night. It was an amazing night. How the hell could so much change in four days? He was the one who brought up a future together. How long had this been going on? I had so many questions. Sobs racked my body, making it hard to breathe. In this moment, I hated him. I hated him so much. I looked at his message once again. His words cut me like knives. *Who the hell is this? Where's my Bryce?* I stared at the message in disgust. I had no idea who this man was. He was not the man I had gotten to know, he never would have done this to me, taken such a cowards way out. The room began to close in on me. I needed to get out. And I needed to get out now. My phone jingled once again. I picked it up slowly. It was Jane.

"How is it going? I wanted to wish you luck tonight!"

"There is no need for that, he's not coming. Apparently he's seeing someone else."

"Whhhhaaaaat the hell? Are you serious? Come over now. Aaron won't mind. If you can't drive, we will get you."

"I'll need a few minutes and then I'll head out. I could use a good drive."

"Okay. We'll be here. Be careful."

I let the phone slip from my hands and there I sat upon the cold kitchen floor. I rested my head against the kitchen cupboard and let the tears fall until I couldn't see. Loneliness sat down beside me. She smiled cruelly and wrapped me up like an old friend. I clutched at my chest, and my heart broke into a million tiny pieces, and as it did, I knew all the pieces would never quite fit back together. Not this time.

Kodaline's *"All I Want"* ran through my head, and the words stung.

"All I want is nothing more than to hear you knocking at my door. 'Cause if I could see your face once more, I could die happy I'm sure. When you said your last goodbye I died a little bit inside. I lay in tears in bed all night alone without you by my side. But If you loved me, why'd you leave me? Take my body, take my body. All I want is, and all I need is to find somebody. I'll find somebody like you. So you brought out the best of me, a part of me I'd never seen. You took my soul

and wiped it clean. Our love was made for movie screens. But If you loved me, why'd you leave me? Take my body, take my body. All I want is, and all I need is to find somebody. I'll find somebody. If you loved me, why'd you leave me? Take my body, take my body. All I want is, all I need is to find somebody. I'll find somebody like you."

My stomach churned and I ran to the bathroom. I hugged the toilet bowl until the moment passed. I sank wearily, pressed against the bathroom cupboard. I let my legs stretch out helplessly before me. I looked down at my stomach and felt a fresh set of tears arise. Maybe I wouldn't be entirely alone in all of this.

CHAPTER 9

I don't remember the drive to Jane's. It's a miracle I even got there in the first place. My eyes were swollen from tears, and there was no sign of them slowing down. I had Eric Church's album cranked. Each and every single song reminded me of him. An ache hovered in my chest and it seemed quite content to stay put. I turned the music up even louder, willing it to drown out my thoughts, and chase away the hurt. *How could he do this to me?* I thought back over the past few months. I could not pick out a single thing that would have led me to believe this would be coming. I pulled over in front of Jane's house and Aaron met me at the door.

His brown eyes filled with sympathy. "I'm so sorry. The guy's a douche, you don't need him."

I knew he meant to make me smile, but I couldn't find it within me. I looked at him sadly and nodded. "I'm sorry to crash your Valentines."

"Don't even worry about it. We weren't doing much anyways."

Jane ran down the stairs. "Oh, Ry, how are you? I can't believe this. I can't believe he could do this to you. What an ass."

I followed the couple upstairs and sank heavily into the lounge chair. Jane paced back and forth ranting. Aaron watched her with quiet affection, smiling softly.

He glanced my way and his features were taken over by sympathy and worry. "Did you tell him?" he asked quietly. Jane stopped in her tracks, hand pausing in front of her mouth.

I wiped away at a silent tear. "No. I don't know if I should at this point."

"Fuck him." Jane roared. "I can't believe this! If I ever see him, he better run. What exactly did he say to you?"

I grabbed my phone and let them read the message. I didn't much feel like talking. I rested my face in my hands and closed my eyes. My head felt so heavy, and it pounded angrily.

"What the hell?" Aaron said confused, "I don't know, this is not right."

"That's it! That's all he gave you?" Jane shrieked.

I had to smile, a little. Jane would always have my back, and I hers, no matter what. You had to love friends like that, they were so far and few in between.

Jane pulled out her phone. "There is no way, no way in hell I am letting this slide. I'm sorry, Ry, but I'm sending him a message."

My eyes burned, so I let them close once more. I briefly heard Jane and Aaron speak in low voices together but I couldn't hear a word that was said. Jane's angry typing filled the room followed by her curses. I rocked the chair back and forth, slowly wishing I could make myself disappear. *What have I ever done to deserve this, to be here? He's left me all alone and I'm scared. He was supposed to be here to hold my hand.* The warm, salty tears fell down my face. That's what hurt the most. He wouldn't be the one to feel the ache of this loneliness, the hurt. He had someone else to fall back on. Someone else's lips to kiss, a hand to hold, a warm body to lie next too. *Fuck you. Fuck the both of you. You called me your china doll, don't you know we break so very easily? I was waiting on forever but all I got was goodbye.* There was no denying, that despite my anger I would miss him. I already *was* missing him. Perhaps what I would miss the most was the idea of him, for this person in front of me now, was nobody worth missing at all.

"Did you respond to him? Do you know who she is?" Jane asked.

I lifted my sad eyes slowly from the gaze on the floor and met hers. Who was *she?* "I'd assume Aiden's mom? He's not the type of guy to juggle many girls at once." *But what do I know? Apparently not much.*

His kind eyes flew into my head and I pushed them out quickly, they were not welcome. *You can't stay here, not now.* "He put in 110% effort wise with us.....I-I just don't know," I paused. "I'd be surprised if it's his most recent ex, he didn't have a single kind thing to say about her. I was left with quite a negative impression."

I bit my lip and thought back to our many conversations. No, I couldn't see that happening. I went on sadly. "Whenever he spoke of Aiden's mom, he had nothing but respect for her," I let out a heavy sigh. "If he went back to her, I'd get it, to some extent. Still, to do it like this though? I never expected this, not from him. I thought he would have felt he owed me more than this." I held up my phone in disgust.

"You have every right to ask him." Jane stated.

I looked at my phone unsurely. I suppose I did, but his text was pretty final. He cut the chord. *Screw it.* "I need to know one thing and then I'm gone. What happened? What changed? I thought everything was fine. I asked, not too long ago if we were heading down the same road. You assured me all was well…you could have given me an out then."

He responded, very quickly. "I ran into my ex and we kinda hit it off again. Nothing changed. I was really into you."

Anger washed over me, erasing the hurt temporarily, it was rather nice. *Nothing changed?* How could he even say that to me? Obviously something had changed.

"He went back to her?! His damn ex! What the hell?" I shouted.

I sat back into my seat, dumbfounded. The one who always looked for a fight? Who had hurt him? Who sometimes scared him? *Yes, I can see the lure.* His text was bullshit. He 'ran' into her, yes, I'm so sure. Did he think I was an idiot? Apparently he did. I'd bet that at some point, a meeting between them had been premeditated. I picked up my phone and held it tightly. As I let the anger take hold, there was so much I wanted to say. But I couldn't say the words, for that was not who I was. I would hold on to my displeasure, the hurt, and let it sit there silently as it tore me apart bit by bit. I really wished I could be a bitch; to be able to speak your mind and let the hatred speak, and not give a damn what you said. There was a reckless freedom in that, one that I could not dance with.

So, instead I simply wrote "I see. Happy Valentines." *Ass.* The hurt washed over me and I let it stay there, for I had nothing left in me at the moment to chase it out.

"He's not worth it." Aaron suggested carefully.

I sighed heavily. Recent events would suggest that was the truth. But my heart, my memories could not agree. I cried then. The strangling ache hit me once again, knocking the breath out of me. For I had lost so much more than the hope of a forever, it felt like I had lost my best friend, and that, hurt me most of all.

I cried throughout the night. I was so glad my brother was not here to hear my heart breaking sobs. Even I had a hard time listening to it. I was sure the other tenants in the house could hear me through the vents, I could care less. I could not sleep. My mind was heavy as was my heart. It was three a.m. and I was wide awake. I sat up and flicked the light on. My eyes landed on the pad of paper and pen that stood on the nightstand. I reached for them and knew a jumble of words would be scribbled on this empty piece of paper soon enough. For what my voice failed to say, my words and thoughts would act as the next best thing, even if I was the only one to read them.

I got lost in a moment, but moments are fleeting.
Hold on to it with a tender grasp,
As the distance it will grow.
Let it bring with you that feeling,
Before time takes it away.
When it comes for time to say goodbye,
Make it fast, make it painless.
I don't want to be left wondering why.
I don't want to be the one to miss you.
Take it all, for I have nothing left.
My heart is so tired,
I don't want to do this again, I can't do this again.
You took a piece,
And it was the best part of me.

I read the words before me quietly, and before I even knew what I was doing, I pulled out my suitcase, and began stuffing clothes inside. I needed to go home. The earliest ferry would be 7:45 a.m.. It didn't take me long to pack and I had a lot of time to kill. I fired up my computer and followed a yoga routine, breaking into sobs throughout. I had a quick shower and glanced wearily into the mirror. *Oh hell.* I looked terrible. My eyes were bloodshot and swollen from lack of sleep and crying. I splashed some cool water on my eyes, hoping it would take some of the swelling down. I studied the reflection looking back at me and I wanted to give the poor girl a hug. Her eyes shone bright from tears, and the hurt and fear etched deep within looked like an assault. An empty loneliness had taken over the once hopeful face. I had to look away for it was almost too much too bear.

The morning was dark and gloomy. Rain fell down steadily, which suited me just fine, let it rain, let it pour. I tossed my bags carelessly in the back seat of the truck and slowly made my way back inside the house. I sat down on the couch and blankly waited for the sun to rise. Maggie sensed my sadness as she sat next to me, whining. She rested her head upon my lap. I stroked her ears slowly. "It's okay, everything will be okay." My voice broke and like the rain outside, my tears fell heavily without a sign of ever stopping.

⌘

I pressed my forehead against the cool glass of my driver side window. I watched blankly at the crowd of people on the ferry. Everyone looked so happy and to my dismay, nobody seemed to be alone. The tears had been coming and going all morning without warning. I ignored the people who walked passed my truck as they glanced at me with inquisitive expressions. I closed my eyes and tried to steer my thoughts into a positive direction. I would soon see my mom, Emma, one of my best friends, and my horse, Tess. I clung to the thought. I had too. The ear buds in my ears blocked out the noise from the outside world around me. I could only hear the music, my music. I let it take me away, far, far away. I let my eyes close.

A strong nagging feeling urged me to open my eyes. As I stared into the vast ocean something caught my attention in the water. I narrowed my puffy eyes, as movement stirred the calm waters. A pod of dolphins broke above the surface. They leapt carefree next to the ferry, playing amongst the waves. For a moment they would disappear, taken under by the blue sea, only to reappear with what I swore, was a smile. I watched them, almost hypnotized. And just as soon as they appeared, they were gone. I took it as a sign that everything was going to be fine, just fine.

Once the ferry docked, I drove down the familiar road toward home and it lifted my spirits slightly. The country roads felt safe, they felt welcoming. I pressed down on the gas a little harder as I made my way up the steep hill that would lead to my destination. Maggie stuck her head out the open window, tongue flapping in the wind. She knew where we were going, she recognized the smells. Truck tires crunched the gravel breaking the silence of the morning. As I reversed into my old parking spot, my mother waited to greet me, her blue eyes filled with worry for her poor, broken daughter. "Mom," my voice broke.

"Oh, honey, I'm so sorry." She wrapped me in a warm hug and we stayed there for a very long time.

I sat on the leather couch holding a mug of steaming hot tea. The warmth was a slight comfort. I didn't have much of an appetite as of lately, and the warm liquid gave a false sense that something filled my stomach. I grew very quiet, as I did when I was hurting. Even in front of my own mother, I had great difficulty crying. But she knew me well. Prying would get nowhere with me. It had to come from me, in my own time. Perhaps that was why I found a great comfort in writing. I didn't have to look anyone in the eyes, it was just my thoughts and a blank piece of paper. I could let the words flow freely, there was no judgment. I found it to be a very therapeutic process.

I took a shaky breath. "I was so happy, Mom."

"I know you were, honey," she said softly.

The tears threatened me once again. "You know what the worst part is?" I nearly whispered. "Whenever I'm happy, there's always a small voice in my head I can't silence. It's always wondering how long the happiness will last this round. I'm always waiting for it to be taken away, it's only a matter of time."

My mother cried then. I could see how much this hurt her as well. Her daughter was officially broken. Another hit, another blow, and she felt it too. For I was her little girl, no matter how old I would get. As her tears fell, mine grew still. I picked up the box of Kleenex and offered it to her.

She grabbed one and laughed dryly. "I should be giving these to you."

I smiled weakly. "I'm okay." *Not really.*

A little while later I stretched out onto my stomach in my old bedroom. A pad of paper was sprawled in front of me. I leaned over and plucked a pen from the nightstand and let the process take over. My hand began scribbling words in a furious manner.

You made it look so easy. There was no looking me in the eyes.

No hesitation; you said goodbye. You cut the final chord.

But you left me here all alone, I feel the emptiness, I shed the tears.

All the while you lie in the warmth of her, how is this fair?

I've been left lonely for far too long.

She won't give you what you need.

Those words are going to hurt, her smile will begin to fade.

When it all comes crashing down I hope it hurts for you baby.

I'll put myself together piece by piece.

Put the armour back on that you so carelessly tossed aside.

I will let my tears fall, I will yell your name.

But I'm going to be okay.

You're the one who lost me.

I stifled back a yawn. I had been up nearly twenty-four hours now. I took a Gravol and smiled softly as I felt the drowsiness set in. I flicked on the fan and let it's steady sound act as a lullaby. *When I awake, please let this all have been some terrible dream.*

CHAPTER 10

It was dark when I opened my eyes. The loneliness was still there, the ache, it cut so deep. A shuddery breath escaped my lips. *Bryce. Where are you? Please, please come back to me. I need you.* I stared up at the ceiling, so many thoughts ran through my head all at once, it was overwhelming. I placed my hands gently upon my stomach. *Are you in there little one?* It was still too soon to take another test, all I could do now was hold my breath and wait.

"You need to eat something, Ryleigh."

I pushed the food around the plate mindlessly. I had no desire to eat, I wasn't hungry. My body's basic needs had altered as of lately. Instead of hunger, I felt hollow from emptiness, my lungs ached with every cold breath that I drew. But my heart…that was the most painful thing of all. It felt so heavy in my chest, an ache had taken hold and it began to grow stronger with each passing day. It was being torn apart, piece by piece. It was beyond broken, and there was nothing anyone could do for it. *His love is such a lonely place to be.* My thoughts then wandered to "it." If "it" was growing inside me, I would need to eat, to nourish the blooming life. And that's what I did. I picked up the fork and slowly began to clear my plate.

⌘

"I missed you so much big girl."

Tess was tied in the alleyway of the barn, the radio steadily played my country tunes. I ran the brush over her thick black coat and felt my fears temporarily fade. This was where I needed to be, right here with my horse in the security that only the barn could offer. This was my happy place, no one could hurt me here. The outside noise began to fade around me, my hurt and fears temporarily disappeared. Right now, when it was just my horse and I, the world made sense. I spoke quietly to Tess, her large black ears flicked back and forth as she listened. I buried my face into her long mane, and threw my arms around her thick neck.

"How could this have happened to me big girl? What am I going to do?"

Tess stood as still as a statue. She seemed to sense I needed her. She waited patiently until the tears stopped flowing. I took a step back to look up at my large horse through tear stained eyes. She lowered her giant head and blew her sweet, warm breath into my face. She brought her muzzle to my arm and nudged me gently. I wrapped my arms carefully around her lovely head and held her for a long time. I hid away in the barn for a few hours before making my way back to the house, trying to enjoy the feeling of being temporarily numb.

My mother and I sat in the living room, a heavy silence filled the room. I wrapped myself up in a blanket and sipped on a mug of tea. My heart began to race, there was no easy way to bring up what I was about to say. I glanced at my mother, knowing she would take it well. She had been a young mother, at the tender age of nineteen. I knew she would be there for me no matter how this was going to play out. She wouldn't judge, she would not give me a lecture, she would just simply be there. I had picked the perfect time to come home for a visit as my stepfather was away on a business trip. He would not take the news very well, he would need a few days to process and calm down.

"Mom…" I bit my lip as her blue eyes fell to me. "I'm late."

My mother's eyebrows rose, her eyes grew wide, and she did not say a word. Not one word. She studied me for a moment, reached for her wine glass and took a long sip. "Oh, honey. You poor girl."

"Mom!"

My mother looked thoughtful. "If this happens, you're world is going to change, forever. But you know," she looked at me again, "you are going to be okay. You will be an amazing mom and you will not be alone in this. Everything will fall into place, it just might take some rearranging, but you will be okay. You are one hell of a strong girl and you know…" her eyes took on a far away look, "you were not expected, but you changed my world forever. It gave me a reason to get up in the morning, to have someone to fight for. I can not imagine my life without you," she bit her lip. "I don't believe there are any accidents, only divine interventions."

I reached for a Kleenex and wiped the tears that had begun to fall. I inhaled deeply and let my lungs ache in protest. Slowly, I released the shaky breath. My hands trembled slightly so I buried them in the blanket and wrapped myself up tighter.

"Have you told him?" my mother asked softly.

"No. I don't know that I should. He clearly doesn't care."

My mother nodded. "It's up to you. But it might help ease some of the worry if you share it with him. This shouldn't fall on just you, he's a big part of this too."

"I know."

My mother grew very quiet then. I glanced up at her and she looked deep in thought. She clearly had something to say, yet she wasn't sure how to go about doing so.

"I'm not made of glass, Mom. You can say it."

She looked up at me and held my gaze seriously. "If you are, I hope you let him in to help you."

I groaned loudly and started to cut her off. She held up her hands to silence me. "Just listen, Ryleigh."

I pressed my lips together and remained silent. "Babies are a lot of work, it's hard. I don't know what happened to him, but from everything I have heard he sounded like a good man, he cared about you. I'm not sure why his head is up his ass now but something about this does not add up for me. It doesn't make sense," she paused.

"But, honey, I would hope for you and the sake of this baby that you two give it a solid go as a family. Wouldn't that be something? That a tiny little one could put you on the same path once again? That would be one powerful baby. And if in the end it doesn't work, at least you know in your heart that you tried, you put forth a solid effort."

A tug pulled at my heart as I remembered the Bryce I had known. That was a man worth fighting for, that was a man worth letting back in. I knew deep down if I was in fact pregnant, he would be there for the baby, no questions asked. I saw first hand how much he loved his own son. *But could he love me, really, truly love me?* I was not so sure. I never wanted to be a burden to anyone, I had always believed that love should be a choice of freewill, not a punishment. Seeing how things ended and so damn suddenly, it left me feeling very lost and confused on the matter. Could I ever trust him again? That I could not answer. For I was not so sure who he was. The man I had grown to care about so deeply, well, I'm not certain he truly existed.

⌘

"How are you feeling?" Emma's blue eyes filled with concern.

"I'm hanging in there." I smiled weakly.

"I bet. I can't believe he did this to you." She shook her head sadly, blond hair swinging. "You were so happy, it was nice to see. What a jerk."

I laughed a little and took a small sip of my Chai latte. Emma and I sat in the quaint little coffee shop that we frequently visited. Many serious talks had been shared here, as well as laughter. Local musicians often came to perform their music; we had spent many a night dancing in this very room. I loved this place; it had a small town charm. The walls were filled with local artists work and soft music flitted throughout the room welcoming those that chose to stay.

Concern filled Emma's features. She was one of my best friends and I really needed to see her. Though she was a petite little thing, she was fiery and bold. Emma didn't hold much back, I don't think she could if she tried. We had witnessed each other fall apart on quite a few occasions, but we were always there to pick each other up, no matter how far away life took us. Emma was the only friend who ignored my protests to stay away while I was at my worst in the hospital. She charged through the door, smile on, and greeted me with a warm hug, telling me that I still looked beautiful.

"Emma," I began slowly. She looked at me with eager eyes and I continued hesitantly. "I might be pregnant," I nearly whispered.

Emma nodded once, and leaned back in her chair. Her face looked deep in thought without a hint of judgment. "Wow. Does he know?"

"I haven't said a word." My eyes fell to a napkin on the table and I began to scrunch it up it mindlessly. "I was planning to tell him on Valentines, but we all know how that played out." I shrugged.

She nodded matter of factly. "Hmm. Do you want to tell him?"

I looked up, torn. "I don't know. A part of me thinks he deserves to know, the other half is confused. At this point honestly, why bother?" I stopped and thought for a moment. "Although it would be nice to share some of the worry. Why should it all have to fall on me?"

She nodded and her face grew serious. "I would then. You'll know in your heart what to do. There is no right or wrong answer in a situation like this, and he is a big part of it. It takes two."

I laughed a little. "Yes, yes it does."

"Promise me one thing," Emma's voice grew quiet. "Please do not take him back. If he steps up, like he should, just be careful. I've been there. You remember after Tom and I broke up? I was a mess. Our relationship ended out of the blue and he left so suddenly as well. I never saw it coming. Taking him back was one of the dumbest things I've ever done. It played out the same, second time around."

But he's not Tom. "I remember. I promise, I will be careful."

"Good." She stood up to give me a hug. "How long are you home for?"

"At least a week."

"Okay. We'll see each other again before you leave. Keep me posted on things?"

"I will."

⌘

What to do? Do I? Or don't I? Why does life have to be so complicated? So many feelings were involved, there was so much that could go wrong...but there were also so many things that could go right. However, this situation felt like a lose-lose kind of thing to me. I tapped my fingers against the kitchen counter aimlessly. *Mark.* I needed to talk to him. How I wished he were closer to me, now so more than ever. I could use his strong arms pulling me into the comfort of his chest. Mark held the gift of laughter, no matter what the world threw my way, he could always put a smile on my face.

"Mark? How are you?"

"I'm good. Away working again but that's nothing new. How are you?"

I found myself reminiscing. Work took him away for weeks to even months at a time quite frequently. While we were together, he would often find a way to get me up to his latest work site. I had grown very familiar with hotels during our time together but I never minded. He always made an effort to see me, and that meant the world to me. I never did mind the drive to find him. We found a way to make it work given the hand we were dealt.

I sighed sadly, that felt like a lifetime ago now. "I'm okay."

"No, you're not. What's wrong?"

I smiled, he knew me so well. "It's been a terrible week. Bryce left me on Valentines, and…well, I might be pregnant."

"Holy shit. First of all, he's an idiot. And second, how are you handling it?"

"I'm hanging in there."

"Of course you are. I really wish I was there. I would give you a hug, keep you close."

"I could use a hug more than ever. I'm a bit of a mess right now."

"With good reason. I'd find a way to make you smile."

"You always could."

"Does he know?"

"No. I don't know if I should tell him."

"It might be best to wait until you know for sure. But then again, I'd throw it at him. I'd want to know…if it was me."

"Yeah, I'm starting to lean in that direction myself."

"Good luck, sweetie. I'm always here if you need me xoxo."

"Thank you, for always being there."

Leave it to Mark, my Alberta boy. His simple words lit a small hope deep within, and at the very least I knew I had some amazing people in my corner. Mark would always hold a very special place in my heart. I let his words embrace me like a warm hug and I hoped the safety of them would last. I think I deserved at least that much, a little comfort was all I was asking for.

⌘

Dear God in heaven I think I might actually pass out. Maybe I shouldn't be doing this. It doesn't feel right. With trembling hands I held my phone. The message was typed, all I had to do was press send, cyber space would deliver it to him. I chewed my lip nervously, I really, really did not want to do it like this, but then again, my plans had gone to crap anyways, so what the hell. I read the message once more with nervous eyes. "Just thought I would let you know that I may be pregnant. Even though you have walked away, you should know as if this is the case, this will impact both of us. When I went to the doctor on Thursday I realized I was almost two weeks late. We did a test then, it was negative. However, I am never late. The doctor said it might be to early to detect so I am to repeat in another week. Was going to discuss in person, but you never gave me the chance. I've been wrestling with this dilemma and losing sleep. Thought you should know. I will let you know either way."

Press send. That's it, that's all you have to do. You have now done your part. Easier said than done. My finger hovered over the "send" icon, my heart pounded unsurely in my chest. Though I was sitting, my knees began to wobble, my legs felt like jelly beneath me. I sucked in a quick breath and tried my best to ignore the deafening heartbeat that rang in my ears. I pressed down shakily on the button that would seal my fate. *Sent.* I let out a breath with a loud whoosh, turned off the phone quickly and tossed it aside. I was not ready to deal with his reaction. I expected him to come at me with bitter, hurtful remarks that would make me feel so very small. I leaned back in the chair and squeezed my hands tightly. Here we go.

CHAPTER 11

Sleep came surprisingly easy. It's amazing how much emotions can exhaust you. I was oddly thankful for that tonight. As my head hit the pillow, the first thought that came to me was not of him. I held my hand tenderly upon my stomach and let it rest there. I closed my eyes tightly and felt slightly disappointed, for I did not yet have a clear feeling if I was carrying a little one with me. *Was I or wasn't I? Shouldn't I feel it? Shouldn't I have some sort of a sense?* It was one of life's many questions that I did not have an answer too.

Sunlight broke through my blinds, gently luring me out a deep slumber. I sat up cautiously and the nightstand that held my phone called my name. I chose to ignore it for a little while longer. *Tess.* I arose with a small smile and pulled on my barn clothes. It was time to feed the big girl breakfast and begin some barn chores. With Maggie by my side, tail wagging, I hauled the grain to big Tess and watched her eat for a moment, relishing in the sound of her happy chews. I pulled myself away, tossed the hay nets over my shoulder and headed out into paddock to tie nets under her favorite trees. As I pulled out the wheelbarrow I grinned. Tess let out happy snorts as she pulled the hay eagerly out the nets. If only all our lives could be so simple.

I busied myself by cleaning out the stalls and paddock, filling waters, and lastly sweeping out the barn aisle. I hung up the pitchfork and dusted my hands together in satisfaction, the place looked good. I glanced around once more and decided the tack room could use a good sweep as well. Once I had the place nearly sparkling clean, I knew there was nothing left to do but check my phone. My heart dropped into my stomach. It was time to face the music.

"Well, that's exciting news. Looks like we're getting married. Yes, please do let me know either way. Everything will be fine, I promise."

I stared at the phone screen, green eyes wide. What the hell is this? That is not the reaction that should be coming from somebody who had just left me for another woman. Not even close. If I thought I was confused before, I was now officially gone. Was this some sort of cruel joke? Or did he actually mean those words? I had been building my defensive wall all night, I was ready for his attack. To my surprise, I found myself growing fiercely protective of the potential little one already. I would let no one speak ill of the innocence that I may be carrying. I read over his response quickly once more. It did not make sense, any of it. I didn't know what to say, how to respond, and so, I said nothing. Nothing at all.

"He said *what* now?" Emma's eyes widened in surprise. I repeated his words and threw my hands helplessly into the air.

My mother looked puzzled as well. "I was expecting him to be a bit of an ass about this. I have to say, I did not see this one coming at all. I'm glad for you though, Ry, at least it's not a hurtful comment."

I rolled my eyes. "I thought I was confused before, but now? I don't even know what to say or think."

Emma frowned. "I'm worried about this, Ry. Just be careful, I know how much you like him, but just remember one thing, and I don't want to sound like a bitch, I just don't want to see you get hurt…" Her words trailed off but I knew she had more.

I nodded at her to go on. She did. "He dropped you like you were nothing. I mean, what can he bring you, honestly? You probably never would have heard from him again if it weren't for this. He should step up for the baby and help you out, that would be the honorable thing to do. But I worry he's going to try to be there for some of the wrong reasons; to ease some of the guilt he may feel just to make him seem like less of an ass."

The words were heavy, but my mind had already been drifting in that direction as well. I knew it was true, I probably never would have heard from him again if it weren't for this. I studied Emma, she had more to say. "What is it Em?"

She looked unsure of how to proceed. "Are you sure he didn't do this on purpose? I mean, nothing he's said is making any sense. It's so, so…backwards."

I thought her words over. He never did hide the fact he wanted children and he had talked about me being a potential mother, but he was going about it all wrong if that was his plan.

"I don't think so…" I said slowly. "He wouldn't have left for someone else, or so I would hope. Excuse me, I have to pee. Again."

I got up and made my way to the restroom. Emma, my mother and I were out for lunch at a semi famous tea house, they were well known for their tea leaf readings. Over the past few days, my bladder had been working overtime. It felt like my entire day consisted of having to use the washroom. I felt a jolt inside, it began to feel like something was indeed settling within me. Two pregnant women, amongst others, were also here at the little café, and to my great dismay, I had noticed that the three of us were constantly using the washroom like clockwork. *Oh dear. Could it be? Could it really be?* I approached our table just as the reader sat next to my mom. She wanted to read her leaves first. The woman began her reading and she hit pretty close on a lot of things. Mom nodded eagerly, agreeing. Emma had never had a reading done before; she leaned eagerly over the table, clearly enchanted.

When it came time for Emma's reading her eyes widened. She grabbed my arm in anticipation, and squeezed tightly. "I'm nervous. I have the butterflies!" she whispered to me. I smiled reassuringly and patted her hand.

As I listened, a chill went down my back. Emma's jaw dropped as the reader picked up on many things Emma had told so few people. Emma sat deep in her chair and looked slightly flustered.

"You're next," the reader looked directly at me. My own heart beat a little unevenly in anticipation. Emma, and my mother's eyes grew serious as they leaned in closer, eager to hear what the reader foresaw.

"Okay." I slid her my tea cup and she stared down at it, rather intently. "Hmm. Are you in a relationship?"

I laughed a bitter laugh. "No."

"Are you sure about that?"

"Yes."

"I'm not. He has a lot of manning up to do, but he's still around," she stared into the cup, deep in thought. "A lot. I see the letter 'B'"

Emma's hand gripped my forearm. I widened my eyes. "Oh, boy."

The reader continued and the hairs went up on the back of my neck. "What's your question?" she asked, staring boldly into my eyes.

I looked, wide eyed from my mother to Emma. They appeared to be holding there breath. "Umm," I began hesitantly, "I-I don't know how to ask? How do I say this?"

She waited patiently, staring, studying me. I twirled my fingers in the air, hoping to find the words. "Well, I guess...do you...do you see a new life around me?"

"As in pregnancy? Yes."

Crap. I began to laugh nervously then, and felt slightly on the verge of loosing it.

"You love kids," she continued. "They don't have an agenda. You appreciate that."

"I do."

"Do you think you're pregnant now?"

"I'm not sure. I-I don't think so..."

"You are. I think it's a boy," she studied me. "You're very close to your brother. You're thinking of naming the baby's middle name after him."

How the hell is she doing this? I had never told a soul, not a single soul. It was true, if I were to ever have a boy, his middle name would be named after my brother, Skyler. If it was a girl her middle name would be a combination of my mother and oma; Rose.

The reader smiled brightly at us. "Enjoy your lunch ladies." She left us sitting in silence, eyes wide.

My mother was the first one to say something, hands in the air. "Well, I don't care what the doctor has to say at this point. I'm sorry, Ryleigh, but I'm convinced you're pregnant."

Emma patted my shoulder reassuringly. I offered a weak grin. Over the past few days, I had begun to feel different, things were changing. An odd sensation had settled over, but I couldn't quite put my finger on it. It left me feeling strangely content. Soon after our lunch was placed in front of us and I looked down at the plate eagerly, I was famished.

⌘

"Surprise!"

My mother and Emma pulled out a grocery bag and handed it to me, smiles bright. After lunch we decided to go back to my mother's to catch up some more, in private. I looked down at the bag suspiciously and opened it. I peeked inside at its contents.

"Oh my God! Girls!" I looked up with an amused expression and began to laugh, really laugh. I held in each hand, a pregnancy test. "Jee, thanks!"

Emma and my mother gave each other a sly grin. "Hey!" I exclaimed. "You guys planned this, didn't you?"

Emma grinned. "We sure did. Now go," she waved her hand, "pee on a stick."

"I'll set the timer!" Mom called out.

I rolled my eyes. "Fine." I took the boxes and headed to the washroom, laughing as Emma began cheering. "Go, Ryleigh! You got this!"

I placed the box on the counter and stared at it. My heart started to thump loudly in my chest. I gingerly laid my hand above my heart. It had been working overtime lately. I grew concerned that it would break through my chest soon enough, or give out entirely from an emotional overload. *Let's do this.* It was fairly simple, pee on a stick for five seconds. One pink line for negative, two pink lines for positive. Easy.

"Start the timer!" I yelled from the washroom. I laid the stick down and watched fearfully, yet full of curiosity. *No, no I can't do this. Not here.* I rose quickly and strode into the kitchen. "I can't watch it. I'll check when the timer goes off."

They kept the conversation light and I tried my best to ignore the butterflies, and the countdown of the clock. *5, 4, 3, 2, 1. Beep! Beep! Beep!* I jumped as the timer went off. It was time.

"Here I go!" I said nervously. I stopped short in my tracks. "What if it's positive?"

"Well," my mother began. "Then the first thing you say is 'Holy fucking shit, here we go.' The rest we deal with later."

Laughter carried me into the washroom where I peeked down at the test, one eye closed. I opened the other eye and picked up the test. Huh, this was odd. One of the result windows had a clear, pink line. The other circle had turned sheer pink. I studied it for a few moments, a little unsure of what it meant. I wrapped it up and tossed it into the trash. "Negative." I said.

"Oh, okay. Well, it might still be too early to tell, that's why we got you a few."

I nodded. "Okay."

Emma glanced at the time. "Shoot, I should go." She gave me a warm hug. "Let me know how this plays out." She gave me a grin and leaned toward my stomach, rubbing it quickly. "Good luck in there little one!"

"Emma!" I shrieked and began to laugh. She smiled and with one last wave she hopped out the door. My hands settled over my stomach and a warm sensation came over me. I had a feeling this was the start of a whole new world.

CHAPTER 12

I saw babies everywhere. Pregnant women, tiny infants in strollers, I just couldn't escape them. It was my own blue car syndrome. It was my last day home before I had to go back to the real world. The trip home had done wonders on my soul. A little pep found its way back into my step, and a brightness slowly filled my heart.

"Dammit, I have to pee again," I muttered.

My mother laughed. "Babies will do that. There's a washroom over there."

I nodded and followed the signs. I found my mom browsing in a center aisle. One of my truck tires had a leak, so I had taken it in to get repaired while the warranty was still good. We busied ourselves browsing through the store while we waited.

"Oh, I want to check their decals here," I said eagerly, turning a corner. "Aw damn!" I exclaimed. The aisle was filled with car seats and baby strollers. "Really?" I shouted.

My mother laughed. "I think the universe may be trying to tell you something."

I sighed heavily, yet a flicker of excitement ran through me. If this were to happen, I could do it without him. I would make it work. I had always looked forward to the day I would be a mom, the circumstances were not ideal, but this child would be beyond loved. The day I held that little bundle in my arms, I would be done for. My heart would belong to him/her forever and always. I browsed the car seats with a new interest. I looked at the prices silently and my mind went into overdrive. There would be a lot of things to price out. Cribs, strollers, car seats, changing tables, diapers, bottles, the list went on and on. *Don't get ahead of yourself. Slow down.* My stomach rumbled with hunger. I rubbed it absently. Soon. Ten minutes later, my truck was fixed and we were on the road once more.

"Thanks for having me over, Mom."

"Anytime. I'm sorry it couldn't be under better circumstances." Her eyes bore into mine. "You will be okay. You're not alone in this."

"I know." I looked up at the sky, smiling. It had begun to snow. The weather report called for a snowstorm to hit tomorrow. Looked like things were starting early.

"Drive safe, okay? Let me know when you're home safe and sound."

"Will do." I gave Mom a tight squeeze and whistled to Maggie. Time to cross the ocean once again.

The snow fell steadily overnight. I awoke to a world covered in a blanket of white and it was still falling heavily. I was ecstatic.

"Come on Maggie. Let's go for a walk!"

I bundled up and stepped into the winter wonderland. The snow fell thick as it twirled and danced among the light breeze. It didn't take long for Maggie's long black coat to turn white. She stopped to shake every now and then, but it seemed to be a wasted effort. As if she too agreed with my thought, she dove head first into a pile of snow. *If you can't beat them, join them.* Maggie flopped happily onto her back and wiggled gleefully in the cool white powder. I smiled at my goofy girl. It was ridiculous how much I loved her. I stared up at the vast gray sky. Today felt like a good day. A great day. I lifted my arms to the sky and twirled without a care in the world.

⌘

It's happened. It's actually happened.

I sat on the bathroom floor, my legs sprawled in front of me. I held the stick in my right hand. A wave of fear hit me cold, followed by a twinge of excitement. Then the fear came back followed by nausea. Two pink lines stared back at me. I reached onto the counter behind me and dragged the container of Tums toward me. I popped two into my mouth and chewed slowly. Huh. What now? I sat on the floor for a very long time, allowing reality sink in. I was pregnant. I carried a little human inside of me. I dropped the stick gently to the floor and placed my hands onto my stomach carefully. *Hello, little one. I don't know you but I can feel you. I think I've felt you for awhile now. Somehow, I love you already. I will keep you safe, I promise.*

My thoughts turned to Bryce, for a part of him would forever be apart of me. Sadness enclosed me, followed by anger. I hadn't heard a damn thing from him. At the very least, he could have asked how I was holding up, if I was okay. But he did no such thing, he left me standing here once again by myself. A quote I had read not too long ago ran through my head. *"It's not about finding someone who won't fight with you or make you sad, or mad. It's about finding the person who will still be there, wiping the tears away, holding you in their arms after a fight, and the one who will never leave, no matter how hard things get."* I shook my head sadly, he was clearly not that person. The happy memories and warmth of him began to fade like an old photograph worn with age. I felt heavy with confusion. Where did my Bryce go? He never would have left me by myself to walk through this scary, unknown path. The Bryce I held close to my heart would be here, holding my hand, walking beside me. What little joy I felt earlier for my little one faded. The tears that hadn't fallen for quite some time, flooded back for I was alone in this life changing moment. He couldn't even bother to care.

"Wow, so it's official then?" Jane asked, wide eyed.

"Yes, I've had two positive tests now."

"Holy crap." Jane studied me. "You seem awfully calm."

I nodded. I felt calm. I had one more good cry and that was it. It was time to pick myself up and pull it together. I was no longer in this on my own. I was responsible for a new life growing inside me. I would be a mother. *A mother.*

I smiled tenderly, and looked down at my stomach with a twinge of love. My life would be forever changed. It already had. "I am," I said softly. "I can do this."

Jane nodded knowingly. "You're going to make a great mom."

I smiled. "Thank you. I have a good one to look up too."

"Yes, you sure do. Have you told him?"

"Nope. Not yet." Anger chose to walk in and I let it. "Not once has he even bothered to ask if I'm okay. I thought he would step up, but he's failing miserably." My eyebrows furrowed. "I'm sure he's with her, keeping himself busy."

"Are you going to tell him?"

"Yes, I will." I sighed. "It's the right thing to do. I grew up without a father, and I couldn't deny my child like that, and let's face it he has every right to be there. I won't stand in the way. Despite what I feel toward him right now, I know he will be an amazing dad. He already is."

A concern crept into my thoughts. "I do worry about Aiden, and how he'll take the news. These things can be so hard on kids…"

Jane looked surprised. "But that's not your worry."

I bit my lip. "No, I suppose not….but still. He's such a cutie."

A car door slammed, ending the conversation. Aaron appeared. "Hey, girls."

Jane stood and met him with a kiss. His eyes took in my expression and they widened. He looked from Jane to me. "Holy shit."

I gave a small smile. "Yup."

"Wow. So, you're going to be a mom? That's huge news. Um, congratulations?"

I forced a tiny grin. "Thank you. Did you guys want to come with me? I was going to look at baby stuff, I'd like to see what's out there. Start getting some ideas."

"Sure thing." We piled into Aaron's car and away we went.

"I feel so overwhelmed." I craned my head back to stare at a wall of baby accessories. "There's so much to choose from."

I looked back eagerly at Aaron and Jane for their own opinions, and I burst out laughing. Aaron stood, shoulders nearly tucked up to his ears, eyes darting back and forth nervously. Jane stood next to him, mouth slightly gaped with one hand on her chest. They kept close to each other and looked ready to bolt at the slightest sound, they were clearly uncomfortable.

"I feel very awkward here," Aaron whispered.

Jane shuffled next to him, shoulder touching his side. "Me too. I would be freaking out right now."

"You guys!" I swatted them lightly. "You're not helping."

I tried to press aside the fear bubbling inside my own stomach when my eyes caught the baby clothing. My heart melted and I nearly ran to the aisle. Tiny booties, bibs, and precious little outfits lay before me. "I think my uterus just skipped a beat," I whispered to myself.

My eyes landed on one outfit, a soft yellow jumper with Winnie the Pooh stitched on the body. The words *Hunny* lay scattered amongst buzzing bees and honey jars. The outfit came as a set with a matching bib and little booties. I picked it up delicately, and I was gone. *Hello little one. I found your first outfit. I can't wait to see you in it. Love, Mom.*

I turned back to my shaken friends. "Isn't this the cutest thing you've ever seen? It's perfect. It will work for a girl or a boy!"

"It is adorable," Jane cooed.

"I'm getting it." I held the outfit up once more and hugged it to my chest. "So cute," I said to myself.

It was late by the time I got home. I met Skyler in the kitchen. "Hey," he said lightly, "where were you?"

I bit my lip, how would I tell him? I looked at the bag I held. I took the outfit out carefully and held it over my stomach, not saying a word. Sky washed something in the sink and he turned to face me once he was done. His eyes took in the scene; his beaming sister holding a tiny, bright outfit over her stomach. His eyes went wide.

"What is that?"

"A baby outfit."

"I know that. But why do you have one?"

I did not say a word. I looked up at him, wide eyed.

Sky grew very quiet, and his eyes grew even bigger. "What?"

"Do I need to say it? Uncle Sky?"

He was about to take a bite of his yogurt. The hand that held the spoon froze halfway to his mouth and it stayed there for quite some time. He lowered the spoon slowly and leaned against the counter, face frozen, big eyes distant.

I killed him. I think he's in shock. Oh, he is so not ready for children. This is terrible!

"Sky? Sky!" I snapped my fingers in front of his face. Nothing. I smacked my hands together with a loud clap. "Hey, come back!"

His eyes moved slowly to mine. He remained silent. He stood tall and slipped past me, reaching for something on the top of the fridge. He turned to me and clutched a bottle of Vodka.

My own eyes grew big and I smacked his arm. "You are so not ready for children!" I exclaimed.

"Hell no, I'm not! Are you?" He leaned heavily against the counter once more, forehead resting in his hand. "A baby? A baby?" he said, almost to himself. He threw back a sip of the Vodka. "I need to use the bathroom." He slipped past me and turned the corner. I could still hear him whispering under his breath. "A baby?"

CHAPTER 13

It was now time to include Bryce in on recent events. I had no idea how he was going to react, but given from his initial reaction, I wasn't expecting a break down, or anger. I picked up the phone to text, and stopped short after a sentence. *Call him. No, I'm not.* I placed the phone upon my nightstand and left the room. I couldn't do it just yet. I paced aimlessly, dodging the dog toys scattered across the living room floor. Did I want him to be here? Did I want him to know? What had he brought to the table as of lately? A whole lot of nothing. I hadn't heard a damn word, not one word since I had last messaged him. But then, maybe he kept his distance from me on purpose, gathering his own thoughts. He was probably sure I hated him and though I should, I couldn't find it within me. *Everything will be fine, I promise.* I remembered the words he had written. I held on to them like a lifeline at the time. But I no longer found comfort in them. Apart of me hoped he would come see me to make sure I was doing okay. But he left me waiting alone. I often dreamt of the gravel crunching as his tires pulled into the drive. I would run to the door and there he would stand with open arms that would pull me in and hold me so very close. But I had let his words go; they held nothing but disappointment.

I sighed heavily and knew it was time to make contact. "I had a positive test." There, message sent. My part was now done.

"Okay. Can we get together at some point to discuss what you plan on doing?"

What *I* plan on doing? Of course, let it all rest on me. "I suppose."

"What day works for you? I start afternoon shifts this week and Tuesday's I have Aiden."

Aiden. I would not let him feel the brunt of this. "Okay. How about Wednesday?"

"You're okay with that? I think in an hour we should be able to cover everything, don't you?"

"An hour will be plenty. What time?"

"Whatever works for you."

"How about we aim for the 10:00 mark?"

"Sure."

"Okay. Did you want to meet here? Or we could go somewhere?"

"I'm not comfortable talking about this in a public place, even if we just sit in a truck and talk."

"Fair enough. Come to my house then, we can talk in the truck."

"Okay. I will see you Wednesday at 10."

Wednesday he would be here, his tires would appear in my driveway after all. Did I really want to see him? Could I look into his eyes and be able to walk away? It had been almost three weeks since we had last seen each other. As time went on, it had gotten easier to breathe without him, I found my smile coming back. Would he just take it all away once more? In two days I would know.

The thought of the upcoming discussion had my nerves shot. I wondered if he was nervous too. I hoped he was. I truly hoped I wasn't the only one in this scenario who felt physically beaten. You can not just toss someone aside like they don't mean anything. Actions have consequences, and now, he would have to face his, and the mess he left behind.

⌘

I sniffed at the air rather unpleasantly. "What's that smell?" I asked Sky who worked at his computer.

He stopped to take a deep breath. "I dunno, I don't smell anything."

My face twisted. "Something smells terrible."

I held my stomach as I fought with a wave of nausea. *Water. I need water.*

I made my way to the kitchen to grab a drink. The smell was much stronger in here. I held my glass under the tap and my stomach took a dive. A can of tuna sat on the counter.

"Found the smell," I called to Sky. Too late, with one hand held over my mouth, I ran for the washroom. I hugged the toilet bowl, and that's where I stayed until it felt safe to get up. I plugged my nose and quickly strode passed the kitchen to my brother. "You have to take care of that can. It's making me sick."

Sky looked rather amused. "Is it now?"

"Please, Sky. If I have to smell it again, I am going to gag."

"Sure, sure. I'll take care of it."

"Thank you."

True to his word, he took care of it. I watched from a safe distance as he rinsed out the can and sprayed down the counter. I let out a sigh of relief. My stomach still danced on the edge as I timidly made my way toward the cabinets and found a box of crackers. I munched on them mindlessly before flopping onto my bed. I was exhausted. I had spent most of my days sleeping. I had never felt so tired in my life.

My mind was in a constant fog. On more than one occasion I had placed my tea in the freezer and eggs in the cupboard. Sky had found it rather amusing, at first. Our kitchen was becoming a regular scavenger hunt for even the simplest items. The amusement wore off rather quickly as Sky loved his food and when he was hungry, he was hungry and needed to eat asap. Maggie found me stretched out on the bed. She pressed herself against the bedside and looked up at me, tongue dangling sideways out of her mouth. Her soft brown eyes stared up me, looking rather helpless. I sighed. I could be a push over at times. I normally didn't allow her on my bed, but today I needed the comfort of someone beside me, and right now I'd have to settle for my dog.

I patted on the mattress loudly. "Come on up girl."

In a single bound, Maggie hopped up. She plopped next to me, and placed her head on my stomach. I stroked her head softly. "What do you think girl? How are you going to be around a little one?" I gently shifted her head onto the comforter. *I guess we'll find out soon enough.*

The next morning, I was up very early. Darkness still clouded the world outside. My stomach was in knots, my heart heavy. In just a few short hours he would be here. I wrapped my arms around my torso and held on tightly, I felt so cold. I knew in my heart I was doing the right thing by telling him. The choice would be his after that. Although my feelings toward him were somewhat filled with bitterness and hurt, I could not deny my unborn child from knowing who his or her father was. No matter what happened from this point on, at the very least I could take comfort in knowing I had done the right thing. With a heavy sigh, I tossed off my blanket and got up. I took a hot shower and enjoyed the embrace as the warm beads of liquid warmed my cool skin. I managed to find a calmness in the sound of the steady water as it beat against the shower tiles. I stepped out and wrapped myself in a warm robe. It was time to get ready for the day.

"You can park wherever in the driveway, all spots are free."

I looked at the clock, 9:30 a.m. He would soon be here.

"Okay."

I held the phone to my forehead, beating it lightly in anticipation. What was there to talk about, really? Did he hope for a particular outcome? I couldn't even begin to hazard a guess. Had he told *her* what was going on? Highly doubtful. She did not strike me as the type of girl who would take that well. I hoped for once he would step up and lead the conversation, for I had nothing, my mind came up at a blank. The familiar ache in my heart was back. I hated him for it. I thought back to all the times his truck had pulled into the drive. Back then, it had been followed by such different feelings and emotions, and they had been much happier....so much easier on the heart and soul. I leaned against the kitchen counter, arms crossed. From where I stood, I had a clear view out the living room window that overlooked the driveway. I would see him pull in. A few moments later, the gravel crunched and the familiar blue pickup appeared. He parked in the spot he used many times before. I did not move. Could not move. My heart thudded unevenly in my chest, my stomach jumped and churned wildly. My hands and knees lightly trembled. I closed my eyes tightly, all this from the sight of his truck alone? What was I going to do when I sat next to him? *Next to the stranger who looked like my Bryce. Help. Give me strength…someone, anyone.*

My phone jingled. "I'm here."

I know. I see you. "Be right there."

I said a silent prayer and pulled on my shoes. I was going to need every ounce of my strength to get through this. *God, if you're listening, please let me get through this in one piece. Do not break me into a million pieces. I can not do that again. Thank you.* The brisk winter air held a promise of snow. The ground was frozen and slick from last nights deep freeze so I chose my steps carefully. I turned the corner, and there I stood in the open drive. My steps faltered slightly as I began to close the distance between myself and the truck. His driver door swung open and he stepped out. His steps were long and sure, but his gaze was focused to the ground. I froze. I could not move a muscle. My eyes burned into him. All the feelings of anger and hatred vanished. They were replaced by a sudden longing, an ache. *You've left something behind.* His brown eyes looked up to my green ones. He looked like a deer caught in the headlights. *Good. Let this be uncomfortable for you. Let it hurt.* I studied his face carefully, he looked tired, worn out, and most of all, he looked confused. I could not say a thing, not one syllable. My mind was empty, fuzzy, and full of cob webs.

"Hi," he began carefully.

I stared back at him cautiously. "Hello."

He took an unsure step toward me and gave me a quick hug. I fell limp in his arms and let my hands fall still at my sides.

He pulled back and looked down at me. "Shall we go in the truck and talk?"

I nodded silently and made my way to the passenger door, the ache growing steadily worse. So much laughter and fun memories were spent in the front seat of this truck. *Not anymore. Not with me.* We slid inside and shut the doors. I pressed my forehead to the glass of the window and stared outside. I could not look at him, he was dangerous and I didn't feel strong enough to resist the temptation.

"You must hate me," he said quietly.

I do. I hate you so much. Yet why do I feel like I need you? "You're not my favorite person at the moment."

"You're not going to punch me in the face, are you?"

Screw you. I'm not her. I met his eyes then, briefly. "No," once again, my gaze settled out the window.

"You've never been here before, have you?"

"No. I have not."

"Okay. Well, I have this whole speech planned out. I'm nervous."

Once again, I said nothing. His eyes watched me closely for something, anything. He continued to study me, and with a quiet sigh he realized he would get nothing. I nestled my hand over my stomach in a slight protective manner, and I waited in silence. I grew slightly impatient as the quiet became deafening. I wanted, needed him to say something. I feared that if the stillness went on any longer, he would be able to hear my heart pounding fearfully inside my chest. I did not want to appear weak in front of him, I had to keep myself together.

He cleared his throat. "The way I see it is we have three options. Option one is my first choice, the one I would hope for," his voice grew quiet, and he stopped.

Curiosity got the best of me. His voice broke slightly as it filled with a small hope. I glanced his way briefly and his eyes drew me in. His gaze took hold of me and held me there. I suddenly felt scared.

"Keep going," I urged.

He nodded, his eyes filled with uncertainty. "The first option is you let me in. I will be there for you and the baby every step of the way. We become a family, and I will be by your side and love you forever with all of my heart." He stopped and grabbed on to the steering wheel and held on tightly.

I had to look away for I felt the threat of tears. I held a hand over my heart. It hurt so much. His words were painful, for there was a time when I could picture us together for the rest of our lives, happy and in love. But was he just saying this because of the pregnancy? I did not want to be with anyone by default, I wanted the person to *want* to be with me out of his own freewill. I broke away my gaze and looked at my hands as they folded neatly in my lap. How could he say those words and act like he meant them? He was with someone else. Kissing her lips, holding her, making her laugh. How dare he tease me like this. For all the while I've been standing here alone and scared. Where the hell has he been up to this point?

I cleared my throat. "What are the other options?" I said rather blankly.

Bryce stiffened like someone had poured cold water down his back. He nodded sadly. "I am not the type of guy who won't bother to be apart of his kids lives. I need to be there for them. Basically, if you try to keep me away I will hound you day in and day out until you let me be there."

I looked at him, eyes wide in disbelief. "I would never do that. I'm not that type of person. I know what it's like to grow up without both parents. I would never do that to my own child."

He nodded quickly. "I didn't think you were."

"I will let you be apart of this child's life. I want you to be there."

"Good, because I will be."

"What's option three?"

He looked uncomfortable. "I will support whatever decision you make. I'm not sure how you feel about the 'A' option…" his voice trailed off slowly.

Abortion. How dare he say that to me. "Get that out of your head. That's not even an option."

He let out a slow breath. "Good."

My hands cradled my stomach gently. *You are safe in there little one. I will keep you safe.* His eyes fell to my hands. His gaze moved up to my face, and he held it rather boldly.

"Can you look at me?" he asked softly.

No. It hurts too much. But I did. I raised my eyes hesitantly and found myself gazing at the man I had fallen in love with. His face softened. His eyes were in turmoil, a lot was going on in that head of his and I was glad. I didn't need to be the only one lost in this.

"How are you doing? Have you been crying a lot?" he asked.

"I'm fine. I won't lie, I had a good cry when I found out, but I'm holding myself together."

"You are a strong girl."

"Yes, I am."

He blew out a breath. "This couldn't have had worse timing. I-I felt like you weren't that in to me. And my ex…she started texting again. I honestly can't tell you why I went back to her. It felt like something I needed to see through I guess. I don't know."

He paused and took a deep, slow breath. "I feel like such an ass for what I've done. I was crazy about you."

Clearly not. Why didn't you ever ask me? "I see."

He looked up at me, brown eyes wide. "Did you feel that way about me?"

Of course I did you idiot. What else could I have done to show you? "Yes."

Bryce looked like he was hit in the stomach. He winced, one hand fell around his torso, the other gripped the steering wheel tightly. He let out a loud breath and closed his eyes. "I didn't know. The timing on this is terrible, if I had known about this earlier, I never would have gone back."

I stared at him, he didn't look like an idiot. How could he have not known? If he was having doubts, why didn't he ever ask me? Instead, he chose to go back to someone else, someone who he claimed made his life miserable. I took a moment to let his words sink in. *If I had known about this earlier, I never would have went back.* Those words damn near killed me, for I had been so worried that as soon as he found out he would bolt, and leave me here alone. I held on to the potential news for as long as I could before I felt the need to say something. If only I had told him sooner…he would still be mine. The irony of it all was cruel for I was left alone in the end anyways.

I shook my head sadly. "I see."

This was too much. I had finally gotten a reason, but it was so disappointing it offered me little comfort. I cleared my throat. "I'll be going to the doctor on Friday to double check the pregnancy test was correct. I'll let you know how things go," I nudged open the door and hopped outside heading for my door.

His door slammed shut and he followed me quickly. "Ryleigh?"

My steps slowed to a stop. *No. Please stay away.*

"I'm so sorry."

I looked at him sadly. He stared back at me carefully, quietly calculating if it was safe to come closer without getting a fist in his face. He took one step toward me. He watched me hesitantly until he was close enough that I could almost feel his heart beating in his chest. *This is going to hurt so much. Please, don't come any closer.* He did. His arms took me in, and this time, mine fell around him, holding him tight. *Why couldn't you have been here sooner? I needed you. I still need you.* Just as quickly as the embrace had come, it was over. He looked down at me, his eyes filled with sadness. I knew I was about to break and I couldn't let him see that.

"I'll let you know how things go," I said softly.

"Please do."

I turned on my heel and walked briskly into the house. I could hold back the flood gates no more. I let out heart racking sobs and sank to the floor. The loneliness, the sting of heartbreak was fresh all over again. Seeing him, feeling his touch only to lose it once more, it was just too much.

"What have I ever done to deserve this? I'm a good person! Why did you do this to me? What do you want from me?" I shouted to no one in particular.

I looked out my window and his truck was still parked in the drive. I watched it for awhile wondering what he was doing, what was going through his head. Finally, his truck roared to life and he pulled away slowly. My eyes fell sadly upon my guitar and a new wave of emotion washed over me. I hadn't been able to play since he left. It hurt too much. He had taken away so much, yet he left me with a tiny, precious gift.

My phone jingled and I picked it up blankly. I was surprised to see a message from him. "If this happens, you need to let me marry you."

My eyes remained frozen on his words. *Need to let me marry you.* I shook my head. *No.* "Marriage shouldn't be a forced punishment. It's a promise between two people."

"Fair enough. But can you see yourself with me for the rest of your life? Because I can see myself being happy with you."

A fresh hurt arose as he pressed the knife in deeper. "I thought I could but I got dropped pretty quickly. Doesn't exactly build confidence. Bottom line, you're with someone else. If for some reason this doesn't work out I disappear anyways."

"I suppose so. I'm so sorry."

CHAPTER 14

My head rested quietly on my tear stained pillow. There was so much I should have said to him. *Choose me. Love me.* But what was the point? Was he only willing to come back because I was pregnant? Or was he willing to fight for me either way? If it was all because of my current situation, then he is not worth it. He's not worth the hurt nor the tears. Why chase something, someone, who will not chase back? It's hard to let go. Sleep would offer me no comfort tonight. I slipped out of bed quietly and turned on the hall light. I stepped into the glow and followed it to Sky's bedroom. It was empty, he was at his girlfriend's for the night. I leaned against the door frame and flicked on the light. Once the baby came, Sky would move into another suite in the house. It had been decided I would stay in the basement, as it had two bedrooms and was the largest of the suites. Sky's room would become the nursery. I looked at his bedroom with a fresh set of eyes. I sat in the middle of the floor cross-legged, daydreaming of how I would decorate. In the corner near the window I pictured a crib with a hanging mobile above. The changing table would stand nearby. I envisioned a dresser in the far corner of the room filled with the baby's tiny clothing. I would have so much fun mixing and matching all the outfits, wondering what my little bundle would wear today. A rocking chair would sit on the other end near the crib where I would sing the little one to sleep, holding him or her safely in my arms. I could almost see the image play out in front of me. But there was one thing missing.

I pictured the scene with Bryce here next to me. His rough hands holding a tender life so gently. I could see the kind smile play on his face as he looked down at a part of him, a part of me. I smiled, I liked this vision. It brought a happiness to my soul and a warmth to my heart. Maybe, just maybe this would all work out. I would have to set my hurt pride aside, but for him I could do it. I would try. I could see a life with him. I had caught glimpses in the past, why not now? We could be happy...very happy. It would take work, but good things in life were always worth fighting for. *Hello, baby. It's Mom. I'm daydreaming of you again. Tonight I'm decorating your bedroom. I'm thinking of a country theme, something with horses. I promise you will like it. You will feel safe here. Sleep tight little one, sweet dreams. Love, your mommy to be.*

⌘

Truck tires crunched in the drive and headlights lit up the room. I glanced around the corner to look at the time, it was just after 9:00 p.m. I pulled back the curtain but it was to dark to clearly see the vehicle. Rain beat against the window loudly. It was a miserable night. A loud knock rapped three times against the door. I opened it slowly, curiously, and there he was. Bryce stood in front of me, soaking wet. He gave me his famous half grin and held out his hand toward me. I looked down and my heart melted for he held a bouquet of sunflowers. The yellow petals shone like the sun, despite the fact they were dripping wet. I took them eagerly and held them close to my chest.

"They're beautiful. Thank you so much," I looked up, eyes bright.

"I should've given these to you awhile ago. I'm so sorry, Ryleigh. I don't know what else I can say or do, but I'm here now, looking you in the eyes to tell you how sorry I am." His hands fell to his side helplessly, his eyes held mine.

I didn't know what to say, so I said nothing. I looked down at the cheery flowers and smiled. I took two big strides forward and pressed my body into his, tossing my arms around his neck. Bryce buried his face against my shoulder and he held for me for a long, long time. We parted the embrace and I slipped my hand into his. He held on tight and I led him inside, smiling.

I awoke with heaviness in my heart. I glanced at my empty bed with dismay. *It was only a dream.* I pulled the comforter against my chest and listened to the steady pounding of the rain against the window pane. My stomach hurt tonight, and I felt nauseous. Morning sickness always found me in the evenings. Tonight was no exception. With a grumble I grabbed the cracker box from the nightstand and chewed on the dry crackers slowly. *Well baby, it looks like it's just us tonight. But that's okay. I promise no matter what happens between your daddy and me, you will be loved by the both of us. That is the one thing, perhaps the only thing at this point I know for certain. And Baby, while you're listening, if you can, please go easy on my stomach. Thanks, little one. Love, your mommy to be.*

The smell of frying eggs and slightly burnt toast woke me. My stomach rumbled with hunger. It was such a contrast, depending on the time of day, as of lately with my stomach. I was either starving or completely nauseous and wanted nothing to do with food. I rose in bed, stretching my arms. I stood and placed my hands across my lower back and tried to bend it as best I could, as that too, had been giving me some discomfort. My lower back possessed a consistent dull ache, one I couldn't ease. After the mounds of research I had absorbed on pregnancy and from what I could expect, the first trimester did not sound like a walk in the park. Between the nausea, exhaustion, and having to run to the washroom almost every ten minutes, it was a wonder a woman could go on with her day at all. I studied myself in the mirror closely, something was different. Oh! I cupped my hands over my breasts quickly and my eyes grew wide. *They're bigger! Holy crap, this is really happening. It's starting!* I opened the door quickly and met my brother in the kitchen as he prepared himself breakfast.

"My boobs are getting bigger!" I exclaimed.

Sky stopped, in mid stir and looked at me with one eyebrow raised. "And I need to know this why?"

"You don't, I just thought I'd share my journey with someone," I leaned around him to grab a piece of toast and grinned.

Sky shuddered. "Please keep me on a need to know basis only."

I laughed. "Sure thing, little brother."

"Speaking of need to know things," Sky started. "I've been doing a lot of research on what you can and can't eat. I'm making you a list, you need to be careful."

I smiled warmly. Sky did not have the easiest time digesting the news of what was to be, but he'd been coming around. Unsure of what to do, he threw himself into research as it comforted him. He was making a not so perfect situation somewhat manageable.

"Well, if I'm going to be an uncle, I want it to be healthy."

I rolled my eyes and began to throw ingredients in the blender for a smoothie. "I eat fairly healthy as it is. Don't worry, I'll be careful." I looked at him quickly. "Thanks for your help."

"Someone has to watch out for you two."

I dropped the banana peel on the counter and gave Sky a quick hug. "Thanks, little brother."

It started snowing early on in the day. The weather network once again called for a snowfall warning, and this time judging from the looks of things outside, it meant business. The world was covered in a white blanket within the hour, and the snow offered no signs of slowing. I watched through the window as the flakes fell every which way. It was beautiful.

"I need to get some food," Sky groaned. "I'm going to the grocery store. Do you need anything?"

Mango! I had been craving mango like there was no tomorrow. "Yeah, I need to grab a few things. I assume we're walking?"

"Yup. There's no way I'm taking my car out in this."

Poor Sky. He still had summer tires on his car and it was not the safest to drive in weather like this. A few years ago he had a very close call while driving in the snow, and it left a mark on him. He suffered nightmares for weeks. To this day, he was not comfortable driving in the white stuff. We lived in a fairly nice area, a semi quiet neighborhood with all the necessities one would need; a grocery store, coffee shop, and drug store all a short walk across the street. We bundled up in our winter gear and began the snowy journey. My spirits soared as I gazed up at the snow-covered trees, the bare branches glistened in white powder. As we stepped into the snow our boots let out a soft crunching noise beneath our feet. *This is perfect.* The roads were no longer visible, the snow had covered them, hiding the pavement from the world. There were next to no tire tracks, many chose to stay inside if they could help it. Our trip was quick and efficient. I stocked up on mango, it made for a very happy girl. Armed with bags of food, we stepped outside as the icy wind picked up. Sky and I zipped our jackets higher as the wind bit at any exposed flesh.

"How in the hell do you find this enjoyable?" Sky grumbled.

I grinned behind my scarf. "I love this! It doesn't happen very often. Enjoy it!"

"I'd rather not. I like my heat. Come on, let's hurry, I'm freezing!"

And we did. With our arms full of groceries and the snow already near our ankles, we attempted to jog home. One of my boots slid out from under me and my arm went up into the air. "Whoops!" I felt myself go down. I dropped the grocery bag and desperately wrapped my arms around a streetlight. I stood at an awkward pose hugging the cold post but it worked. It was enough to keep me upright.

Sky stopped impatiently. "You all right?"

I bent over and snatched up the grocery bag. "Yup. Let's go home!"

It was an easygoing day. Sky worked on his computer for most of the day, and I enjoyed another winter walk in the snow with Maggie. I flopped on the couch, feet hanging over the edge as I read a book. Night had fallen and the world was still white, the snow continued to fall. Sky and I had planned to walk to the Sushi place for dinner, and I counted down the hours until then. I adored Sushi, but I read raw fish was not good for the baby, so tonight I would settle for chicken or veggie rolls.

Sky's phone jingled, and as he read it a concerned look grew on his face. "Oh no. Chelsea's stuck at the sky train station. There are no more busses running. There's no way she'll make it home tonight."

Chelsea was Sky's girlfriend. She had bussed out to Vancouver for the day and her plan had been to catch a bus home after her event was over. Unfortunately for her, the busses stopped running due to the weather. She had made it halfway home, but she was still a good forty five minutes away.

"She might try to get a taxi to our place for the night," Sky said with concern. "Is it okay if she stays over tonight? We could wait for her and go out for Sushi together?"

"Of course she can come over. That's going to be an expensive taxi ride though," I said slowly.

Sky furrowed his brows. "It will be. I don't like the idea of her in a taxi in this weather. I'd pick her up but there's no way my car could go in this. I'd slide all over the place and the stations forty minutes from here…" His voice trailed off, deep in thought.

"I can get her," I offered. "My truck ploughs through the snow. I'm okay driving in it."

Sky's face lit up. "Really? Would you?"

"Of course. Let her know her ride is on the way."

Sky sent a quick text. "Okay. Let's get ready for an adventure!"

I started the engine to let the truck warm while Sky helped me sweep the snow off the windows. "Okay, that ought to do her," I said happily. "Let's head out."

Sky hopped in nervously and rubbed his hands together. "You sure you're okay doing this? The roads look bad and it's coming down pretty heavily."

"Piece of cake." I smiled and flicked on the radio. I put the truck in neutral, flicked on the four-wheel drive and waited for it to click into gear. Once I heard the 'click' I stuck it into drive.

"Here we go!" I stepped on the gas lightly and the truck began to cut through the snow covered roads.

Sky sucked in a deep breath as I turned the corner and ventured onto the freeway. I glanced at him quickly, his body remained rigid as he gripped onto the sides of the seat.

"You doing alright, there?" I asked.

"Yup. I'm glad I'm not driving. This stuff scares me."

I laughed. "Poor brother."

I drove cautiously and kept my eyes ahead. We took it slow and steady but we still had the odd slide. I felt bad for my brother, he appeared to be holding his breath the entire time. He sat nervously, eyes wide, and I almost heard him count down the time until we reached our destination. I pulled into the station and we drove slowly looking for Chelsea.

"There she is!" Sky exclaimed, relief in his voice.

I pulled the truck next to the curb, and stopped in front of Chelsea. She was bundled up like an Eskimo. She was a tiny thing, barely 5'3. She had shoulder length black hair and happy brown eyes. She looked so tiny next to my brother who towered over her.

She ran to the truck and hopped in quickly. "Thank you so much!" Her voice was heavy in gratitude. She began to unwrap her giant scarf. "I was worried I would be stuck here for the night."

"No worries. We wouldn't let that happen to you," I waved my hand at her.

"Both hands on the steering wheel!" Sky snapped.

"Sorry."

"How about I treat you guys to Sushi? It'll be my thank you for picking me up."

Sky and I agreed with great enthusiasm. Today shaped up to be a near perfect day after all.

CHAPTER 15

"Ryleigh?"

I turned away from the batter I was mixing. "Yes?"

Sky and Chelsea stood in the doorway, engaging in a silent conversation with their eyes, one I could not follow. I placed a hand on one hip. "What's up guys?"

Chelsea nudged Sky. "Give it to her."

"Okay, hold on." Sky pulled a book from behind his back and handed it to me. "Here you go. We saw this in the bookstore and we thought it might help. I like how it's written, it's easy to follow and it kinda feels like a diary entry."

I looked eagerly at the book. I grinned as I read the title '*Pregnancy, a Beginner's Guide.*' I flipped through the pages and smiled. The book was perfect. It gave a week by week guide of the baby's growth and development, as well as what the mother should expect for her own personal changes. It contained a thorough list of foods to enjoy/avoid, exercises, and a checklist of things to do before the baby's arrival.

I hugged the book to my heart. "Thank you! It's perfect. I love it." I gave them both a warm hug.

Chelsea grinned. "If you need any help at all, I can always babysit. I'm good at changing diapers too."

I smiled. "Thanks. I might have to take you up on that offer so I can sneak in a nap or two."

"Anytime," she said happily.

It had been two days since Bryce and I had last seen each other. I hadn't heard anything from him, but I wasn't surprised. That seemed to be the way things worked lately. He would disappear until I contacted him with some news. I began to feel like a secretary. It bothered me. For someone who had brought up marriage and wanting to be a family, he sure wasn't making much of an effort. My stomach curdled at the thought, he was probably with *her*. What did he think he was doing? How could he sleep at night? How could he look her in the eyes and act like nothing was wrong? Was he able to kiss her lips and hold her without any thoughts of me entering his mind? And all the while I'm here alone, carrying his child. It frustrated me to no end. He made no sense anymore and I had officially given up trying to figure him out. If he wanted to be a part of this, of us, he was doing a piss poor job. So I let the hope go, and looking at my circle, I realized I would never quite be alone. I had a supportive mother, brother, and friends who would be there, and had been there every step of the way. This child would be loved by not only me, but those around me. The thought comforted me. I did wonder who he had in his corner, if anyone. I realized I never once asked if he was okay, how he was doing. Did he tell anyone? Was anyone standing beside him to help him through any of his worries, or fears? I suddenly hoped for his sake, he did. No one should be left to deal with something like this alone, and I would know. A small part of me felt guilty for never reaching out to him, but then again, why should I? He had given me no reason too.

⌘

I devoured the book. It was full of neat descriptions and helpful pointers. I had a lot of work ahead of me still, and this was all before the baby would even arrive. I began a list of things I would need: baby outfits, bottles, stroller, car seat, changing table, wash cloths, diapers, the list went on and on. It was overwhelming to look at it all, so I decided to tackle it piece by piece, break it into small sections, purchase a bit here and there and before I would know it everything on my list would be checked off. I stretched out on the couch eagerly reading the book.

"Fascinating. Did you know you may start to respond to touch, baby by weeks nine to twelve?" I turned the page. "Oh! How exciting. Through weeks fourteen to sixteen, you start to hear the world around you. Soon enough you will actually hear me, little one."

I laid my hand against my still flat stomach, by the third month, I would get the little baby bump. *I can't wait to hold you in my arms.* With each passing day, I grew more and more content at the thought of motherhood. I would soon be stepping into a brand new unknown world, and I couldn't wait.

It was a bright new day, the sky was blue, and the sun beat down warming the cold ground. It was mid morning when Jane called to check on me. We decided to meet up at the lake and take the dogs for a walk.

"You look good, Ry...so are there any new developments with Bryce?" Jane asked somewhat hesitantly.

"Thanks, I've been feeling pretty good lately...almost happy." A slight frown appeared. "No, nothing new with him."

Jane shook her head in slight distain. "What is he doing?"

I threw my hands in the air. "Don't ask me. For the life of me, I could not tell you. One minute he talks about being a family, yet he disappears. I guess he's waiting on me. I'm not entirely sure."

"Is he still with her?"

"Most likely."

Jane raised an eyebrow. "So he's waiting for the doctor to give the green light that all is a go and then what? He'll be yours, and only yours?"

"I don't know. Jane, this whole thing is so unbelievably messed up." I stopped briefly. "I could use him here with me. It would be nice for him to walk me through this a little bit. But instead..." I shrugged my shoulders. "I don't know, he seems to be caught up in his own world I suppose..."

Jane made a face. "This is a complicated place to be, I don't know how you're managing this, but you are and I'm proud of you. Have you shared any of your worries with him?"

"No. I don't feel like I can. He's not mine, and I don't know...a part of me thinks he's only saying reassuring things to make himself feel better."

Jane nodded. "Perhaps. Honestly, Ry, I can't offer you much insight on this one here, nothing has made much sense. It seems to be one extreme to the other."

"I'm glad I'm not the only one who's left feeling a little confused."

Jane gave a short laugh. "No, you're not. But you know...you are not alone in this either."

"I know."

"I'll even go to the doctor appointments with you," she offered quietly. "You shouldn't do this by yourself. I know you can, but I won't let you."

I smiled, she knew me all too well. "Thank you. I've actually been thinking of inviting him along to my appointment on Friday."

Jane looked caught off guard. "Okay. Well, if it makes you feel better by having him there, then go for it." Her tone was less than impressed.

I sighed heavily. "Jane, you know one way or the other, he will be in the picture. You have to accept that."

She made a face. "I know. I will, I promise. I'll do my best, but you know how I am. I hold grudges and he really hurt you. I saw you that first night after he left you."

I winced slightly. Valentines day...that had been a horrible, unexpected slap in the face. "I know."

Jane perked up a bit. "Let's not go down that road again. Let's think happy thoughts. Oh!" her hands flew together. "Just think of all the little outfits you get to choose from! I call hosting the baby shower!"

I laughed and let the happy feeling take me over. "Deal."

I have big dreams and fickle thoughts.

I was made for more than this.

I long to be free and able to breathe.

Find me in my place where the light can't reach,

I long to find my home.

This is going to break me in two.

I will forever curse the day I lost you.

The porcelain smile, it will shatter the mask.

I long to go home, I need to find my home.

Such a carefully composed statue of elegance.

Time will wear it down as she waits for no one.

I long to find my home.

This is going to break me in two.
I will forever curse the day I lost you.
The porcelain smile it will shatter the mask,
I long to go home, I need to find my home.
Find me where I go when I'm alone
Take me by the hand and I will follow
Just don't lead me into the dark, I need to be able to see.
I long to go home.

I tapped my pen against the notebook as I read the words I had written. Sometimes I just needed to write. Words and thoughts rattled around in my brain quite often and I needed to get them out. I always felt a quiet satisfaction when my jumbled thoughts came together so neatly. Writing had always soothed me, and tonight I needed something, anything to help me feel at ease. Tomorrow morning was my doctor's appointment and I don't know why, but I was nervous. I had been feeling rather ill lately, but that was nothing new. Perhaps it was the simple fact that this step would make everything that much more real. After tomorrow there would be no going back.

I read the letters scribbled on the page once more and felt somewhat content. Sleep tempted me, and I gave in without a fight. I laid the notebook onto the nightstand, reached forward and flicked out the lamp. *Good night, Baby. Tomorrow is a big day for us. Sweet dreams. Love, Mom.*

⌘

My leg would not stay still. It bounced restlessly as I waited for my name to be called, releasing me from the holds of the waiting room. I tried to entertain myself by flicking through the magazines laid neatly on the table. I must have went through six of them, but I wasn't paying attention to any of the pages. My mind was elsewhere. My thoughts were taken up by my potential child.

"Ryleigh?"

I looked up eagerly as the nurse behind the desk called for me.

I stood. "Yes, right here."

"Great, come this way."

I followed her to a private room and she shut the door behind me quietly. "You're here to confirm a pregnancy, correct?"

"Yes."

"Okay, this will be quick. If you could just pee into the cup, we will have the results very shortly."

I nodded. "That I can do. I have to pee all the time as it is."

She laughed. "That's a good sign."

I grabbed the cup and made my contribution. I found my way back to the room and waited…and waited some more. I let out a loud sigh, and once again my foot bounced restlessly. The doctor entered the room abruptly, causing me to jump in surprise.

"Sorry about that," she said apologetically. "Congratulations, it looks like you're expecting."

In that moment, hearing those words officially I felt like I would indeed pass out. I leaned forward in the chair and braced my hand against the exam table that lay next to me. I don't know why I felt so taken aback for I had accepted it days ago. I would never forget that life changing moment as I sat on the bathroom floor staring down at a piece of plastic, knowing my world was about to change forever. The range of emotions that had been showing up lately were tiring. My mother's words flitted through my head. "*Holy fucking shit, here we go.*"

The doctor must have noticed for she leaned forward and tapped the top of my hand. I looked up at her wide eyed. She smiled. "I know it's a lot to take in, isn't it?"

I nodded. "Y-yes."

"Is this good news?"

I thought about it for only a split second and met her eyes confidently. "Yes, it never seems to be the 'right' time, does it? I know everything will work itself out."

"Good. Let's have you book an appointment for later this week for a more thorough exam."

I nodded and stood. "Thank you."

"See you soon."

A slow grin spread over my face, and though I tried, I could not wipe it away. I booked the appointment before I left and stepped out of the clinic, smiling wide.

"So I have some news." I pressed send and waited for cyberspace to deliver the message to Bryce.

"Oh?"

"Yes, I'd like to discuss it in person, if that's okay?"

"Of course. When can we meet?"

"Whenever works for you."

"How about Monday morning? Your place? 10:00?"

"Sounds good. I will see you then."

And there it was. The date was set and I would soon repeat those words. *I'm pregnant. I am pregnant.* Even to my own ears it sounded so strange, like something out of a fairy tale, so foreign, but exciting all at the same time. My stomach twinged and I flinched slightly, nerves were doing me no good. I needed to do something that would calm me. *Baking.* Soon enough, I found myself in the kitchen, pulling out the ingredients I needed to bake cookies. I decided on peanut butter chocolate chip. I began to cream the egg and peanut butter together, watching it turn silky smooth. Next I added some honey, mini chocolate chips and a tablespoon of flour, I had a very special recipe. I created it awhile back now and it seemed to be a household favorite, they never lasted long.

Baking calmed my soul. It was one of the few things in life I could control, how the final product turned out. Whenever I found things spinning out of control, I would often find solace in the kitchen. Today was no different. I popped the cookie sheet into the oven, set the timer, and began to tackle the dishes. The smell of fresh cookies wafted throughout the house. The aroma of baked goods always made the house feel cozy and warm. The timer beeped. I took out the sheet and gently placed the cookies on a cooling rack. Afterwards, I found myself heading for bed, exhaustion had hit me like a ton of bricks and my stomach started to hurt; sharp cramps rippled through like a wave and I hugged my sides tightly hoping they would go away. I dug out my heating pad, and placed it on my stomach gently. I was asleep in a matter of seconds. I dreamt of Bryce. They were memories of when I called him my own.

"Can I ask you a favor?" One of his messages had read.

"Of course."

"Can you please send me a picture of your pretty face?"

That was when we started dating. Around that time I began to think he was different, he was special. I remember how happy I was back then. It was like coming home after being away for too long. My second dream, or memory I should say, was the last time I saw him, the last night he held me in his embrace. I remembered as we laid next to each other as Kip Moore's *'Hey pretty girl'* played in the background. He had looked at me with such love. *"If you give me a little girl, I will play this song for you."* I never would have guessed that would have been our last night. I didn't see it coming. If only I would have known. I would have held on for as long as I could.

Our laughter floated through my thoughts. He looked at me with a thoughtful expression from across the table. "You know what we don't have yet?" he asked.

"No. What would that be?" I said, chin resting on my hand.

He smiled and got up quickly, grabbing his phone. He crouched beside me and held the phone in front of us. "We don't have a picture of us together."

I smiled softly. "You're right, we don't." I grinned back at him and leaned my face next to his.

"Say cheese!" He tapped his phone and the flash went off, capturing our smiles, and the last happy moment we would ever share.

⌘

Something was wrong, I awoke in pain and tenderly began to sit up. I didn't feel very well so I made my way to the washroom. My heart sank into the pit of my stomach, there was blood. I had read that spotting was quite common in early pregnancy, but I knew this was something else entirely. I sank onto the bathroom floor and cried until I could cry no more. *I cried in this very spot when I found out I was carrying you, and I will cry here knowing I couldn't keep you.*

CHAPTER 16

I sat in the doctor's office alone. The room felt cold and unwelcoming. Loneliness found me once again. She sat next to me, smiling a cold and bitter smile. *Haven't I lost enough? When will it ever be enough? Why me? Why does it always have to be me?* My thoughts fell to the baby's first outfit I hung in my closet. The sting of hot tears appeared as they fell freely down my face. I placed a hand over the top of my stomach, the tiny person growing inside me would never be placed so lovingly in it after all. A sob escaped my lips and I held it back. *How do I mourn you, little one? I never really knew you but I felt you growing inside me. I am so sorry, so sorry I couldn't hold on to you. How could I lose you? I had already fallen in love with you.* The door swung open and the doctor came inside, a sympathetic look drawn across her face. She pulled up a chair and sat next to me. She reached out and patted my arm in a comforting manner. I drew in a shaky breath and closed my eyes, feeling the tears slip down.

"I'm so sorry, Ryleigh. I know my words will offer you little comfort, but these things, they just happen. Nobody knows why."

The doctor rattled off medical terms. I looked away blindly and felt myself slip out of my body. Her words began to fade, I saw her lips move but I heard no sound. I felt strangely numb, yet there was a sharp, severe pain that shot through my heart. I didn't know how people survived this. An emptiness settled over me and in that moment, I felt like I had nothing left in me, nothing at all.

Something the doctor began to say caught my attention. I put my swollen, sad eyes on her and tried my best to listen to her meaningless words. "From my best estimate, I would assume you were about five weeks along, so we won't need to perform a scrape, your body has taken care of things."

I closed my eyes tighter. I hated my body with everything I had in me. *Traitor*. The doctor continued. "Once again, I'm so sorry. I'm sure your partner will be able to offer you some comfort. In times like these it's important to talk to one another."

I looked at her with blank eyes. No, he would not be able to offer me anything. I knew in that moment I would be left alone to deal with this, again. He would not stick around to be there for me. He would not offer me a shoulder to cry on. He would simply place the situation in the back of his mind and move on. He would leave me here with my heart forever broken, scattered across the floor. I got up slowly, without saying a single word. I walked my tear stained face through the waiting room, acutely aware of the many sets of eyes that watched me. I pushed open the door and stepped outside into the fresh morning air. I looked up at the sky and simply began to cry.

On Sunday night, I knew I would never see Bryce again once I delivered him the news. I wouldn't be able to say the words I longed to say, so I decided to do what I did best; write. It didn't take me long to come up with the words, for they were weighing heavy on my heart and my mind. I left my hurt, anger, and sadness on that paper. It was a piece of me he would always have with him, if he chose to keep it. I stared down at the sheet for awhile. I needed him here with me, but I knew how this was going to play out. He would choose her. I folded the paper up delicately and left it on the night stand. I closed my eyes and prayed for a dreamless night.

Monday morning came. I don't know whether to say it came fast or slow. My days were filled with an ache I never even knew could exist. It burned me to my very core. You see, when your life falls apart, the world does not slow down and wait. It keeps on moving and expects you to catch up. But I could not, I was done. Bits and pieces of me lay around in tiny broken monuments. I did not want to feel anything, I just wanted to sleep, and hoped I would feel better when I awoke. Gravol became my best friend. It would numb the pain for a bit and help me sleep. Sleep was good, I welcomed it, for when I slept I couldn't feel anything. But then the dreams found me. I couldn't make them stop. They were a cruel taunt of what I had lost. For you see, I began to dream about babies. I dreamt of the precious child I would never come to know. Some nights the little one was wrapped in a tiny blue blanket, other nights it was pink. I had held the little one so proudly in my arms as I gazed down with nothing but pure love. I awoke in tears quite often, with my hands upon my stomach. Sleep had once been my companion, but now I feared it.

Has time officially stood still? I drummed my fingers nervously on the old kitchen table. He would be here soon. Clearly not soon enough. My heart raced in anticipation and my vision grew slightly hazy.

The jingle of my phone grabbed my attention. I hesitantly glanced at the screen. A new message from him. "Good morning. I'm at McDonalds. Can I grab you anything? Tea?"

Damn him. He's not making this easy to hate him. I picked up my phone and declined politely. I sucked in a breath, he would be here in five minutes and I would be forced to have the single most difficult conversation of my life. The sound of tires pulled my attention. My heart skipped a beat as my eyes fell on his old blue pickup The silver toolbox shone brightly in the bed of his truck. This was it. The moment I could no longer put off.

Another jingle from my phone. "I'm here."

I grabbed my phone. "Be right there."

I pulled the hood over my head and took a deep breath. I picked up an old grocery bag that held a very precious item inside and stepped out into the rain. Turning the corner and dodging the puddles, I came into his view. Country music blared from his truck. *He's nervous too.* Music was a big part of his world, it was a comfort to him, as it was for me. His door swung open and he stepped into the rain. *Bryce.* I swallowed quickly, he still made my heart race.

His dark hair was tousled, his hands in his jean pockets. "Hey," his voice was thick with uncertainty.

"Hi." I said back just as quietly.

Bryce walked over and gave me a quick, polite hug. I returned the gesture and broke away quickly.

"Did you want to talk in your truck, or…" I let my voice trail off.

His eyes fell to me in a studious gaze, trying to read me. I straightened my posture and put my shoulders back. I was good at hiding my thoughts. He wouldn't find them, no one ever could.

His chocolate eyes looked expectant. "Sure. It's warm in there." I looked up, and that half smile I had always loved so much played on his lips. "And it's dry in the truck."

I nodded quickly and tightened my grasp on the grocery bag I held firmly. "Sounds good to me."

I quickly made my way to the familiar vehicle and hopped in with a slight ache. This would be the last time I would ever sit here. I glanced to him slowly. He looked nervous, his hands held onto the leather steering wheel and he stared blindly through the windshield. His chest rose up and down in a slow, very controlled manner as he took a deep breath in. My head fell back on the worn out bench seat and I let the bag fall to the floor. This was it. There was no going back. He turned to me slightly, his eyes lit up with faint hope.

The threat of tears brewed behind my green eyes. I couldn't look at him. Not yet. I sucked in a sharp, quick breath. "So, the doctor guessed I was about five weeks along…" *Finish the sentence. You can do this!* I glanced once more his way and brought my gaze to his. "It didn't take, I-I lost it."

And there it was. Those awful words stumbled out of my mouth. My voice. Even to my ears it didn't sound real. How could such a terrible thing, an awful loss happen to me? To us?

Bryce let out a loud breath like he was punched in the stomach. His back stiffened and his hands fell helplessly into his lap. "What? I-I don't understand."

I kept quiet and nodded slowly. I held my gaze absently out the window and watched the rain ripple the puddles. I had a few days to absorb this horrible news, he was hearing it for the first time. I kept my gaze low. "They say early miscarriages happen quite often."

My words held no comfort. My voice sounded bleak and dead, it mimicked what I felt inside. His eyes burnt into me. I lifted mine to meet his all the while studying him. In that moment I realized that this had really hurt him too. I watched as the hope and joy drained with his color. The sharp stab of pain tore through me once more.

"What does this mean for you? Are you okay? Do you have to go through any procedures?" Genuine concern filled his voice. I don't think he realized it, but he leaned closer to me now, almost as though he cared.

I again looked away. "No. It was early enough that I'll be okay. No need for any medical assistance."

"I-I'm so sorry that this happened. I don't know what to say."

I once again felt my eyes burn with emotion that threatened to break me. "Me, too." My voice grew so very small and sounded nothing at all like my own.

Silence filled the small space between and it was deafening. Two people who fit so neatly together were now miles apart. My eyes landed on the white plastic bag by my feet. I leaned forward and picked it up delicately. I traced my fingers gently across the plastic surface surprised at how much this hurt.

I cleared my throat. "I bought our baby's first outfit."

A sad smile appeared. "Yeah?"

His brown eyes fell on the bag with an eager interest. I placed the bag between us, and as I let it go, the emptiness hit me. "I didn't know if it was a boy or a girl so I got something neutral. It's yellow." I smiled slowly. "I thought it was a happy color." I met his eyes and once again saw the hurt. I pushed the bag closer. "You should take a look. It's really cute."

He nodded, and with trembling hands he gently unwrapped it. His eyes grew glassy as he held up the little outfit with the words *Hunny* and Winnie the Pooh etched over the soft fabric. It was more than an outfit, it was a hope of a new delicate life. A part of him, and a piece of me joined together.

He cleared his throat and with his forefinger and thumb gently traced along the stitching. "It's very cute." He glanced at me. "You have good taste."

I looked at my faded sneakers. "Thank you. Do you want it?"

He looked surprised. "Are you sure? You don't want it?"

"No." I could feel his stare and my voice grew weak. "I can't look at it."

His voice grew soft. "Okay. Yes, I'll take it." His eyes took it in slowly and then with his calloused, hard working hands he delicately placed it back into the bag. The silence again grew thick and heavy. I needed to leave.

"So, I guess that's it." My hand reached for the cool silver handle and I popped the door open, and stepped out into the rain.

Footsteps sounded behind me. I turned to face Bryce. He looked helpless, his eyes were shadowed with an emotion I hadn't yet seen on him. It was quite the contrast from the usual man I had gotten to know; happy and free. With what might be the last ounce of my strength I lifted my gaze to meet his. It could possibly be the last time I would ever lay my eyes on him. There were no words left, both of us held on to a different hope, and they had been ripped away from us. He stepped closer and wrapped me up tightly, drawing me in. I placed my arms around him snugly and breathed him in. I let my head fall heavy onto his shoulder. I could no longer hold the tears back, they trickled down my face. There were so many things I wanted to say. *Please stay here with me. Don't walk away. Please stay. Choose me.* He held me for a long while. Neither of us spoke, there was nothing to say. Familiarity sparked deep within…it was security. When he held me like this, so tight yet tender, I had always felt loved. But it was not meant to be. We both took a careful step back, looking at each other, this was the end. A torn man looking back at a broken girl.

I placed my hand into my pocket and felt the paper inside. My hand clasped around it and I pulled it out. This common piece of paper held the words to all of the things I could never say out loud. This was for his eyes, a glimpse into my head and my heart. "Here," I extended my hand in a helpless gesture. "This is for you. You know how I like to write."

He accepted it gracefully and stared down at the folded paper with curiosity. The faintest of crooked smiles tugged on his lips. "Thank you."

I gave him a sad smile and nodded. I turned gently on my heel, and without looking back, I walked away from the only man I ever loved. The only man who had taken nearly every piece of me and broken it. When his hands would open the note, inch by inch, piece by piece, this is what his eyes would read.

"The cold crept into my chest taking me down. For a moment I could feel nothing, pushed to the point of tears as you made your point. What was the point? I am nothing but who I'll always be. Quiet and guarded, you left me standing alone. You made it hurt. The dance is always the same, the faces they never change. Such a cruel game.

I remember the day our eyes met as you walked over to say hello. There was a softness in your eyes and a kindness in your touch. A promise that never came to be. You needed a little more, I think. I would never be enough. Was I ever enough?

I took it like a strong girl but I crumbled and fell crying to the ground as the force broke me. I hoped you would show your face, but I didn't hear a word you said. All I could hear was my own heart beating, taking it slow. The heaviness it hurts. Yours was just a selfish need to make for another empty night. You were never enough; I was never enough.

I remember, head down, the day I found out. You left something behind, a part of you became a piece of me. A son or a daughter, I would have loved them well. You asked if I could find happiness with you. I think my answer would have been yes. I grew content with a new arrival but it was not meant to be. I cried as they told me the little life had faded out of me. And I was alone. A new title and role stripped away in a matter of seconds. I could've used you as a friend who would be there to hold my hand. I am but a small girl trying to make sense of this. An ache for a life I will never know. I have never been here before. So wrap me up slowly and tell me that this will all be okay, before I'm left here watching you walk away.

-Ryleigh"

I walked slowly to the house, feeling more alone than I ever thought humanly possible. It physically hurt, every breath was labored, every heart beat a struggle. I sat down limply on the couch and my phone jingled. I looked at it slowly, it was Bryce.

"I hate to be rude asking questions after I left but I won't stop thinking it unless I ask. You didn't get an abortion, did you?"

That comment would normally have hurt me. How dare he think I could do such a thing. *If you knew me, really knew me you wouldn't have felt the need to ask that question.* If he was here, if he had chosen to check in every once in awhile, he would have known how much I had already fallen in love with my unborn child. The comment slid off of me rather easily, I was already growing numb. I picked up my phone to respond.

"No, I could never do that. Ever. I've always wanted to be a mom and I started to let myself grow excited. I would have loved the little one with everything I had. Things would have worked out. Listening to them tell me I lost our baby was the hardest thing I've ever had to hear. I've never been here before. I don't know what to do right now. I try to be a positive person, but right now I'm a little broken."

"I know from a guys stand point it's pretty devastating. But I can't even imagine how it would feel from the mothers. If there is anything I can do to help, please let me know. I'm so sorry, Ryleigh."

What could he do to help? How much of an effort would he be willing to make? All I needed, all I wanted was for him to sit right here next to me. He didn't have to say a word, all he had to do was simply be here. *We leave so much unsaid. The words we ache to hear are the words we never seem to say.* I was stuck in the dark and I wasn't quite sure how to find my light. I grew tired of this place, yet I was not sure how to move forward. For I was mourning the loss of someone I never held, never met. What the fuck was I supposed to do with that? The single person who played a large role in all of this was the one I needed the most, but he was not here. The harsh bitterness I had grown to hate reared it's ugly head once more. It didn't seem fair that he could go on with life in a seemingless, effortless manner. He had someone else to go home to each and every night, and that hurt me. That hurt so much. How could he think I was going to be okay? My heart ached at the lonely thought, did I really mean so little to him after all?

I couldn't let myself get stuck here. I wouldn't let myself get stuck here. There had to be something I could do, anything, to help ease some of the burden. For some reason, I wanted to remember this day, the look on his face as I told him I lost one of the most precious things I've ever held on too. I wanted to remember the sadness as it filled his eyes, it let me know he felt it too. And I needed to hold on to the memory of him holding me for one last time. Though no words were spoken, the embrace had been enough. In that small moment, I felt tied to him. I felt like he cared, and for once, we faced something together.

I needed to write. And so, that's what I did. I picked up my lap top and I let my fingers hit the keys and watched as the words appeared in an easy manner across the screen. I started with today's events, and felt a slight flicker of hope as some of the weight slid off of me. It was my form of therapy in a sense, I could say whatever my heart desired and there would be no one to tell me I was wrong or shouldn't feel this way. As odd as it sounds, it felt like I had a friend sitting beside me, encouraging me to go on. I wrote for hours, once I let my thoughts out of their confinements, my fingers could not keep up to the flow of memories that wanted to escape. Nearly three hours had passed since I started writing and I needed to stop. I stretched out my forearms and circled my tight wrists. The ache had left me for awhile. I knew it was only a matter of time before it crept up again, but I was glad I could find an escape, no matter how momentarily. I sat back into the cushion and scrolled to the beginning of my work. This was the fun part; reading.

It was just after eleven p.m., the house was silent and still, all except for me. I paced the room anxiously. I could not get Bryce out of my head. The way he looked after I had told him the news, the way he studied at me as I slipped out of his grasp. I chewed my lip thoughtfully. I had kept quiet for so long. I had not yelled or screamed, I had not set out to cause any sort of fight whatsoever throughout recent events; that was not who I was. Yet I could no longer ignore the tiny voice in my head saying to fight, to stand up and say something to him. I needed to give him an opening, and I hoped he would take it.

Earlier in the day, when he looked at me, touched me, I saw no hate nor disgust. I saw *my* Bryce, and the way he used to look at me with such tender affection. He had once been good for me, two paths made to cross. He felt like home. We had talked about a future, maybe it wasn't too late. I blew out a large breath, I had lost so much already. What else did I have to lose at this point? Absolutely nothing. If I didn't say something, anything now, I knew I would regret it forever. I looked at the clock once more. He'd be working the evening shift. If I sent the message now he would get it within half an hour. I tapped my fingers restlessly on the phone. What to say? *Say what you need to. Lay it all on the line.* And so, that's what I did. I hoped it would be enough.

"I want to thank you for coming by today. It was not an easy thing for me to do, but I felt it should be done in person. This whole thing has been very hard on me. I'm sorry I never asked how you were. I've probably lost more than I ever thought possible. I hate being vulnerable. I was confused and hurt when you left, it seemed so sudden. I'm just going to say it, and this is scary for me, but I miss you. If you feel at all the same, I'd let you in. Life is short. It's simple really, find those who make you happy. If you've found it, then you're a lucky man. If you have your doubts, you know where to find me. I had a good feeling with you. Maybe it was just me, but hell, I can't not say anything. I've spent so much of my life being quiet. How many good things have I let slip by? That's all I've got. If not, I will take a step down to one side and bow out."

Sent.

I blew out a breath of relief. I had said my peace. It was up to him now. I held my breath and hoped for the best. I flicked out the light and laid down quietly, waiting. My phone lit up the dark room as it jingled. My heart dropped to my stomach, this was it. It had to be him. I glanced nervously at the phone, it was Bryce.

"No problem. I don't think this could have had worse timing. I feel like such a prick for what I've done. You are very special to me. But I didn't think you felt the same and I've made my choice and gone back to her. That note you gave me made me cry like a baby. You are very talented with your writing. I wish things could have worked out differently. If you ever need anything don't be afraid to contact me."

And there was my answer. He did not want me. He had someone else now. He made his choice. After everything we had been through in this short time, I can't say I'm surprised at how this would end. For he had left me alone to face my fears and uncertainties along the way. If he really wanted to be with me, he would have already done so. He could make the simple choice to leave her like he had done so long ago. He had the power to make a change, but he chose to stay. Rejection hit me like a bullet, it was fast and the force shattered me all over again. My stomach turned at the thought of them together, creating a future, having babies of their own. Her in a white gown, walking down the aisle as he stood waiting with a warm, welcoming smile on his handsome face. *That could have been me.* There was nothing left for me to do, I was done. A heart wrenching sob escaped my lips and I did not hold back. Tonight, I would cry alone for everything I had lost and could not get back.

CHAPTER 17

It was time to get a little drunk. Jane and I decided to have a girls night; a night with no men, no drama, just us girls. We could get everything off our chests and there was only one rule; no judgment. It was a night of freedom, a night to laugh, a night to pretend that everything was all right. It would be all right.

"Just leaving my place now. Be there in 20 minutes, be ready! I'm so excited!"

I read Jane's message and found I could smile. "K! Let me know when you're here!"

"Will do."

My plan for tonight was simple, to laugh, and I mean, really laugh. And to get drunk, to feel comfortably numb. Two simple rules, and they were two pretty damn good ones at that. I applied lip gloss and ran my fingers through my hair one last time. I nodded with satisfaction, at least I looked cute tonight. The swelling in my eyes had gone down immensely, and my face had some color back. I looked like a half decent human tonight.

My phone jingled, I smiled a little and was pleased to find a twinge of excitement ran through me. "I'm here!"

I grabbed my jacket, said a quick good night to Maggie, and ran out the door. Rain fell heavily from the sky. I dodged the puddles as best I could before I slipped into the shelter of Jane's black Honda. "Whew, what a mess out there."

"It is gross." Jane turned to me quickly. "Sooo, are you excited?"

I didn't even have to think twice. "Yes! I need this so badly."

Jane nodded triumphantly. "I know. There's this great sports bar downtown and the games starts at seven. It should make for a good night."

"Sounds good to me!"

I didn't follow hockey the way Jane did; she was a hockey fanatic. However, I did not care. I was glad to be out of the house and I would find comfort in the noise of others tonight. Anything to pull my attention, I would welcome gladly. We entered the bar and I immediately felt my spirits soar. The place was jam packed. Large crowds gathered to cheer at the big television screens. Everyone seemed to have a drink in their hand, and a smile on their face. We found a table in the midst of it all. We climbed into our bar stools and ordered food and a drink to get the night started. The drinks came quickly, Jane and I raised our glass and tipped them together.

"To girls night!" We shouted.

I took a long sip of the cool beverage and smiled. *Ah, alcohol, make me feel happy tonight.* Jane offered to be the designated driver, so while she was limited to two drinks, I, on the other hand, was a free girl.

"So, how are you doing?" Jane asked as she munched on a french fry.

"I'm feeling good!" I was already on my second drink.

She laughed. "Yeah I bet. But other than that, have you heard anything from him?"

"Nada." I took another long sip and flagged the waitress down. "I'll have another please." She nodded and bustled away. I giggled. "I'm starting to feel very good indeed."

Jane rolled her eyes. "Yeah, well, at least your entertaining when you're drunk."

The game started and Jane's focus went up to the TV screen. I watched curiously trying to see what all the fuss was about. The game grew intense. It was now a tie. People in the bar cheered and screamed for the home team. Strangers became united. I watched with amusement and decided to join in on the fun. I picked up on the players names fast and began to cheer. Jane looked thrilled as she and the man sitting next to her began to scream at the TV. I slid off the bar stool to yell out a players name and decided I would cheer for him in particular. A large group of guys at the table next to us began to cheer and stood beside me, pumping their fists. With a drink in one hand, I made my way around the tables close to my own, and decided to cheer with random strangers. The game was now in the last period. The excitement and tension in the room grew thick. The noise was deafening, I loved it. I found my way back to Jane and leaned next to her. With three seconds left in the game, our team gave a mighty effort and scored the last goal. Random strangers gave me swift, tight hugs and shook me with happiness. I won't lie, I was pretty tipsy by this point so I went along with the excitement in the room quite enthusiastically.

"That was an amazing game!" Jane shrieked.

I pulled my drink closer. "It sure was. What a game!"

"Wow," Jane said again, "I think I'm going to celebrate and get dessert. You?"

"Oh, yes," I said, wobbling in my stool slightly. I leaned forward and gripped the table. "Only mine will be a blended dessert. Make it good and strong!"

Jane laughed. "Oh, Ry. I have to say, it's nice to see you smiling at least."

I grinned. "Oh hell, I feel fantastic right now," I began to giggle at nothing in particular and Jane joined in.

It was not hard to have a good time here. The room still buzzed from the earlier game and it was contagious. A small tug tore at my heart at the thought of going home to an empty house. I reached for my drink and took another sip.

Jane's cheesecake arrived and her eyes went nearly twice the size. "Oh my god. This looks amazing. You might have to help me eat it."

"That I can do. Hold on, smile for me! You look so happy, it's cute!" I pulled out my phone to snap a picture. I glanced at it. "It's a good one."

My blended drink arrived next and I ate the cherry first. I don't know why, but my thoughts had suddenly drifted to my baby's first outfit. Regret washed over me. Why had I been so quick to get rid of it? I thought back to the day I found it, I had been drawn to the tiny thing. It was the first purchase I had made towards accepting my world would be forever changed. And now he had it. Another thought crept into my head, and I did not like it one bit. If they were to have a child together, *she* would be the one to call it her own. *She* would be the one to place her child in an outfit that I had chosen for my own with such loving care. *No, no, no. I had chosen it for my own little one, not theirs.* After I had purchased the outfit, I hung it on the coat rack along my bedroom wall. I had admired it almost every night before I fell asleep where I would dream of my son or daughter nestled in the soft fabric. It was meant for no one else.

"Ry? Where did you go?"

I looked across the table at Jane's quizzical expression. "Oh, sorry," I sighed and rested my chin on my palm. "I was just thinking of how I wished I kept the baby's outfit."

"You gave it away? Aw, it was so cute!"

"It was. And yes, I gave it to him."

Jane spoke matter of factly. "Ask for it back. He'll give it to you."

I bit my lip, I couldn't see him being an ass about it. He knew I was hurting, not that he cared. I wouldn't demand it back, I'd ask for it politely, like I always had for everything else. *I will, I'll do it. He did say if there's anything I need to never be afraid to contact him. I think this counts?*

I dug through my purse and found my phone. "I may have a strange favor to ask you."

To my surprise, he responded almost immediately. "Yes?"

"This may sound rather odd, but if you haven't done anything with the little outfit, I'd really like to have it back."

"Of course you can have it back. This isn't your way of saying 'Just kidding. I'm still pregnant?'"

That caught me off guard. Did he think I was hiding something from him? The ache returned to settle over my broken heart. "No. I just need it back."

"Okay. I can bring it to you Monday morning."

"Sure. Around 10?"

"Can do."

"Thank you. You have no idea what this means to me."

"Anytime."

"He'll drop it off Monday morning, no problem."

"Good. I knew he would." Jane nodded, and handed me a spoon. "Okay, help me eat this monster." I reached for the utensil and helped her, gladly.

Before we headed back to my place, we made a quick pit stop at the grocery store. "I need Gravol," I moaned as I pressed my forehead into the cool window of the passenger seat.

Jane winced. "Sorry. I shouldn't have let you had those last couple of drinks, I guess." She pulled into the parking stall.

"No, they were delicious. I needed this tonight. I just need some back up supplies."

"Okay. Can you get out of the car by yourself?"

"I won't know until I try." I opened her car door and climbed out. "Oh boy," I muttered under my breath. The world swayed, ever so slightly. I shut the door behind me and took a few careful steps forward, Jane was right by my side. I waved a hand carelessly at her. "I'm okay, just a wee bit wobbly is all."

Jane grinned. "All right. I'll catch you if fall." She looked at the time. Almost midnight. "I think they consider Gravol a narcotic. They might have them locked up."

I groaned. "Well, we're here. Let's double check."

We headed to the pharmacy section, and sure enough, my prize was locked behind a protective case. "Aw, sorry, Ry. They're behind the case, I can see them here."

New hope sprang into me as I studied the barrier closely and smiled. Lucky for me the Gravol was at the end of the case. All I had to do was reach behind it and I should be able to drag it out. I leaned closer to the shelf when the world got wobbly. "Jane!" I held out my arm. "Hold my hand, keep me steady!"

She did, wide eyed and slightly confused. "Ry, what are you doing?"

"I need my damn Gravol," I muttered and reached inside. With my middle finger, I was able to reach the nearest box and drag it to the small opening of the barrier. "Got it!" I gripped down and slid it through the small crack. I turned to face Jane, smiling triumphantly.

"Ryleigh!" She started to laugh, and I joined in. "I hope they sell it you." Jane whispered nervously as we waited in the checkout line.

"Shh, shh. I got this." I approached the teller happily and immersed in small talk. She rang it through with no problems. I am either extremely charming, or she really didn't care. We hopped into Jane's car and buckled up. She flicked on the radio and turned it up. We sang and danced in the car until she pulled into my driveway.

"Thanks for tonight, Jane. I had a blast. I needed this so much."

"No problem, it was a lot of fun. We need to do this again, soon!"

"For sure. Drive safe!"

"Yup. Enjoy tomorrow," she said with a sly grin.

I winced, ah, the morning after. I would be useless tomorrow. I waved a quick goodbye and watched Jane pull away. I made my way carefully and slowly into the house. I brushed my teeth, rinsed my face and slipped into an old T-shirt. Before I climbed into bed, I tossed back a glass of water with an Advil and Gravol. Sleep should come easily tonight. I flicked on my fan and crawled under the covers. I was asleep before my head hit the pillow.

⌘

I could have spent the entire day in bed Sunday, but it was too nice of a day to waste. The sky, a bright blue, tempted me to come outside and enjoy what it had to offer. I peeked through my blinds and sighed heavily, and snuggled deeper under the covers. It was warm in here, dark and cozy. My body felt limp and lifeless and my head had a slight ache. I closed my eyes with every intention of going back to sleep. A soft, yet steady noise drew me to uncover my face. I propped myself onto my elbows, listening intently. Birds chirped, I hadn't heard that sound in quite some time. It was the promise that spring was near.

"Time to get up," I mumbled to myself.

I forced my heavy body out of bed and stretched slowly, trying to wake my muscles. I began daydreaming of a steaming hot shower that would make me feel somewhat human. Heading for the washroom, I gave Sky a half hearted wave and flicked on the shower. I stepped inside and stood under the glistening hot liquid for quite some time. I stepped out and slipped into clean, dry clothes. I felt refreshed and was pleasantly surprised as a burst of energy had found me.

"Come on, Maggie, let's get out of here for the day." I picked up the truck keys and my dog bounced at my side. "Want to go for a truck ride?" I opened the back door and Maggie shot out like a black bullet.

I had mixed feelings as I drove out to the Park. *It was one of the places I had been with him.* I sighed heavily, and flicked on the radio, hoping to quiet my thoughts. A familiar song came on and it tugged at my heart. With a curse I changed the radio station, some songs still hurt to much to listen too. I wondered if music had the same effect on him, for he had always said his memories were tied to music. That's one of the big drawbacks when you grow close to someone who has many of the same interests as you; once it's over, you have so many reminders of what you lost.

I pulled into the park, clipped the leash onto Maggie, and slipped the ear buds into my ears. I turned on the Ipod and pressed play. I found myself walking along the very same trail we had explored together; I was heading to the old farmstead. *Do I really want to go there? Yes. Yes I do.* It was one of the most beautiful trails in the park, and I felt strangely close to him here. I was greeted by feelings of comfort and the tender ache of longing. I couldn't let his memory haunt the things I enjoyed forever. I would have to face them, and over time, the hurt would slowly fade. Or so I hoped.

The day turned out to be beautiful. A sweet, warm scent lingered in the air that held the promise of new life that would come to bloom. The tall grass in the open fields gently swayed, birds perched on the trees high above and sang a quiet, happy song. Maggie trotted next to me, tongue out to one side, tail wagging. She was in her bliss and I held on to her pure happiness. The music played upbeat tunes in my ears and I breathed in the fresh air deeply into my lungs. I forgot how much I had enjoyed taking Maggie out, it was calming being outside in the quiet. There were no time constraints or noise of the busy world. I felt simply free. Maggie and I followed the large curve in the trail, and just around the corner lay the old farmstead. I watched it come into view slowly, and began to head toward the attraction. I cut across the field and came upon the large wooden barn. I picked my way to it slowly, and let my finger tips trace lightly across the wooden beams. I could feel the grain in the wood, it felt rough beneath my delicate hands.

"This would be such a nice location for engagement photos. Don't you think?" I smiled a little at the memory. Bryce had stood against the barn, carefully scouting it out. My eyes intently took in the scene as well. *"Yes, I agree. It has a rustic feel here, it's so peaceful and beautiful. It feels like a different time."*

He had looked back at me, brown eyes bright as he strode over to stand next to me. *"Let's remember this spot."*

I had stared up at him, eyes dancing. He had given me such hope for a future, stability…a best friend to walk by my side. *"Deal."*

Sadness had found me once again. My hollow eyes slowly took in the farmstead, its beauty momentarily clouded by things that would never come to be. I shivered slightly, for the warmth of this place had faded. I felt like an intruder, as if the ghosts of those who used to work these fields were restless and I was no longer welcome.

"Come on, Maggie, let's get out of here."

Today seemed to be a trip down memory lane. It seemed like an unconscious decision for I did not plan to go in the direction my feet were so intent on leading me. Maggie and I walked at a brisk pace now. I felt jumpy and on edge, we were almost at the old racetrack now. *Why? Why here?* The trail ended, and Maggie and I crawled under the old gate. I unclipped her leash and let her wander, checking out the many smells that drew her this way and that. I stepped onto the old cement track and sat with crossed legs. It was so quiet here. The track wasn't on the main trail so I didn't expect to run into anyone. I pulled the Ipod out of my pocket and turned up the volume. I did not want to think. Maggie was just up ahead on the grass following a scent that intrigued her. I uncrossed my legs and let them stretch freely. I focused my gaze on the track, it seemed decently clean and dry. I laid myself down gently and crossed my hands behind my head, letting them act as a pillow. I focused my gaze on the great blue sky that towered above. My eyes tried to make shapes of the big white fluffy clouds as they lazily danced across the sky. I smiled softly, this had been one of my Oma's favorite past times. The memory took me back to childhood where she would lie with us kids in the sweet summer grass, helping us create character's in the sky. *I miss her so much.* Childhood had been a much simpler time. What I wouldn't give to be a kid again, even if only for a day. To view the world through such innocent, fresh eyes.

I lay on the track for quite some time. I watched as the dark sky moved in, slowly but surely overtaking the blue. Hot breath brushed on my skin. I gazed up as Maggie sat her large, fluffy body next to mine. She stared at me with innocent eyes. She seemed to be wondering what I was doing down here on her level. I reached up and ruffled her ears. "Ready to go home pretty girl?"

I stood, and clipped on Maggie's leash and we began the long walk to the parking lot. The clouds above opened wide and let the rain fall steadily. I slowed my pace and let the rain wash over me, soaking me from head to toe. I ran my hands through my tangled, wet hair. *Wash away my hurt. Wash away the loneliness. Take it all, for I have nothing left.* Half an hour later, I found my truck standing alone in the parking lot. I was pleasantly surprised I had an old towel in the backseat. I plucked it from the floor and gave Maggie a good towel dry. She hopped inside and snuggled on the old blanket I spread across the floor. Before getting in myself, I slipped off my soaked jacket and wrung out my tangled hair. I hopped inside, turned the key and the engine started. I let it run for awhile before turning on the heat. The radio was on the country station and Lee Brice's *"I Don't Dance"* came through the speakers. *"You waltzed away with my heart."* I blew out a loud, angry breath. I hated feeling like this. Tomorrow I would see my Bryce, only he wasn't mine anymore. I had no claim to him, he did not want me. A part of me thought about sending him a text to leave the outfit in the mailbox so I wouldn't have to see him. I hated watching him leave. He was always leaving these days, and after tomorrow, there would be no reason for him to ever come back.

⌘

This was the final act. And I was not ready. Monday morning came much too soon. It was 6:30 a.m. and I was wide awake. The pent up, nervous energy began to grow and build within my bones. I needed to find an outlet that would help relax me. Normally in situations like this, I would find comfort in the barn, but that wasn't an option here. I settled for the next best thing, a workout. I completed a quick circuit and the excess energy left my body. I hopped into the shower, dressed, fixed my hair and was dismayed to see that it was only 8:00 a.m.

I didn't have much of an appetite but figured I should put something in my stomach. I threw some fixings into the blender for a smoothie and drank slowly, all the while watching the time. It wasn't exciting, but I decided to clean the kitchen to tear my eyes away from the slow ticking of the clock. Once that chore was out of the way, I settled for the distraction of being outside. I needed the fresh air against my skin. I grabbed my iPod and walked out to the truck. I plugged the iPod into an adapter cable, placed it in my stereo, and cranked the music up. I tidied up the inside of the truck, and once that task was done I checked the fluids under the hood. I found an old milk crate and placed it by front hood so I'd have something to stand on that would allow me to reach the engine. Against the backdrop of the music, I didn't hear Bryce pull into the drive.

I jumped, startled as his voice rang in my ear. "Everything okay with your truck?"

I looked down on him in surprise, he actually seemed to be concerned. What did it matter to him? I stepped off the crate. "Everything's okay. I'm just checking the oil and what not."

I took him in slowly, he looked terrible. His hair was tousled and it looked like sleep hadn't found him for awhile. He gave me a half hearted smile, but it did not reach his eyes, they looked empty and dark circles formed underneath. I forced my eyes to his but I could not find my Bryce within them, he was no longer there.

"Well, I'm glad your trucks okay," he offered.

"Me too."

He looked away and kicked at the gravel with the tip of his boot. "I'll get the outfit."

I watched him turn for his truck. He opened the door slowly and leaned inside. He stood back cradling the package in his arm. He looked broken, he seemed to know that this was the end. He walked toward me slowly, eyes still on the bag. He stepped in front of me and hesitated. "Here," he lifted his hand to me hesitantly.

I took it and held the delicate item against my chest. "Thank you. I really appreciate this."

He looked up at me, brown eyes vacant. "Why did you want it back?"

"I needed it. I wasn't ready to let it go."

He nodded and rubbed the back of his neck. "Yeah, I get that."

He looked away quickly and held his focus downwards. I fixed my gaze on him, taking him in for the last time. *Goodbye my Bryce.* Tension hung heavy around us. He lifted his eyes to me, mouth sewn shut. We both stood helpless, yet said nothing. *Don't go, please. Stay here with me. Say something, give me something, anything.* I bit my lip unsurely and let my eyes fall to the ground. My voice had left me, I simply did not have the strength or bravery within me. He cleared his throat and stepped in to give me a quick hug. We stepped back, all the while looking at each other.

I'm not sure where the anger came from, but it was suddenly there. How could he have said all those things about our future, and not mean them? He hated his ex. I remember his exact words, and before I knew it, my voice cut through the silence. "Hey Bryce. Remember this? I don't know how you look at things, but the way I see it is this. You really need to like the person you're going to be with. You'll spend a lot of time together and you want to look forward to those moments, being with that person. Not dread them."

He backed away slowly, but I continued. "Does she make you laugh, Bryce? Does she make you smile?"

He said nothing. I watched as he slipped into his truck. I did not move, I pressed myself against my own truck and hoped it would keep my trembling legs upright. He fired up the engine and without a single glance my way, he reversed out of the driveway and I watched him drive away, leaving me behind for the last time.

CHAPTER 18

Seconds turned into minutes. Minutes turned to hours, hours into days. Some days I felt like I could breathe again, others I could not escape the ache that would take hold of my heart and knock the breath out of me. I wished I could trade it in for a new one, a stronger one, one that had never known the ache of a loss. I went on with my days like nothing happened, or so I would try. I threw myself into work, workouts, visiting friends, anything to keep myself busy. It was in the quiet of the night I would fall apart, when the house grew silent, and everyone was snuggled deep inside their beds held by the warm embrace of a pleasant sleep. I had nothing to occupy my time, sleep seemed to have forgotten about me. For although my mind and body were tired, I could not find the peace of a good slumber. I lay awake, and regrets and the 'what ifs' would taunt me. If only I had told him sooner that I was late, he would have stood by my side and I wouldn't be left here. I wouldn't have gone through all the heartbreak and hurt alone. He would have given me his shoulder to lean on, his arms would have kept me safe and warm. Looking back on everything, what did I have to show for it? Absolutely nothing but a broken heart.

I let my mind wander to the 'what ifs' and a vision slowly came into play. It was the day I found out I was late. I left the doctor's quickly, shaken up and sat in my truck left alone in the confines with my jumbled thoughts. That awful voice crept into my head. *He's going to leave you.* But this time, I would do things differently. I shook that voice out as quickly as it had entered. *No, he will not. He will stay, he's different.* I turned the key into the ignition and began the drive to his house without a second thought. I would let him in. I would share one of the most uncertain, scariest moments of my life with the man I had fallen in love with. I found a place to park near his house, and with an unsteady hand, I knocked on the door.

He opened it up and looked at me in surprise. "What's wrong?" concern filled his voice.

I took a shaky breath. "I'm late."

His face drew back in surprise. He composed himself rather quickly and took me by the hand. "Come here, everything is going to be okay." He led me inside and I followed willingly, knowing everything would be fine, just fine. I would not have to be alone in this after all.

I let the vision fade away into the air, there was no point in hanging on to something that was never to be. Things had to get better, and I suppose they slowly were. I didn't cry every day, although I often felt the sting of loss. My heart ached almost all the time, but I was getting good at ignoring it. Music was a sore spot, a lot of the songs stirred a pain that hurt my very soul. So many memories, so many promises that would never see the light of day. But yet, I was trying. I got out of bed every morning, put on fresh clothes and carried on with my day, as slow as some could be. I missed sharing my day with him, little moments here and there that would've put a smile on his face. One of the things I missed the most was the contentment in knowing that someone was out there waiting to see you, counting down the days and hours until they would be with you.

A memory flitted through my head and I found it brought a smile to my face, even though my heart felt differently. Bryce and I were both stretched out on his bed. Music played in the background as usual. He was in a silly, happy mood that was contagious. I stretched out on my back and stared up at the ceiling, laughing almost uncontrollably. Bryce popped upwards and placed himself on top, hands pressed flat on the mattress on either side of my head as he kept the majority of his weight off of me. I wrapped my arms around his neck and smiled warmly.

He grinned, a fire playing in his eyes. "Are you ticklish?"

Oh no. I knew where this would go. "Umm, why no, no I am not."

He laughed. "I don't believe you." He traced his hands lightly down my side and I tensed, tightening my grip around him. His smile broadened. "You are!" he exclaimed. "I knew it." He studied me quietly and raised a brow. "I have you just where I want you."

"No, please, no." I squirmed desperately, trying, and failing to get out of his grasp. But it was too late, for he held on tight, I was stuck in his hold. And so, he began to tickle me. I laughed, almost to the point of tears, begging him to stop. He seemed to find such joy in teasing me. He gave me false hope of freedom and I sat up, back faced to him trying to crawl away. He quickly slipped his hand around my waist and pulled me into him. I eventually laid limp in his arms, knowing it was a loosing battle.

He took pity on me and craned his neck to look me in the eyes. "My ticklish, cute girl."

I looked upwards smiling. "Picture me waving a white flag right now. I surrender."

He laughed another bright laugh. "Okay" His lips met mine softly. He pulled away slowly, grinning. "I don't know about you, but that was fun."

I rolled my eyes. "For you maybe."

I watched as the memory slowly faded away in front of me and wrapped my arms around myself slowly. What happened to us? We never fought, we never got on each other's nerves. We fit so nicely together....we were just beginning. The time that we had spent together brought a smile to our faces, another memory to hold on too, another plan for the future. I had been searching for someone like him for a very, very long time. I wiped the tears that started to fall, at least for a little while, I got to feel like the luckiest girl in the world.

⌘

I curled up on the couch, and hugged my knees towards my chest. I listened to Sky excitedly describe a new work project he had begun to tackle. His voice grew quiet and he turned to study me. "You okay, sis?"

I looked at him slowly. "I guess. I miss him."

Sky shook his head. "Don't, he's not worth it. You miss the idea of him."

I looked at him rather blankly. "I suppose."

Sky shook his head again and frustration filled his voice. "I am so tired of all these assholes hurting you. That's it, next time you bring someone here, it's going to be a whole different experience. Being nice doesn't seem to be cutting it."

I looked at my little brother, who really wasn't so little anymore. I had never seen a protective side of him before. "So you won't have a beer with just anyone then?" I teased.

"Oh, I'll still have a beer, it just won't be the same experience as last time. No more nice guy on this end."

I stared back at my brother, and felt so proud of the man he had become. He was honest, trustworthy and upfront. He would always be there for those he loved and never back down from a fight. Sky treated his girl like she were a treasure. It was so nice to see that there were still a few stand up men in this world, and I could call one of them my brother. Yes, looking at Sky, I was so thankful he was nothing like our father who was famous for leaving a string of broken hearts and promises. One of the clearest memories I had of the man was his backside; for we were always watching him leave.

"Come over."

I looked down at my phone as I read Ben's message. He heard the news through the 'friend phone chain' and decided I needed to get out of the house. I sighed heavily. I wasn't sure how festive I was feeling, but anywhere would be better than here.

"Sure, I'll be there soon."

"Good!"

I threw on my jacket and slipped into my shoes. It was a short drive and I pulled into a free spot in the driveway. I hopped out of the truck and let myself in the front door. Jared's house held an old comfort for me tonight.

Ben strode out of his room and smiled when he saw me. "Hey, Ry! Glad you're here."

I smiled. "Me, too."

"Hey. I'm sick," Jared's voice came around the corner.

Ben laughed. "No, he's not. He's hung over."

I raised a brow. "Ah, I see." I peeked around the corner. Jared sipped soup at the kitchen table.

He raised his eyes to meet mine and smiled. "Hey, you." He glared at Ben. "Being hung over still counts as sick."

I laughed. "No it doesn't. That's self inflicted, sorry."

Ben grinned. "Ha!"

I pulled up a seat next to Jared. He studied me closely, and when I feared he could see too much I broke eye contact. Jared didn't call me out on it, instead he simply changed the subject to a lighter topic. I silently thanked him for the gesture. I watched with slight amusement as he began going over, in great detail, a truck he planned to restore. His blue eyes danced as he went on to describe his plans. I watched him with a small smile and studied his face. I had always liked it when he let himself get scruffy, and tonight, he wore one of my favorite looks. I turned my gaze to the table and pushed away an old longing.

"We're out of beer," Ben stated. "Not good.."

"What? No." Jared's head popped up. "We need to do a liquor run before they close."

I shook my head and smiled. Ah, the simple life, where your worries consisted of running out of alcohol. I was glad I could sit in on it, if only for a night. My eyes fell to Jared's bedroom and he noticed. His gaze fell to my face. I met his eyes slowly and he looked thoughtful. I gave a shy grin and shook my head in a silent 'no.' Jared had always held me close when I spent the night, and if he wasn't holding me, his hand would be placed upon me just for the contact of simply being there. I could use that feeling more than ever, but this was something I needed to walk through on my own. I had to move forward, and I would.

"I guess we should get a move on then, boys. It's almost eleven."

Jared looked down. "I'm in my PJ's. Do you think I need to change?"

Ben laughed. "Naw, come on let's go."

We stepped outside and began the short walk to the store. I stood in between the guys and listened to their hearty banter and found myself smiling along to their mindless chatter. It was good to be drawn away from my silent sorrows. We made it to the store and stepped inside.

Jared gave a somewhat self-conscious glance back at us. "Is everybody staring at me?"

Ben grabbed a box of beer. "You're fine."

I smiled and raised my voice slightly. "You look pretty sexy in those PJ's. Plaid's the way to a girl's heart."

His eyes grew wide and I burst out laughing. He came closer, towering over me and placed his hand over my mouth. "Shh, you're such a brat."

I wiggled loose and grinned. "You bring out the worst in me."

The guys grabbed their liquor and I was surprised I didn't feel like joining in. Once we got back to Jared's place, I made myself a cup of tea instead. I didn't feel like dealing with the consequence that tomorrow would bring from a liquid filled night. I plopped down next to Ben, and rested my head on his shoulder, sighing heavily. He gave me a knowing smile and hugged me tightly. I left my head on his shoulder for quite some time before I straightened up.

Ben got up to grab another beer and Jared scooted closer and extended his palm to me. I looked down at it and noticed a scar where his palm met his wrist. "I don't think I've ever shown this to you, have I?"

I looked at it closely, and traced it with my finger. "No, what happened?"

"I was eleven years old and I tried to chop a piece of wood with an axe. I missed," he shrugged half heartedly.

"Oh ouch. That's a bad oops."

He laughed. "Yeah. I was thinking about our camping trip last summer and I don't remember showing it to you then. I was busy with the axe that weekend, ha!"

I smiled. "You made me nervous. As the night went on, you got pretty loaded. I thought for sure a limb was going to come off."

He laughed. "Well, I sure as hell wasn't going to let you do it. You would have lost something for sure."

We both laughed, and I agreed. Ben joined in. We talked about all our close calls and 'what if's.' Topics turned to our hopes, dreams and dreading turning the big 3-0. Where had the time gone? I let my mind take me away and hoped everything would be okay. I said goodnight to the guys and pulled out of the driveway. It was well after midnight and the roads were quiet. I began to drive home at an easy pace, I was in no hurry. The stop sign was in the distance up by the church, when out of nowhere a set of tail lights came straight for me. A driver attempted to back out of a driveway and clearly did not see me. I slammed on my breaks but they came at me too fast, I knew we were about to collide. The car's rear end headed toward my door with a decent amount of speed, and in a last ditch effort I cranked my wheel a hard left, turning the back end of my truck closest to the oncoming car. I felt the impact as the car collided with my rear tire followed by a crunch. *Fantastic.* I quickly placed the truck into park and hopped into the middle of the dead street.

A woman in a party dress ran out quickly. "Oh my gosh I am so sorry! Are you okay?

"Yeah, I'm fine."

I walked to the rear of my truck and began to assess the damage. There was some minor paint scrapes above my rear wheel but I was more concerned about what I couldn't see, if there was any damage done to the wheel axle. *I'm going to need to make a claim and get them to assess my truck. Lovely.* I looked at her car and winced. Her car had taken the brunt of the damage, her tail light was cracked and her rear end was freshly crunched. I noticed she had a passenger in the front seat who seemed to be pretty content to stay put. "Are you guys okay?" I asked.

"We're fine. I'm so, so sorry."

I sighed heavily. "No problem. I'm glad I have a truck." I smiled weakly. "We should exchange information."

"Of course."

I leaned in my front seat and began to dig for my papers. I was surprised to see I trembled slightly. As far as collisions went, this was my first and I considered it to be pretty minor, yet it shook me. We exchanged our information and I hopped back into my truck and made way for home. All I could think of was how much I wished I could talk to Bryce.

⌘

Today was a big day; it would be the first day trying to heal an ache I couldn't stop, a blind faith toward fixing what was left of my heart. For today, I would fulfill some empty promises on my own. I needed to try and let go, to prove to myself that no matter how much I hurt, I would be okay. I would put myself back together, piece by piece. I may not fit together like I used to, but I'd place back what I could, as best as I could. It started with the guitar. I had been staring at it for far too long, it was time to play. The guitar leaned against my bedroom wall, where it had been for weeks. I traced my fingers across the smooth finish carefully before picking it up. I sank to the floor and placed it in my lap. The hollowness in my chest began to throb but I willed myself to press through. *Do it. Play. Play for yourself. Don't let him take this away from you.* And so I did. I ran my finger down the strings and let the music seep into the walls. I pressed my fingers down along the frets, creating notes. I strummed the strings in unison and hummed along. I let my eyes close and felt the music wash over me. I found the smallest of comforts in the moment, and though it was small, it was an ember burning, and ember's could be brought back into a fire.

I awoke early the next morning, I decided to rise with the morning sun. I ate quietly as to not disturb Sky, got dressed, grabbed the keys to my truck, and slipped out the door. I hopped up into the front seat and pulled out my GPS, punching an address into the screen. I was going to see the Alexandra bridge today. Bryce spoke of it a few times and it was somewhere he wanted to take me. It sounded beautiful, like a wonderful photo opportunity. I had my heart set on seeing the place, and so, today, without him, I would. The drive would take me a few hours, but I was always one for road trips. I liked to drive, especially when the scenery was beautiful and with good music to listen to, made it all the more enjoyable. The truck roared to life breaking the silence of the still morning. I pulled out of the drive and headed for the freeway. I turned the music up good and loud where I sang to my hearts content. I tried to ignore the ache in my chest, it had become a daily chore, but deep down I knew this was something I'd have to go through all on my own. The sun began to rise. It lit the sky on fire with pink and orange before burning off just as swiftly as it had come on. The sky grew brighter with every passing second, it was going to be a beautiful day. Hints of blue still hid under the early morning clouds, but the hope of a bright day was present. My spirits soared slightly, just like the morning clouds, happiness lay somewhere deep inside of me, I just needed to find it once more.

The highway took me out of the city limits. I was glad to see the buildings and clutter of the city in my rear view mirror. *That's where you belong.* Once I broke through the views of concrete, wide open space greeted me. Tall trees towered along the side of the road and the mountains came into clear view. They possessed an awing beauty. I let my eyes eat hungrily at the view before me. I couldn't help but give a sidelong glance at the empty passenger seat. *This was supposed to be our day, our trip…and here I am, all alone. Bryce.* I stepped down on the gas pedal, pushing the truck faster, hoping that like the city behind me, I could leave my broken heart and lonely memories in the dust.

The road began to twist as I started to climb in elevation. There was no one else on the road, so I slowed the truck and took in the serenity around me. The Fraser River lay below, and today under the sun, it sparkled like a blue diamond. The old bridge came into view, I found a quiet spot to pull over and I turned the truck off. Loneliness once again found me and struck me in the heart. I took a forced breath, grabbed my camera and hopped out of the vehicle. My feet crunched on the loose gravel before me as I began the walk down the incline, heading toward the bridge.

The Alexandra Bridge had been built in the 1800's, used as a connection for the Cariboo Wagon Road. The original bridge had been destroyed by the rising of the Fraser River, another sturdier bridge was built in 1926 and to this day, it still stood. The suspension bridge was built along the footings of the original; the large concrete arches on either side came out the rock bluffs. The iron bridge lay over the wild river below contained by the silence of the mountains and one hundred year old trees. I could almost picture the pioneers using the structure as their horses and mules pulled the wagons and supplies. The history of another lifetime was heavy in these parts, and I drank it in eagerly.

I picked up my camera and switched out my standard lens for the zoom.

I began snapping pictures, capturing a memory that wasn't quite what I thought it would be. As I looked through the lens, a part of me kept hoping to see him here next to me. I could picture his smile, lighting up his face.

"Didn't I tell you? It's amazing here, isn't it?" I could almost hear the excitement in his voice.

"You sure did. You're right, I love it! Thank you for bringing me here."

A broad smile would appear on his face. "You're welcome. I'm getting to know you pretty well," I could see him extend a hand. "Come on, follow me."

And I would. I would have followed him anywhere. In this particular scene, I knew where we would end up; sitting on the tailgate of his truck, music pouring from the open windows. He would hop up and pat his hand for me to sit next to him. I would. And there we would sit, taking in the view around us. It would have been the perfect day. But I was alone. I found myself staring into the vast openness around me and grew cold. I looked into my viewfinder one last time and took the final shot. I made my way back to the truck and slid inside. I flicked the music on and listened quietly. I stared into the quiet confinement around me and let the tears fall. For today, I had come to a place where no one could find me for a reason. I placed a hand over my now empty stomach and felt the ending of a life. Today, I was trying my best to let go. *I am so sorry, my little one. I tried so hard to hold on to you, I wasn't strong enough, but my dear, I held on to you for every second of your being. Goodnight, my sweet one. Mommy will love you to the moon and back.*

I let my head fall heavily against the seat. I would always keep the little one's memory with me. Every year on March third, I would feel a twinge in my heart as it marked the day the little life slipped out of me. A part of me would be forever changed. I had stumbled across a quote and written it down. I pulled the piece of paper out of my pocket, and with a deep breath, I stepped outside once more. I sat on the hard ground and unfolded the paper. I stared at the words and cleared my throat and began to read aloud a passage. *"How very quietly you tiptoed into our world, silently, only a moment you stayed. But what an imprint your footprints left on our hearts."* I read it for Bryce and I, even though he was no longer here. It seemed like a fitting thing to do, for the man I had loved would have mourned the loss. I stared at the paper once more, and with trembling hands, I tore it into tiny pieces and blew it into the wind. I watched as the small white flecks got carried away. I stared until they were swallowed amongst the valley below. I wiped at the tears and slowly found my truck. I turned on the engine and carefully drove back to the main road. I had nowhere in particular to be, so I made a last minute decision to take the back roads home. As I drove past miles upon miles of farmland, I found myself coming to a crossroad. I pulled off slightly to the side and got out of the truck.

I breathed in the sweet air and heard the faint mooing of cows in the far off fields. The large maple trees swayed in the breeze, the tall green grass shone under the late sun. My GPS lost it's signal, but today, it did not bother me. To the right, a herd of horses grazed peacefully, their tails swished in unison, trying to keep the early spring bugs at bay. I watched them for a long while. I stared out into the fork in the road. Where do I go from here? Would this ache, this hurt ever truly go away? I knew I was lost, the question was, would I ever find my way to where I belong? Or am I one of the unlucky few destined to always be left searching for a way on my own?

The sun began to set. Darkness would be here soon, covering the light of day. I looked to the sky and let a few tears escape the corner of my eyes. Goodbye, my Bryce. I hope you always keep a small part of me with you, for I fear I will always have a piece of you with me. I hope when I enter your mind, it will bring a smile to your face and a warmth in your heart. I hope the day comes when I can think about you and it won't hurt so much. I truly hope that one day, I can smile and be glad that for awhile, you were mine. Perhaps our paths will cross again one day and we will remain on the same road. I did not know, for I could not for see what the future would bring. As of now, my future was uncertain. I had a lot of healing left ahead of me, but I would not give up. I would rise each day with the sun, and lay my head as the darkness falls. My lungs would open with each breath, and my heart would go on with a steady beat. I would do my best to sing like no one was watching, laugh like I had something to laugh about, and keep dancing, dance until I forget you.

You can't love with a fear of it always coming to an end, this I know all to well. I will love again, in time, and I will love with everything I have in me. I hope he is worthy, and will stand by me through the good and the bad, even when I need to fall apart. One day I hope to hold a child in my arms I call my own, their little heart holding a strong beat and the man I love by my side. Yes, the future was so full of questions and offered no guarantees. Life would take what it wanted when it wanted. It will throw you down paths you could never foresee and they might not all be good. Life is a journey and you need to find the light amongst the darkness, and know deep in your heart the sun will rise again; it has too. I hoped the darkness of my tunnel would be nearing it's end soon.

Small buds had begun to bloom on the trees, I took comfort in it. Spring was bringing with it a fresh, new life from the dead of the winter. Hopefully I, too, could rise from the ashes. Time would tell. I climbed back into the truck and turned the key. I turned left, for it looked like the road less traveled, and that my friends was something I knew all too well.

Katt Rose

is an aspiring writer who has a love of music, animals, and writing. Katt worked in the health care field but she could not silence the stories inside her head. Once she began to write, she knew there would be no turning back. She was home.

A message to my Readers

If you enjoyed "The Loss", please leave me a review on my Amazon page, the more reviews the easier it is for others to find me. You can also check out my other books there as well, or check out my website at

http://kat-rose-c1r1.squarespace.com/